P9-BYV-206

Praise for Kate Johnson's *Ugley Business*

"Move over Stephanie Plum, Sophie Green has arrived. ...Ugley Business is a great story full of action, smart remarks, lots of British humor and characters that I wish I could meet. As I previously said, Move over Stephanie Plum. Sophie is here!"

~ *Jan Crow, ParaNormalRomance Reviews*

Praise for Kate Johnson's *I, Spy?*

5 Stars   "I absolutely LOVED the story. Sophie is an awesome character, full of life. She has a quick and sarcastic sense of humor that made me laugh out loud. Did I tell you how much I liked her?"

~ *Anne Chaput, eCata Romance*

4.5 Stars   "If you like the Stephanie Plum series, I believe you will like I, Spy? as it has a similar feel to it. This book is modern, quirky, ironic and sassy. I can easily see how this will spin out into an excellent series."

~ *Janet Davies, Once Upon A Romance*

"This book has everything! Kate Johnson has created a wonderful set of characters. This is one book which if were in print, I would have on my keeper shelf!"

~ *Jan Crow, ParaNormal Romance*

4 Stars "Kate Johnson tells an outrageously funny story... I Spy? was one laugh after another. It is good to see that a ditsy blonde can save the day and when Luke and Sophie finally hook up readers will just not believe where! I Spy? is one hot read and too funny for words. Readers enjoy!"

~ *Alisha, TwoLips Reviews*

Ugley Business

Kate Johnson

A Samhain Publishing, Ltd. publication.

Samhain Publishing, Ltd.
512 Forest Lake Drive
Warner Robins, GA 31093
www.samhainpublishing.com

Ugley Business
Copyright © 2007 by Kate Johnson
Print ISBN: 1-59998-718-X
Digital ISBN: 1-59998-470-9

Editing by Jessica Bimberg
Cover by Scott Carpenter

This book is a work of fiction. The names, characters, places, and incidents are products of the writer's imagination or have been used fictitiously and are not to be construed as real. Any resemblance to persons, living or dead, actual events, locale or organizations is entirely coincidental.

All Rights Are Reserved. No part of this book may be used or reproduced in any manner whatsoever without written permission, except in the case of brief quotations embodied in critical articles and reviews.

First Samhain Publishing, Ltd. electronic publication: June 2007
First Samhain Publishing, Ltd. print publication: October 2007

Dedication

To everyone at Stansted Airport, especially the crew on check-in. I miss you...but I don't miss the hours!

Prologue

The way I see it, life is made up of choices. Yes or no; black or white; this week, next week, some time, never.

Like, do I tell people on MySpace that I get up at three-thirty in the morning to do a job I hate, I live in a flat smaller than some people's wardrobes with only a small tabby cat for company, and I haven't had a real boyfriend since I found my high school sweetheart porking the tart from down the hall two months into my English Lit university course?

Or do I tell them that I pay half the going rate on my rent, have access to any and all government files, own a gun and am sleeping with the most gorgeous man I have ever seen in real life?

That I am, in fact, a spy?

Hot lips brushed the back of my neck. "Are you going to spend all night writing that thing," Luke asked, "or are you going to come back to bed?"

Choices, choices.

Chapter One

Sometimes I wish I could make Luke my alarm clock. Would I rather be wrenched from blissful sleep by the frightened shrieking of the digital monstrosity that skulks on my bedside table, or by Luke Sharpe licking my neck?

"Wake up," he murmured.

"I don't want to."

"Wake up or I won't—" he broke off, and I didn't get to hear the next bit because he came back with, "There's someone at the door."

"Don't care."

"Could be important." His mouth moved lower and if I had cared before about the door, I pretty soon stopped.

"It'll be a...a delivery or something," I mumbled. "Postman..."

"Mmm," Luke agreed, unable to perform a verbal manoeuvre any more complicated than that because his mouth was currently engaged in other activities. Then he lifted his head. "Sophie?"

I meant to say yes, but only managed a sort of breathy squeak.

"How many people have keys to your door?"

"What?"

"Who has a key?"

What the hell was he talking about?

"Why?"

"Because they've just unlocked it."

"Oh." Then, "*What?*"

Luke laughed at me as I shoved him away. It was my mother. I knew it. "Put some bloody clothes on," I hissed, but it was too late. The bedroom door opened and my best friend Angel was standing there, mouth open, staring in disbelief.

I stared back, my face burning, and Luke, still laughing, flipped the covers over me and addressed Angel. "And you would be...?"

Angel blinked at him. "Shocked and impressed," she said. "You?"

"Amused and embarrassed." They both looked at me.

There were no words.

"So this is why you're always late," Angel said, shaking her head. "You want me to wait out here?" And she shut the door, retreating into the living room.

Luke fell about laughing. "God, you should have seen your face."

"This isn't funny!"

"Yeah, it is. Come on, Soph, she's your best mate."

"Exactly, and she'll therefore be very hurt that I haven't told her I've been sleeping with you for two months."

"So don't tell her it's been that long." He swung himself out of bed and I got distracted for a moment. Luke is perfection, at least until he opens his mouth. He's all long, lean muscle, tight and toned, sinewy and sleek like a racing horse or a big cat. He wandered into the bathroom, saying as he went, "Lie, sweetheart. It's what you do."

I stuck my tongue out at him as he shut the door, and stumbled out of bed to grab my dressing gown and go apologise to Angel, who had never met Luke in a formal capacity (not since he stopped pretending to be Italian when he was working undercover at the airport) and who had no idea that I was anything other than a bored passenger services agent, just like her.

She was lounging on the sofa, reading my *Cosmo*, and she raised her eyebrows at me. "Wait," she held up a hand, not taking her eyes from the page, "I'm just reading how to better my orgasm. But then you might be able to give me a few personal tips...?"

I could overhaul *Cosmo*. Sleeping with Luke had been educational, to say the least.

"Look, Angel, I'm so sorry..."

She shrugged. "You'll be forgiven if you buy me a white chocolate mocha and tell me every single detail."

I blinked at her, and she rolled her eyes.

"We were going to go shopping?"

I smacked myself on the head for that. "God. Of course. I forgot... Just give me ten minutes..."

Angel laughed at that, and I suppose she had a point. It often took me ten minutes just to locate my hairbrush. I'd never left the house in under half an hour in the two years we'd known each other.

"Have some coffee," I said. "I'll buy you the mocha when we get there."

"With cream?"

I nodded distractedly and went back into the bedroom. Luke was pulling on a loose T-shirt that hid the gun tucked into his jeans belt.

"You're going?"

He looked up. "Three's a crowd. And besides, methought I heard the word 'shopping'."

"Methinks you heard right. I planned it weeks ago and totally forgot. Sorry."

"It's okay." He pulled me into his arms and kissed me. "I'll see you later?"

"I'll give you a call."

And then he was gone, the door slamming shut in the breeze, and Angel was sighing with delight.

"My God, Soph," she said, "I'm bloody jealous of you."

"Mmm," I said. Sometimes I was even jealous of myself.

"How long has this been going on?"

"Not long," I said as casually as I could. "It's all kind of sudden." I looked up at the clock. "Speaking of sudden..."

"I think we said we'd pick Evie up at ten," Angel said, following my gaze to the clock. "T minus two minutes."

"Shit." I threw her my mobile. "Send her a text that we're—I'm—running late."

She looked over the sleek Nokia. "New phone?"

Bollocks, bollocks. That was my work phone. "I'm, er, switching over," I lied, tossing her my old Siemens. "I'll be really quick."

Actually, I was impressed with myself. I flew in and out of the shower, wrapped myself in a strappy top and pedal pushers, added shoes and threw my makeup into my bag, and we were off. Sophie Green, gal on the go.

We took Angel's car—she has a Mini Cooper S that goes very fast. I have a Land Rover Defender called Ted, who is bile green and who I adore unconditionally, but who only goes up to eighty-five miles an hour.

Come to think of it, I guess that says something about us. Angel is cute and tiny and reminiscent of a Sixties classic. Her mother was the ubiquitously famous, glamorous, unforgettable, original sex symbol and gay icon, IC Winter. Angel looks just like her but in miniature—same golden curls, perfect curves, flawless skin that tans at the mention of sunshine, huge blue eyes and curvy little mouth. She also lives up to her name. She is a complete darling.

I, like Ted, operate on a rather larger chassis, come from solid, unpretentious stock, look like a lick of paint would do me some good and never fail to save the day. Well, actually, I've only ever saved the day once, but the day has only been in danger once while I've been around to save it. So to speak. But what I mean is that I somehow lack the glamour Angel wakes up with every morning. She never has fat days and can quite happily leave the house without a smudge of makeup. Not so me.

But I do have something she doesn't—Luke—and she never stopped asking me about him. But you see, the thing is, I can't tell her anything. Luke is a secret agent. He's the one who hired me. At the moment, he's the nearest thing I have to a boss. And the government agency we work for is so tiny and secret that I can't even tell my own mother about it. Not even Tammy, my tiny little tabby cat, knows of its existence, which is mean, since her life has been in danger because of it.

Even worse was when we picked up Evie, and Angel asked her if she knew anything about my new boyfriend.

"Boyfriend?" Evie's ears pricked up and she leaned forwards through the gap in the front seats. "You never told me you had a boyfriend!"

"No, well, I don't," I muttered.

Angel sent me a look of deep sarcasm. "Let me guess, he's just a friend who takes some highly vital medicine which you spilled all down you and he had to lick it off or he'd die?"

I glared at her.

"Do I want to hear this?" Evie asked doubtfully.

"*I* don't want to hear it," I said.

"Come on, Soph," Angel said, "if he's not your boyfriend then what is he?"

A very good question. Luke is my working partner but also my superior. I suppose the closest word would be mentor, although that implies wisdom and patience and kindness, none of which are attributes Luke has in abundance. He's also my lover, we spend every night together and every night is amazing, but by no stretch of the imagination is he my boyfriend. No siree.

"Look, it's complicated," I said, and both girls looked horribly disappointed. "I don't want to talk about it."

"I would," Angel said enviously, because despite being the most desirable thing on the planet, she's also very shy and under permanent romantic scrutiny by all the tabloids and celeb magazines who have nothing better to do than wibble on about IC Winter's daughter's love life. Or lack of.

"What's he look like?" Evie asked, and Angel jumped in.

"Gorgeous. All muscly and burly—"

"He's not burly," I interrupted. "I hate muscles. He's lean. But very strong."

"Mmm," Evie said.

"He has blond hair and great cheekbones. A real ten," Angel said admiringly.

Hey. I'm sleeping with a real ten. Go me.

"So why didn't you mention him before?" Evie wanted to know.

"Because..." I had no answer. Because he's a spy and officially speaking, he's hardly supposed to exist? Because I really don't have any words to describe our relationship at all?

Because I didn't want you to hate me for breaking out of the singles club and getting the great sex that you're missing?

"Oh my God," Angel said, "is he the married one?"

"The *what?*" Evie cried.

Ahem. When I first met Luke and had to undertake an undercover mission or two, I may have told Angel that I was going on a date with a married man, so I couldn't tell her anything about it.

"No," I said, "he's not married. But he's really private and this is early days, so I don't want to start trying to explain it when I'm not sure where it's going."

Yeah. That sounded good.

"But we're your *friends*," Evie said, clearly hurt, and I felt rotten. But I was determined not to cave, even though it cost me a lot in white chocolate mochas.

We were in Faith, watching Evie try on a pair of pink striped mules with clear Perspex heels when one of my phones bleeped in my cavernous bag. I carry a huge bag around with me because I need to be prepared for all eventualities. Therefore I have sticking plasters, sewing kit, green-dye defence spray, emergency makeup, deodorant, moisturiser, toothpaste and brush, spare underwear, water bottle, notepad and coloured pens, Italian phrase book (that's a very long story), military ID and two phones, both with battery-powered chargers. Oh, and my SIG-Sauer P-239. And bullets.

How Luke gets by without all this crap, I have no idea. He just grabs his phone and keys and goes.

I hauled out the phone. It was my Nokia, the work phone, and there was a text message on it from the man himself.

New boss confirmed Karen Hanson. MI6 bigwig. Coming in tomo. U want the honours?

Not likely. Showing our new boss around the tiny but still unfathomable SO17 headquarters? Luke had spent the last two months trying to explain to me how the place worked, but I still didn't get it. Probably this had something to do with the fact that, as the other SO17 agents were still recovering from awful injuries sustained in my one and only big takedown, me and

Luke were the only people in the place. So we got a little distracted. By each other.

I texted back, *No, I'll let you have the privilege.*

He replied in seconds, *OK then but u have 2 pick Maria up & look after her.*

Oh, joy.

It's not that I don't like Maria. I do. It's that I'm totally intimidated by her. That and the fact that it's my fault she's spent the last two months in hospital, recovering from bullet wounds that were inflicted because I was too incompetent to look after myself.

I texted back a disconsolate affirmation, and looked up to see Evie paying for the shoes.

"How many pairs of shoes does she have?" Angel asked me.

"Oh, I don't know. A few dozen. Maybe a hundred."

"Seriously?"

"Don't you?"

"Well, yes, but most of them were my mother's. When is she ever going to wear them?"

"Angel, you sound like my brother."

"Well, he has a point. Couldn't she spend the money on something else?"

"Like what? She lives at home and doesn't have a car."

Angel wrinkled her pretty little nose. She has money, lots and lots of it, and I sometimes wonder why she bothers to work for Ace Airlines, because they pay in peanuts whereas the royalties from the films her mother made and the songs her father wrote, would keep her in Faith shoes for a very long time. Actually she could use the Faith shoes as door-stoppers, the money she has, and wobble around the house in Manolo Blahniks. But that's Angel. Both tiny feet firmly planted.

I ought maybe to explain that Angel and Evie come from opposite sides of the friend divide. I went to school with Evie and have known her for years. We failed our GCSEs and our A levels together. I met Angel on my first day at Stansted Airport, working dreadful shifts for Ace Airlines. She, like me, has no great ambition and has worked there for far longer than anyone in their right mind ever would, because neither of us can think of another job to go to.

Well, actually, I have another job, but I can't bloody tell anyone. And because of the amount of people who use Stansted Airport, I have to stay on there so I can legitimately keep an eye on anyone SO17 wants me to.

Shoes bought, we wandered up to the mall food court, where Evie bought a Happy Meal, Angel got Chinese and I got a low-fat sandwich, steaming with resentment that Angel inherited the thin and tiny gene, whereas I got the tall and curvy gene. I eat about half the calories Angel does, but I don't know if there's some sort of osmosis going on, because she stays effortlessly tiny and perfect and I have to do sit-ups.

Well, I should do sit-ups. I never have. Lately Luke and I have been burning off a lot of calories...and you didn't want to hear that. Okay.

Angel got a call from one of the many, many men who are in love with her, and like the polite child she is, dashed off to answer it out of earshot. Evie and I sat there chatting, waiting for her, both wishing we hadn't eaten so much (I may have helped Angel finish some noodles), when suddenly someone tapped me on the shoulder and I looked up into sweet hazel eyes, shiny hair and a dazzling smile.

"Harvey!"

Harvey is one of my favourite people in the world. When I first met him I thought he was a felon, but it turns out he's CIA and therefore on my side. Actually he sort of saved my life. He's absolutely lovely—clean-cut, all-American, tall and broad shouldered and impeccably mannered.

"Thought I recognised that hair," he teased, twirling a lock of my hair, which was currently a darkish blonde. I had to dye it a while ago when I was in disguise, and so far every time Harvey has seen me it's been a different shade as the dye gradually washes out. "Haven't seen you in weeks. How've you been?"

I grinned. "I've been great. You?"

"I've been great too. Thought I'd stay in Britain long enough to see the sun."

"Well, here it is. And it'll probably be gone tomorrow, so make the most of it."

He smiled. "How's your leg?"

Ah, yes. My leg. Two months ago, on the same night Harvey saved my life and Maria nearly lost hers, the person I was trying to capture slammed a piece of splintered wood into my thigh. It hurt like nothing on earth, but it got me off work (Ace work) for a few weeks while Luke hindered my recovery in bed. As far as Angel and everyone at Ace is concerned, I fell down the stairs at my parents' house. My parents think it happened at work. Christ knows what would happen if Angel and my parents should ever decide to discuss the topic.

"It's fine," I said, but refrained from slapping it for proof, as Luke was in the habit of doing. It still wasn't perfect and when I put in an appearance at the airport, I made a show of hopping around on crutches. It wasn't that bad, but I liked the sympathy.

Harvey was glancing between me and Evie, and I nearly smacked my head again. Of course. Harvey has perfect corn-fed Ohio manners and was waiting to be introduced. Evie, pretty starved of good-looking men, was slavering for a mention.

"This is my friend Evie," I said, "Evie, this is Harvey. He's, uh, a friend of Luke's."

Some of the warmth vanished from Harvey's face at that. "Luke? That still on between you?"

"Very much so," Evie answered before I could. "Angel walked in on them in bed together this morning."

I closed my eyes in embarrassment. Something very nearly happened between Harvey and me, but, well, Luke sort of got there first. At the time I was too distracted by people trying to kill me, but now I can't believe I had two such gorgeous men in competition over me.

"And who's Angel?" Harvey asked politely, not looking at me.

"My friend," I muttered. "From the airport. She's…" I waved a hand, "…around somewhere." I cleared my throat. "So Harvey, what are you doing here?"

He shrugged and looked a little embarrassed. "I'm here with a girl."

We both looked around, Evie with an expression of disappointment. "Where is she?"

"She went to the bathroom."

"Must be some girl to get you to come shopping."

"She didn't tell me it was shopping. I thought Lakeside was like a country club or something."

I laughed in delight. "Harvey, you're adorable."

"Yeah, that's what she said." He glanced over at the ladies. "There she is. I'd better go."

Evie and I zoomed in on the girl in question. Blonde hair, black roots. Dark lip liner with too much gloss. Heavy makeup. Tight white tracksuit and platform trainers.

"Oh, Harvey," I giggled, "she's such a Shazzer!"

"A what?"

"An Essex girl."

"You're an Essex girl," he replied, confused.

"No, I just live in Essex. I don't have shares in lip liner." I shook my head. "Go and have fun with her, looking at white knee-high boots."

Harvey gave me a mock-glare, but he was smiling as he walked away. He's just too sweet to be offended by anything.

We attacked the shops again, Evie's theory being that you shop better on a full stomach. If this was true then I was going to shop incredibly, because I'd eaten rather more noodles than I'd thought and needed to walk at quite a speed to burn them all off. I bought some teeny tiny little skirts and shorts, to make the most of the unexpectedly hot weather (it was the end of June, but still Britain. I began every day in the expectation of clouds and rain, just so I wasn't disappointed) and got changed in the ladies. When I came out Angel was wincing.

"What? Are my legs too fat for this skirt?"

She shook her head. "They look great, except for that big scar and all the bruising."

I checked in the mirror. Actually I thought it made me look pretty cool, a talking point. Scars are sexy.

Besides, it wasn't that big. Only a few stitches where the splintered wood had rammed in.

"I didn't realise it'd been that bad," Evie said, coming out and washing her hands. "You never said there were stitches."

Hadn't I? Surely not. I'd told everyone about the stitches and all the painkillers I was on. I'm a glutton for attention, okay?

But not this much attention. I didn't want to have to tell them all the details. I couldn't remember them all: after all, they'd been totally made up. I averted my eyes and they fell on a newspaper lying on the counter. The headline read "Top-up fees too much? Tenth prof found murdered." Tenth? What about the other nine?

Oh, well. There are too many professors in the world anyway, right?

We made our way home, dropped Evie off and started back to my village, but on the way Angel casually asked, "Do you want to come back to mine? We could have some wine and watch DVDs all night."

"You mean stay over?" *What about Luke?* My body panicked, but my mind said, *Take a damn day off. You can survive one night without him.*

Ah, but could I? Time to find out.

"You're not working, tomorrow, are you?" Angel asked, and I shook my head.

"No. I'll stay. Sounds fun."

We went back to my house to pick up my things and feed Tammy, my tiny baby tabby cat, who was sitting by her food bowl, looking plaintive, doing her best to convince me that, contrary to my memory, I hadn't fed her in at least a week, so could I give her about three pounds of food to make up for it?

"Nice try, Tam," I said, dropping Go-Cat into her bowl, "but you're too glossy for the waif look."

Tammy gave me a dirty look and inhaled her food. I poured out some milk for her as compensation for being left on her own (not that she'd even notice), and she demolished that, too, before disappearing through the cat flap to go and find a nice juicy mouse for dessert.

I pressed the play button on my answer phone and my mother's voice rang out. "Hello, love, it's me. Just wondered if you were going to put in an appearance this week. We haven't seen you in ages. We're having tuna for tea tomorrow. And it's always nicest the way you cook it."

This was true, but also rather blatant. I made a mental note to call her back later, before I got too smashed, and carried my sleeping bag out to Angel's car.

"I'm sorry, Ted," I said as I passed him, "I'll take you out tomorrow, I promise."

I swear he gave me a reproachful look.

"You really talk to your car that much?" Angel asked doubtfully, putting my bag on the backseat.

"He gets cranky if he's ignored," I said, patting Ted's khaki flank reassuringly.

"That'd be the battery," Angel cracked, and I wondered where she'd learnt so much about cars. She had to ask me for advice when she bought the Mini, and I was tremendously flattered that she bought what I recommended. Well, what my brother Chalker helped me to recommend.

We drove up to her house playing No Doubt at top volume, but I had to switch it off out of respect when we pulled up in her driveway. Because, appropriately for someone with such a name, Angel lives in a converted church; well, more of a chapel, really, with a small spire and everything. Her bedroom is in the semicircular apse, her bed on the dais where the altar used to be. Her guest room is in the Baron's Gallery, a relic from when the village still had a baron back in the sixteen hundreds. She's not entirely sure how old the church is; presumably it says so somewhere on the deeds, but Angel has never seen the deeds, because she just inherited the place from her mother who renovated it as a charming little getaway.

My mother won't go near the place. She thinks it's creepy, and I suppose sometimes at nights it can be. She says it's like a set in a horror film, but she never listens when I point out to her that, really, a church is likely to be extremely safe from the unholy creatures of the night. When you think about it.

I chucked my sleeping bag on the floor where the choir used to be and went out to the kitchen, which is in the north transept and has the original font as a sink. Angel was unpacking all the crap we'd bought at Tesco on our way home—

ice cream, doughnuts, Pringles and dip, large packs of Smirnoff Ice which I'd have to mostly decline, because I wasn't allowed to get drunk in case there was an SO17 emergency.

I got a text message from Harvey just as I put the Pretty Woman DVD in the player. *Who was that girl you were with? The blonde,* he'd written, no preamble, so he must have been serious. I glanced over at Angel, who was beheading Jelly Babies, and wondered when Harvey had seen us together.

But before I could send a reply, my phone rang and Angel looked up. "Miss Popular," she teased.

"It's Luke," I apologised. "You watch the film, I'll only be a second."

I slipped through the intricately carved screen that separated Angel's bedroom from the rest of the church, and sat down on her four-poster bed. Her mother did several hammy horror films, and Angel loves the theatricality of her house. She has velvet drapes and everything.

"What's up?" I said into the phone.

"Where are you?"

Nice to hear your voice, too, I thought, but said, "Angel's. I'm staying over."

"Oh," said Luke. "Right." Then there was a little silence. "How come?"

I frowned. "Because she's my friend and she asked me, and because I haven't had a girlie night in for months."

"Oh," Luke said again. "You're not going to get drunk, are you?"

I sighed heavily. Ever since I got really drunk this one time ages ago, and nearly gave the game away to Harvey (before I knew he was CIA), Luke has had a thing about me drinking. He says we should have one unit a day so we don't turn into complete lightweights, but can still operate a car totally legally.

"Yes," I said. "I'm going to get really, leglessly, tearfully, stupidly drunk. And I'm going to throw up."

"Ha ha." He paused again, and when he came back sounded persuasive. "Are you sure you wouldn't rather have a night in with me?"

"Yeah, 'cos that'd be a change," I said.

"Come on. We can watch films and eat ice cream and stuff."

"Can we do face masks and talk about orgasms?"

"We can do better than talk about them," Luke said silkily.

"Yes, well, so can me and Angel. We're going to have pillow fights," I said airily. "In our underwear."

"Where does Angel live?" Luke wanted to know, and I smiled.

"I'm not telling you."

"I could find out."

"No doubt, but you're not coming over. She has very secure locks on her doors and she'd be really pissed off if you broke one of her stained glass windows."

"Heartbreaker," Luke said.

"For Christ's sake, I'll see you tomorrow," I said, but secretly I was pleased, really pleased, that he missed me that much.

"No," he said, "you won't. You're rehabilitating Maria and I'm fetching coffee for Karen Hanson."

Bollocks. "Well, I'll see you tomorrow night, then," I said, and he sighed disconsolately. "If it helps, I'll talk about you all night," I offered, and he laughed.

"Nothing classified."

"Is our sex life classified?"

"No, in fact I'm rather proud of it. Tell Angel every detail."

I hung up smiling. It was hard not to feel smug when I thought about a god like Luke actually wanting me in return.

I came back into the nave, where Angel has a sitting room set up, but she was kneeling in the window of the south transept, peering hard through the wobbly glass. She has secondary glazing set up inside, but on the outside the windows are hundreds of years old. Preservation orders and all that.

"Angel?" I said, and she jumped. "Are you all right?"

She nodded, but she looked white. "I just...I thought I saw someone out there."

"Not another misplaced Christian?" She's always getting people wanting to come and pray in her house.

"No." She didn't smile. "No, I..." She sighed. "Sophie, if I tell you, will you promise not to laugh?"

I nodded. "Of course not," I said, and then got confused with myself.

"I think I have a stalker," Angel said, and I didn't laugh, because Angel is prime stalker material. She's always getting wacko fan mail from people who see her and think IC is still alive, and occasionally some mad fan tracks her down and knocks on her door. Angel usually hides until they go away, occasionally calls the police. She's never had any big problems before. But that doesn't mean she'll never have any.

"Have you seen him before?" I asked, because the fans are nearly always male.

She nodded. "Well, I think so. I'm not sure. It's just that sometimes when I leave the house, I just get this feeling that someone's watching me. And last week I came home and," she dropped her eyes, "it sounds ridiculous, but a pair of my knickers had gone missing from the washing line. I looked in the bushes and things in case they'd got blown away, but I couldn't find them."

"You think someone took them?"

She shrugged. "I don't know. I don't want to be paranoid. It's probably nothing. I'm just getting jumpy, what with the

Trust Ball coming up and everything. It always attracts some nutcases." She shook herself. "Let's watch the film."

I followed her into the sitting room, but I wasn't convinced.

Chapter Two

It was later, much later, after we'd lounged around talking about the crappiness of work and the unreliability of men and how impossible it is to get a date these days—somehow managing to avoid telling her how Luke and I met, and that we've never actually been on a date—after the lights had gone out and I eventually settled into sleep, lying on a spare quilt with the sleeping bag open over me like a blanket, because it was too hot to snuggle down inside a ten tog...it was as late as this when I was nearly asleep, that I thought I heard a noise and ignored it.

I know, I know, bad spy behaviour. But I live with Tammy, who's a noisy bugger when she wants to be, and my flat backs onto the car park, and the boiler makes odd noises in the middle of the night, and I thought it was probably a tree tapping against the window.

But then I heard Angel calling my name in a panicked whisper.

"Did you hear that?"

"Hear what?"

"Tapping on the window."

"Thought it was a tree."

"There aren't any trees at this end."

"A bird?" I suggested hopefully.

"I think there's someone out there," Angel whispered, frightened, and it suddenly struck me how lonely it must be to live out here, totally alone, no neighbours for a mile in either direction, not even any parents to run to when you got scared, like I always did.

I had my gun in my bag, and the thought crossed my mind that I could go out there and shoot the bugger if I wanted to. I was allowed.

And then I thought, it's probably just some drunk who'd got lost. Or some kids out for a smoke.

"It's probably nothing," I said, "but do you want me to go and check?"

Angel shook her head rapidly, sitting up in bed surrounded by a halo of blonde curls. "You can't! All on your own? Sophie, he could be dangerous."

Well, so could I. In the right circumstances.

"I'll be okay," I reassured her, pushing back the sleeping bag and looking for my sweater as we heard another tap.

"I won't let you go outside," Angel said, and then there was a flash, like from lightning, from the window nearest me, and I jumped. It wasn't lightning weather. That had been a camera flash.

"How about we call Luke?" I suggested.

Angel's church was on the outskirts of a tiny little village, a couple of miles up the road from where I lived. Luke's flat was not half a mile from my own, he could be here in ten minutes. Less if he ignored the speed limit, which he usually did.

But, "Soph, it's the middle of the bloody night," he mumbled when he picked up.

"This is important."

"Are you okay?"

"Yes—"

"Is Angel okay?"

"Yes—"

"Then it can't be that important."

"It bloody can be, you stupid fuck," I hissed, just to get his attention. Also because we'd been watching *Heathers* and the language always rubs off on me. "There's someone outside."

"Is that illegal?"

"It is if we can hear them. Angel owns the acre around her house. We keep hearing taps at the window and it's not a tree or a bird and she won't let me go out to see. So can you come over to see? Please?"

Luke sighed. "What do I get for this?"

I glared at the phone. "Oh, for God's sake," and I cut him off.

"Is he coming?" Angel asked meekly.

"No," I said. "Not now or for the conceivable future."

"Oh," Angel said, as my phone started ringing again. Luke.

"Where are you?" he asked, and I smiled, and ten minutes later saw him creeping round the outside of the church. He'd parked at the end of the drive so the intruder wouldn't hear the car, he was dressed all in black, and he was stealthy and incredibly sexy.

"So, what," Angel asked as we watched him disappear round the north transept and we crept up to the pulpit to watch, "does he do this often? SAS training or something?"

"Mmm," I agreed, "something," because Luke had SAS training. Eton, RAF, SAS and now secret services. Actually, that much on its own is a turn-on.

"So how do you—" Angel began, and then my phone started to vibrate. I'd been clever enough to switch the volume off, so as not to alert the intruder.

"There's no one here," Luke said, "except me. And I'm fucking freezing. Let me in."

"He says it's clear," I told Angel. "Can he come in?"

She nodded and fetched the keys from the entry hall to let Luke in. He raised his eyes warily to the gargoyles and ancient stone, and stepped over the threshold.

"Seriously," he said to Angel, "a church?"

She nodded. "With a name like mine it's sort of a given."

He smiled, spied me and came over. "Was there really someone out there, or was that just an excuse to see me?"

I rolled my eyes at Angel. "It's a good job you have vaulted ceilings, or his ego wouldn't fit in here. Yes," I said to Luke, "we definitely heard someone. And I think I saw someone, too. Out on the south side. In the bushes where the crypt is."

"The what?" Luke said.

"The baron's crypt," Angel said, unconcerned, going over to the kitchen and switching the kettle on. "Don't worry, it's been empty for centuries. Ever since the church stopped being used and they relocated all the bodies to the cemetery in the village."

Luke looked doubtful, but he nodded anyway. "You get a lot of people wandering around your garden?"

"Yes, but not usually at night," Angel said. "Tourists and hikers. People taking pictures."

"Speaking of which," I said, and told Luke about the camera flash.

He sighed. "Police," he said. "You need to tell them. Write down everything that happens as it happens, anything unusual, but don't confront anyone, even if you think you'll be okay." He paused. "You want me to stay?"

Angel nodded shyly. "I don't want to trouble you..."

"Hey, I'm already here. And Sophie owes me anyway."

Sophie did not owe him anything. I frowned distrustfully. "We're sleeping in Angel's room," I told him. "She's the one who needs protecting."

Luke looked mardy, but he nodded anyway. "You are going to owe me big time when we get back to yours," he said, and I nodded tiredly.

"In the morning." I yawned. "Save it for the morning."

"I intend to," Luke said, and took the mug of hot chocolate Angel offered and followed us into the bedroom with a wolf-like grin.

I woke alone, wondering why my arm was numb and my bed was empty. And then I remembered that under the quilt and the carpet was a stone floor, and that when I'd drifted off to sleep Luke had been there with his arms around me.

I sat up. Angel's bed was rumpled but empty, and I could hear voices through the carved screen. When I peered through the gaps, I saw Luke lounging at the big oak table, and Angel clattering around in the kitchen.

"Nice of you to join us," Luke said when I shuffled out in my shorts and camisole. "Coffee?"

I took the cup from him and inhaled the contents. "More."

Angel refilled it, smiling, and I drained it in seconds. Now I felt I could speak.

"Better," I said.

"Two syllables," Luke said admiringly, peeling an orange. "That must be strong coffee."

"Shift-strength coffee," I said. "You get up at three-thirty in the morning and see how many cups you need to stay coherent."

"So this is what passes for coherency?"

I glared at him and picked up one of the hot croissants Angel had just put on the table. "Don't you need to be going?"

"Ouch," Luke said. "I don't need to be there until ten."

"It's half nine now."

"Yes, and it'll take me fifteen minutes to get there."

I stared. He was wearing yesterday's black T-shirt and jeans. He looked edible, but not very professional.

"You're not going like that?"

"Why not?"

"Don't you want to look..." I searched for a word. "Smarter?"

"I'm smart enough, thanks," Luke said, popping a piece of orange into his luscious mouth.

"Do you have a big day at work?" Angel asked politely.

"New boss," I said quickly.

"And what is it that you do?" Angel asked, and Luke narrowed his eyes at me.

"I'm a roofer," he said, because he lives above a roofer's yard. And it might explain the muscles. "Long hours. All weathers. Very strenuous." He stood up. "And now I'm going to go. Make myself look smarter."

"Don't you be late now," I said.

"Or you," Luke replied, eyebrows raised. Oh, bollocks, yes, Maria.

I saluted him. "Sir, no, sir!"

"See, that's the kind of obedience I like." He grinned, running sticky orange-juiced fingers through my hair and kissing me. "I'll see you later?"

"I'll call you," I agreed.

"Just not in the middle of the night this time." He thanked Angel for breakfast and loped out, looking sexy, while I stared longingly after him. Our first platonic night together. It's all downhill from here.

Angel was watching him go, too. "God, you're a lucky cow," she sighed. "Not sure whether I should offer you a pain-au-chocolat or not, now."

"What did I do?"

"Got a sexy boyfriend."

"He's not my boyfriend."

"Could have fooled me," Angel said, and I thought, *yeah, me too.*

I washed the orange juice from my face, despaired of my hair and got dressed, leaving on the pretence of an unspecified family obligation, and Angel drove me home.

"If you hear any more funny noises..." I said as I got out of the car, and she smiled.

"I'll call you. Or maybe I'll just bypass you completely and call Luke," she winked.

"Careful."

"Thought he wasn't your boyfriend."

"He's not..."

"So what is he, Soph?"

I sighed. Beats me. My partner. My mentor. My lover. But not, for some indefinable reason, my boyfriend.

"He's just Luke," I said, and even to my ears it sounded stupid. "See you, Ange."

"See you."

I let myself into my lovely little flat where Tammy was wailing, looking hungry, despite the lacerated squirrel that lay, headless, by the washing machine.

"Did you bring me a present?" I said, and she gave me a suspicious look. "Or is it a private trophy? Well done, baby."

She looked pleased with herself. I know I shouldn't encourage her, but a) squirrels are noisy buggers, b) they're about twice her size so that's quite an impressive feat, c) they're going to get squashed by a lorry even if they're spared by Tammy, and d) she's a cat, and doesn't understand me anyway.

I fed her properly, marvelled at how much food a tiny little body like that can hold, wished I had the same metabolism and stripped off to take a shower and get the damn orange juice out of my hair.

And when I was halfway through washing my hair, got the fright of my life (well, one of them) when something slammed against my bathroom window.

I switched off the shower and, mildewed curtain pressed against me, peered cautiously at the window. Nothing.

Heart hammering, I reached out and opened the window.

There was a stunned pigeon wandering around on the ground.

"Stupid bird," I muttered, then looked up to see one of the guys who I think lives upstairs, watching me, and hurriedly shut the window. What was this, a free show?

Hair washed, as clean and fresh as the weather would allow, I got dressed, collected my keys, locked the million different locks on my doors and windows, including the metal shutters that turn the flat into a furnace, and left. Paranoid? No. Someone threw a firebomb through my window a couple of months ago.

I drove up to the hospital and went straight to Maria's ward. SO17 doesn't stretch as far as private healthcare, so she was in a room with a teenager who had appendicitis, a woman swathed in bandages who had crashed her car while talking on a mobile phone, and an old lady who had something indefinable and distinctly smelly wrong with her.

"Thank God you're here," Maria said loudly when I turned up. She hates hospitals and had got more and more belligerent since she woke up in ICU. She was dressed, lounging on her high bed, reading a magazine and looking horribly bored. "They wouldn't let me go until someone came to collect me."

"Well, here I am." I picked up her bag. "Ready?"

"I've been ready for about a month," she grumbled, swinging to her feet and only wincing slightly. She was hit with a bullet in the abdomen and had to have her wrecked appendix yanked out. She also had to have a patch of hair at the back of her head shaved off so they could sew up the bloody wounds she got when her head slammed into a wall.

I, of course, have felt almost Catholic guilt ever since it happened, despite that I'm officially C of E. I still feel like it's all my fault, even though Maria and Macbeth, the other agent involved, have repeatedly told me that they knew the risks when they took on the job.

Sometimes I wonder who told them about these risks, because they didn't tell me. The nearest I got was Luke telling me he'd have to kill me if I ever breathed a word of SO17's existence to anyone.

We wandered out of the hospital and Maria gratefully breathed in lungfuls of fresh air. "God, I hate hospital air," she said. "It makes me feel ill, and I didn't need to be ill on top of everything else."

Trying hard not to grovel, I put her bag in the back and asked if she needed a hand up to the high cab.

"No," she said with slight scorn, "I've been working out while they weren't looking. I'm as fit as I was before. Well," she amended, wincing, "nearly."

Ted is a rather basic model of car with no stereo, electric windows or alarm, but he has a ghetto blaster under the passenger seat, and Maria managed to get it tuned to something decent as we chugged on home. She lives in town in a huge old house that she bought before starting on her crippling SO17 salary. Maria used to be in the SBS and is as tough as they come.

She is also really annoyingly beautiful. She has dark hair so glossy you can see your own, less glamorous reflection in it, huge dark eyes and skin that would make a makeup artist redundant. She has a perfect figure that must have prompted the invention of the word "svelte", perfect teeth, hands, legs, everything.

I glanced at her hands. Messy cuticles. Hah!

Then I tried to hide my own nails. We can't all be perfect, can we?

"So," Maria asked, after she'd settled on the beach towel that protected her from getting stuck to Ted's vinyl seat in the summer heat, "what have I missed?"

I shrugged. "Got a postage stamp? I'll write it down for you."

"That quiet?"

"Pretty much. I went to stay with my friend Angel last night and we thought there was an intruder, but Luke couldn't find anyone."

The camera flash bugged me, though. I'd swear it wasn't lightning.

"Speaking of Luke..." Maria glanced sideways at me, and I refused to bite. "Sophie, what's going on between you?"

When did everyone get so nosy? When did my love life become so interesting?

Oh, yes. When I finally got one.

"Nothing," I said, but I'm a terrible actress, I'll never ever make a good spy, and Maria was shaking her head at me.

"I've seen you two when you come to visit. All those little glances, can't stop touching each other... You wouldn't fool my grandmother, and she's deaf and blind."

"It's not serious," I tried, and Maria snorted.

"We're talking about Luke, right? The only serious relationship he's ever had is with his SIG."

This is true. The gun goes everywhere with Luke, and you do not touch the gun. My baby is Tammy. His is his SIG.

"Exactly," I said. "We're just having fun."

"You're sure that's all?"

"I'm not made of metal and I don't have a slide latch, so I'll never capture his heart," I said lightly, although I wasn't joking.

Luke is fantastic and we have an incredible time together, but I'm not sure if I could cope with being loved by him. I think my head might explode or something.

We pulled up at Maria's house and I took her bag inside. The place was light and airy—or would have been had it not been locked up for two months. Luke and I had been round once or twice to check up on the place, stack her mail so that the front door could be opened, make sure nothing was leaking, but it was still mostly hot and airless inside. Maria went around opening windows and brushing dust away with her fingers. Her house, like mine, has lots of secure shutters and locks, but all of them on the inside so as not to look weird. Or spoil the period detailing, as the case is for Maria's house. I'm not sure a twelve-year-old flat can have period detailing. I have socks older than that.

She was just debating whether to walk to the shop or drive to Tesco for something cold and sinful to drink, when my phone rang.

"Why didn't you answer before?"

It was Luke.

"I switched it off in the hospital, like a good girl. And then I was driving."

"You're a paragon," Luke said drily. "Where are you now?"

"Maria's. We've just got back."

"Can you come up to the office?"

Eek. "Both of us?"

"Yes. And—" he lowered his voice, "—try to look respectable."

"Is she scary?"

"That doesn't begin to cover it."

Marvellous. I ended the call and turned to Maria. "All work, no play. We have to go and present ourselves to the new boss."

"Fantastic." Maria was wandering upstairs. "Just let me get changed. My clothes smell of hospital."

She came back down in low-slung jeans and a tight black top that rode up to show the new scar on her stomach. Not respectable entirely, but a clever reminder of why she'd been off work. "Let's go."

It only took her about half an hour to lock everything up, and then we were off, rattling up to the nondescript airport business park, where SO17 has its office. The sign by the door reads "Flight Services Inc.", and once you get past the swipe card entry there's a normal-looking inner and outer office inside.

Luke was waiting in the outer office, fiddling with the leaves of a pot plant. "I said respectable," he said, looking me over with an expression of despair.

"This is as respectable as I get," I said. "Anyway, isn't Macbeth coming?"

"Yes, but—"

"Next to him I'll look like a paragon of virtue."

Macbeth was Maria's protégé, a huge black man who looked as if he'd be more at home at the door of an exclusive club. He could break through pretty much any lock and, he said, disable a car alarm in two seconds. I fully believed him.

However, Luke did not obviously fully believe me. I didn't see why. In my mind, denim shorts, a cotton camisole and sandals are very respectable in late June. I glanced over myself. Maybe the chipped polish on my toenails wasn't too fetching. Or the biro'd shopping list sweating off the back of my hand. Or the cheap sunglasses pushed up into my hair, which was starting to revert back to its usual scruffy blonde.

Luke, of course, was looking immaculate in chinos and a white shirt. Bastard.

"Shall we go through?" he said, gesturing to the closed door that led to the director's office.

"I feel like I'm on detention," I said.

"Not yet," Luke replied ominously, opening the door for us to go through.

Karen Hanson sat at her desk, dressed in an expensive grey suit, her dark hair in a perfect chignon, her manicured hands holding a heavy Parker pen. Her age was hard to tell; she looked like one of those women who was very careful with herself and therefore could be anywhere from thirty-five to fifty-five.

Maria and I exchanged glances. Now I sort of wished I wasn't wearing five-year-old denim shorts and five quid sandals.

"Maria de Valera and Sophie Green," she said, looking up at us in the right order. How did she know that?

Oh, yeah. File photos. Right.

"I'm the new director of SO17. My name is Karen Hanson, you can call me Karen if you want or One if you're more comfortable with that."

One was our old director. His name was Albert, but we figured One had a more Bond-ish sound to it. Plus it was easier to store him as One in my mobile, with everyone else as numbers according to seniority. He was shot and killed not long after I started working for SO17.

"I've been in Saudi for six months working undercover for a sheikh suspected of connections with Osama Bin Laden. In case you're wondering, he was cleared. I've trained with the SAS and been with MI6 for ten years. I am married with two grown-up children who have no idea that I'm not the oil company executive I have always told them I am. The existence of SO17 came as a surprise to me, and it must continue to be a surprise to everyone else. I expect total complicity in keeping this organisation top secret, as well as your full loyalty and cooperation. Do you have any questions?"

I barely had any brain functions left. This woman was my own personal nightmare.

Maria raised her hand, a clever move that showed off her scar. "Will SO17 be getting any additional funding?"

Karen Hanson shrugged. "I will try to secure some extra funds, especially in the light of your recent activities, but MI6 has plenty more things to worry about than your pay packets."

"I didn't mean pay packets," Maria said with a cut-glass smile, and I took a very small step back, "I meant *funding*. For equipment. Weapons. Surveillance. Perhaps someone to man the lab?"

"I will do that," Karen Hanson said. "I am a qualified doctor."

What a surprise.

"Miss Green," Karen Hanson clipped, and I jumped. "You have nothing to say?"

"Not right now," I said cautiously.

"Nothing wrong with keeping quiet." She shuffled some papers, and I wondered what they actually were. Did everyone in a high-powered position have papers to shuffle when they want to change the subject? Was it one of those things you learn in management school? "Now, a new job just came in. Surveillance and possible personal protection."

"You mean bodyguarding?" Maria frowned. "With all due respect, Mrs. Hanson, SO17 doesn't take on contract work."

"Does SO17 want to be paid?" Hanson asked waspishly. "Then SO17 takes on contract work. It's not a breach of security, the client already knows of our existence. Her parents were agents."

Even though her own kids didn't know of the agency? I glanced at Maria and saw she was thinking the same thing.

"When do we meet the client?" Luke asked. He'd been standing to one side, evidently having exhausted all other questions and arguments this morning.

"Agent Five is escorting her in. They should be here any minute now."

"I thought I was Agent Five," I said in a small voice.

"No, you are Agent Four," Karen Hanson said dismissively.

Ooh, a promotion. Probably because the old Four is currently serving a life sentence, having shot the old One, as well as several other people. I started hoping the number wasn't jinxed.

We stood there in silence for a bit. Then, "Did you show her the lab, Luke?" Maria asked.

"First thing," Hanson said, before Luke could speak. "I'm impressed."

"Shame it was ordered to the spec of the person who shot your predecessor," I said idly.

"And why should that be a problem?" Karen Hanson's eyes, which I hadn't noticed before, were pale blue and horribly penetrating. She swung her gaze on me, and I took another step back.

"Well, because she was a psycho," I mumbled.

"You think that usage of the lab will turn me into a psycho?"

I looked helplessly up at Luke, but he was trying not to laugh. No help from him, or from Maria, who was avoiding eye contact with everybody.

"I think that someone as unbalanced as Alexa clearly was, was not likely to have installed a lab that could have been used for wholly sane purposes," I said. "The cattle prods alone are a sadistic and rather unnecessary addition."

I caught Luke's eye and he gave me a mock-serious nod, as if he agreed completely.

"And the manacles," I added, looking straight at Luke to see if he'd bite. And apparently he's not perfect, because he did bite.

"You didn't think they were sadistic last week," he murmured.

"No," I said, "not them. You, maybe."

Maria had one hand to her mouth and the other on her flat stomach, trying not to laugh. Karen Hanson's eyes swung between me and Luke like a blue searchlight.

"I'm not going to ask," she said, the very tiniest hint of a smile touching her lips.

"We're not going to tell," Luke replied, his smile more overt.

Maria turned her face away, shoulders shaking.

Thankfully, at that moment the outside door opened, we heard voices, then the inner office door swung open and Macbeth walked in, immediately filling the room.

"Agent Five," Hanson nodded. "Did you have any problems?"

"Yeah. Had to go back for sunglasses," he said, voice deep and rumbling, barely betraying a smile. Macbeth seems big and scary, but underneath he's a bit of a pussycat. A pussycat with claws, mind. Maybe what Tammy wants to be when she grows up.

"This," Hanson said to us all, "is our new client. Angelique Winter," she added, as Macbeth stepped aside, Angel appeared, looking pale and fragile, and I felt light-headed.

Chapter Three

Thoughts and shocks crowded into my head, everything from *Angel knows we exist* to *Angel's parents were agents?*

And then, *Maybe she really does have a stalker.*

And then, *She knows I've been lying to her.*

Karen Hanson had started talking, but she stopped when it became clear no one was listening. I wasn't paying attention to anything, my gaze rooted on Angel, my mind whirling.

"Sophie?" someone said. "Soph? Are you all right?"

It was Luke, touching my arm, lifting my chin and turning my face to his. I wrenched my gaze from Angel and let it linger on Luke.

"I—I'm—"

"You're SO17?" Angel squeaked.

"We are," Luke said. "You know about SO17?"

"My parents..." Angel began, and trailed off.

"Her parents were both agents," Karen Hanson supplied.

"IC Winter was a government agent?" Luke said in disbelief.

"You're IC Winter's daughter?" Maria stared.

"IC and Greg Winter were both agents," Karen repeated. People tend to forget Angel's dad. He was a bigger earner than her mum, but not half as famous. "She in MI6, he in MI5. Both had a lot of useful contacts."

There was a long silence. We all stared at Angel.

"Well," Maria said eventually. "Bugger me."

Macbeth looked her up and down thoughtfully.

"The stalker," I said to Angel, recovering. "Is that why you're here?"

She nodded. "It's been going on and on. That's why I asked you to stay. I'm frightened to be alone. I—I didn't tell you about the dropped calls, the letters, even e-mails. I got a call from someone who's writing a biography of my mum the other day. She said she's getting harassed by some guy—or it might even be guys. There's something he wants, but he never says what."

"And you can't think of anything it might be?" Maria asked. "No debts or anything?"

Angel shook her head. "Not that I know. Everything was in the black when they—when I—it's all clear." She looked up at me. "How long have you been a secret agent?"

"Two months."

"Since—oh my God, since you went to part time, since that thing with the baggage belt—" she clapped her hand to her mouth.

"It's okay." Luke grinned. "The thing with the baggage belt was what got Sophie hired."

Angel shook her head. "Wow."

"So, what," Maria asked, "are we supposed to be guarding her?"

Hanson shot her blue gaze at Maria, who didn't flinch. "You, Agent Two, are off active duty until I am satisfied that you are totally healed." Maria opened her mouth and Karen held up a hand to head her off. "You will stay here and investigate possible perpetrators via the computer."

Maria glared at her mutinously and muttered something foreign under her breath. She has grandparents from all four corners of Europe, and speaks the languages accordingly. But apparently so did Karen Hanson, because she returned Maria's glare with a cool glance, and replied in the same language. Maria burned, but said nothing.

I was *scared.*

"Agent Four," Hanson said, and Luke had to nudge me. "You will guard Angel at work. Be her shadow. Notice everyone who notices her."

I couldn't help an eye roll.

"Is there a problem with that?" Hanson asked me crisply.

My main problem was that I didn't want to work Angel's twelve hour shifts. "Well, have you seen Angel lately? Everyone notices her."

Angel blushed prettily. Karen Hanson gave me a glacial smile. "Then you will have to be vigilant."

I made a face at Luke, who grinned. Vigilance is not my strong point.

"Agent Three," Luke looked up at the summons, "your time will be divided between personal protection at Angel's home when she is there, and background work at the airport if it is needed. You still have your green pass?"

Luke nodded and took it out of his pocket to show her. All airport workers have a security pass, mostly for purposes of identification and to get in and out of the car park, but if you work airside you need it for access. The pass, along with its individual PIN code, can get you in and out of all the doors that your specific job requires. Passenger service agents like Angel and myself have green passes, which access most areas. Police, and by extension Luke and me, have red security passes, which access all areas.

When I got involved with SO17, it was through Luke, who was working undercover for Ace as a PSA using the alias of Luca, a flirtatious Italian. He'd dyed his hair brown and wore contact lenses, and his accent was authentic enough to confuse genuine Italians.

I saw Angel looking at Luke curiously, and when he showed her the pass, her mouth dropped open.

"You're Luca?"

He nodded.

"The whole time and that was you? Sophie, did you know?"

I nodded.

"Wait—you are really Sophie, aren't you?"

I laughed. "As far as I know."

"Agent Five," Hanson turned to Macbeth. "I understand that security is one of your specialities."

Huh. Wish I had a speciality.

Macbeth nodded, smiling widely, and Hanson went on, "You will be responsible for securing Angel's property and guarding it when she is absent. Be discreet, this goes for all of you."

I closed my eyes for a second. Macbeth, as big as at least two normal people with the demeanour of someone who's going to cause you immense physical pain; me, five foot ten with my blonde hair and big boobs (I'm sorry, but I get noticed); and Luke, who is basically one giant pheromone. Not exactly what you might call covert.

"You will all need copies of this," Karen Hanson gave us each copies of Angel's roster. "Four, your schedule has been changed accordingly. You will be on check-in when she is, and at the gate when she is."

I nodded.

"Let's recap. Two?"

"I'll be here doing Internet searches," Maria said gloomily.

"Three?"

"At home when Angel's at home. Maybe sometimes at the airport too." Luke looked pissed off at this, and no wonder—he'd got the longest hours. But then he was the most highly qualified.

"Four?"

"Angel's slightly larger shadow."

Karen cracked a smile at that. "Five?"

"At home when she ain't there."

"Right. There is to be a firm crossover. She doesn't escape your sight. Understood?" We all nodded. "Then off you go. Mission starts immediately."

She picked up her pen and started writing again and we all turned to go like dismissed schoolchildren. Then something occurred to me.

"What if Angel wants to go out? Shopping, or to the pub or something? Is she going to be quarantined?"

Karen Hanson smiled. "Well done, Four. And since you're so observant, you can escort her whenever she leaves the house."

Luke grinned and pulled me out of the room before I could complain.

"And that's what you get for being concerned," I grumbled as he shut the door.

"It's very sweet of you," he kissed my forehead. "Well. Angel. Where do you want to go?"

"What am I, a Sim?" Angel said. "I need to go home. And think about all of this."

"So I guess I'm coming with you," Luke said.

"And I need to do some shopping later," Angel said.

"So that's me, too."

"And I need to come and secure that chapel of yours," Macbeth said. "Who has air-con?"

Ted didn't, so I drove him back to Angel's alone, trying to think, while Macbeth took his latest motor, an Alfa 159, and Luke drove his undercovermobile, a silver Vectra. Angel got in Luke's car, judging it to be the safest, but not by a huge margin. I think she was more shaken than she let on. She had said once before how she hated guns. Now she knew she'd be travelling with one wherever she went—or if she was with Macbeth, with half a dozen.

And she wasn't the only one who needed to think. I had to fit into my head not only the global knowledge that IC and Greg Winter were spies—not an actress and a songwriter, but *spies*, like me (well sort of)—but that Angel knew about SO17. I didn't have to lie any more. I could tell her about me and Luke. I could talk to someone about it all.

Despite the hot, still air inside the car, I felt myself breathe easier.

Back at Angel's house, all was chaos. Macbeth had driven off somewhere unknown to gather some security equipment of dubious legality, and was now drilling holes in the ancient stone of the church, fitting enough microphones and cameras to cover a talk show. The electric drill droned on and on and there were wires everywhere as he connected everything up.

Luke went around checking locks on doors and windows and told Angel to get metal shutters fitted to them all. Angel protested loudly that this was a fifteenth century church and that she wouldn't be allowed because of its Grade I listing, but Luke paid no attention.

"Do you want someone to break into your house?" he asked, and Angel made a face.

"Well, no, but—"

"Get the shutters. They'll roll back into the wall—"

"But the walls are ancient!"

The argument was stopped by Macbeth, who came in and said to Angel, "You should get some shutters on these windows. Fifteenth century glass ain't cheap to replace."

Angel then got into a conversation with Macbeth about fifteenth century glass, about which he appeared to know an astonishing amount, and Luke stretched back on the sofa and looked up at where I was leaning over the balcony of the baron's gallery, watching it all.

"You okay up there?"

I shrugged and nodded.

"Bored?"

More shrugging. More nodding. I was too polite to say, "Yes, out of my mind."

"Want me to come and keep you company?"

Before I could shrug and nod again, he'd disappeared under the gallery and started up the narrow stone staircase that winds up to the gallery. It's a big space, twelve feet by nearly thirty and open to the room below, although there are heavy drapes that can be pulled across for privacy.

Luke straightened up as he came through the low doorway and regarded me with his head on one side as I sat on one of the guest beds.

"What?" I said.

"You look hot."

"Hot as in sweaty and exhausted, or hot as in—"

"Hot as in," Luke said, smiling lazily. "Although I could make it sweaty and exhausted, if you want."

I rolled my eyes. "Angel and Macbeth are down there."

"So? We're up here." He started towards me slowly. "We could be quiet."

"The hell."

"Okay, they could listen in."

I smiled. "No, Luke."

He put on a hurt face. "No last night, no this morning. Come on."

"Tonight?"

He nodded. "You'd better—"

Oh, shit. "No, bugger, I'm going home for tea. I promised."

Luke scowled. He pulled me to my feet and kissed me, long and hard, the sort of kiss that didn't usually end with me still being clothed. And this was no exception: Luke already had my shoulder straps pushed down to the point of indecency.

He only stopped when Angel belted out a dirty whistle, to the accompaniment of Macbeth laughing.

"Get a room," she called up, and I blushed.

"We've got one," Luke called back. "Your guest quarters aren't very private, Angel."

"You shouldn't be standing by the edge."

He looked back at me. "She's right, you know." He pulled me back over to the bed. "Over here's better."

"I am not having sex with you while there are other people listening in!"

He made a face. "Spoilsport." He glanced back at the door to the stairs. "What's upstairs?"

"Upstairs?"

"Yeah. The stairs go up as well as down. Angel?"

"We can still hear you."

"What's upstairs?"

"Delicate things."

"I think it's storage," I said.

"Storage is good." To Angel, he said, "We're going to have a look around."

"Okay, but don't break or, you know, stain anything."

Blushing hard as Luke laughed, I let him pull me up the tiny spiral staircase and into Angel's attic.

Jesus, it was like a treasure trove. All of IC's dresses were stored here in garment bags, the windows totally blacked out so the fabrics wouldn't fade in the sun. Greg's guitars were all here, too—the Gibson Les Paul, the Fender Strat, the Hoffner violin bass, the Simon & Patrick—boxes of music, sheet and vinyl; memorabilia, movie posters and concert tickets; boxes and boxes of photos.

"Jesus," Luke said.

"I know."

"We can't have sex here."

"We can't?"

"It'd be sacrilege."

I stared. "Sex in a church doesn't bother you, but sex in full view of Greg Winter's Gibson is sacrilege?"

"Hey," Luke said severely, "he wrote 'Heartswings' on that guitar."

Men.

Instead of getting sweaty, we got dusty instead, looking through all the boxes for something that Angel's stalker might want. But we didn't find anything. Or rather, we found lots of things. The guitars alone were worth about the same amount as my flat. The piano downstairs in the south aisle, the one Greg had used to write the mega-famous "I Don't Know Why", had been valued in the millions. Looking under some old cardboard boxes, I found a safe.

"That could be interesting," Luke looked at it.

"You going to break into it?"

"No," he went to the stairs and yelled down, "Angel, can we look in your safe?"

She didn't answer and he went farther down to yell over the gallery. She called something back up and he re-emerged in the doorway, shaking his head.

"Women."

"What?"

"The combination is her birthday." He frowned. "Do you know it?"

"Do I know my best friend's birthday? No."

He gave me a look, and I rolled my eyes. "Of course I bloody know." I gave him the full eight digit number and the safe rolled open.

We stared.

"Jesus," Luke said.

"I know."

"Fuck me."

"Later." I reached in and took out a velvet case. "Recognise this?"

He frowned at the diamond bracelet. "Should I?"

"And this?" I took out a necklace that probably had about the same worth as the entire village.

"That looks familiar..."

"I wore it to the Buckman Ball. Had to get it professionally cleaned before I could give it back."

Luke looked impressed. "You wore IC Winter's diamonds to the Buckman Ball?"

"I did indeed." I stroked the huge pear-shaped, brilliant cut central diamond. We'd had some good times together. Maybe not at the ball, but certainly afterwards...

"Sophie?" Angel's voice drifted up the stairs, and I blinked. Luke blinked too and I wondered if he'd been remembering after the Buckman Ball too. Hard to forget.

Very hard.

"Sophie?" Angel was in the little arched doorway now. "I did tell you about tonight, didn't I?"

Still thinking about the night of the ball, I gave her a blank stare.

"I'm working."

Beside me, Luke groaned. "You are?" I said.

"Six through six."

"All night?"

"That's the shift I usually do. First of four."

I closed my eyes. Twelve hours at the airport. It just might kill me.

"What time is it now?"

"Five," Luke said. "Just gone."

We'd been up here that long? That has to be the longest me and Luke have ever spent alone together without taking our clothes off.

Looking at him, I could tell he was thinking the same thing.

"No," I said. "I have to go home and take a shower and get changed and go." I stood up, dusting myself off. It was so hot up in the tower, the backs of my knees were pooled with sweat and my clothes were sticking to me.

I glanced at Luke, who never seemed to get sticky and sweaty, just moist and dishevelled and, in both senses of the word, really hot.

Definitely a shower. A cold one.

I went home, took the coward's way out and texted my brother that I wouldn't be home for tea, and got in the shower. When I got out, no cooler, my mobile was ringing. My old mobile. My mother.

"Hi," I said, dripping onto the carpet, "did you get the message I sent Chalker?"

"Yes," she said, "but I thought I'd ring and check."

But why? This is what I don't understand. I sent a message that said I had to go into work so wouldn't be home for tea. Simple. Clear. What was she clarifying?

"They're really short staffed," I said. "There's like, a, er, stomach bug going around the whole airport. So I'm going in with Angel. To help her out." A thought occurred to me. My dad was a huge IC fan. "Mum, you know all those books Dad had on IC Winter?"

"Yes," she said doubtfully.

"Do you know where they are?"

"I think they're in the conservatory. Or the loft." Not much difference. "Why?"

Oh, yeah. Why? What is it with my mother and "why?"?

"Well, it's just, it's just...Angel wanted to have a look."

"Angel wants to look at books about her mother?"

Not a good excuse. I don't know how I haven't got fired yet from SO17. "Yeah. A sort of objective point of view. You know Angel."

She didn't, not really, but she still said, "Oh, okay. I'll get them out for you. Will you be coming for tea tomorrow?"

The first of four shifts. Six through six. "Not unless you start tea at about four," I said. "I'm on nights now."

Like a nurse or a paramedic or something. Cool.

"Oh." She sounded disappointed, and I suppose it has been quite a while since I went back there. Properly, I mean, not just to pick up a shirt or something. "Well, you'll be getting overtime, won't you?"

Not a chance in hell. "Erm, yeah. Night shift pay. Look, Mum, I've got to go. Got to pick Angel up."

But when I got there, Angel shook her head at my car. "Vinyl seats and no air-con?"

"You can open the window," I said.

"So what happened to a 'neat and tidy appearance'?" she quoted from our uniform guidelines.

"Sophie's never been neat and tidy," Luke said cheerfully, coming out of the church behind her and trying to ruffle my damp, pulled back hair. I ducked, and he grinned. "Got everything?"

I had my gun and my warrant card and my red pass and my military ID. And a slightly illegal stun gun. And a loud defence alarm that shot green dye all over an attacker. I hadn't yet found a use for it—maybe if I wanted to go into camouflage I could try it. Maybe not. The can says the dye lasts for seven days on the skin.

"Have fun," Luke said, kissing me lightly on the lips and stepping back quickly before either of us got carried away.

"Doubtful," I said gloomily, and he smiled.

"You love your job, remember?"

Right now it was hard to even remember saying that.

Angel explained on the way to the airport that most of the overnight flights were not Ace, who never flew after eleven at night or before six in the morning, but chartered flights for holiday companies. Our actual employer was not Ace, but a handling company called Air International, who supplied PSAs like us, as well as ramp and dispatch and baggage services. Ace was their biggest client at Stansted, but there were others, like the charter airlines, who only had one or two flights a day. Mostly these were handled by the twelve-hour staff like Angel, who were there to greet the midnight arrivals from the Canary Islands or Tel-Aviv.

This last one made me nervous. There were reasons why flights to the Middle East had their own gate with a separate scanner. I didn't want to handle those flights.

Look at me, a bloody secret agent and frightened of a planeful of people who have probably never been in the same country as Osama Bin Laden.

I texted Maria on the way in to see if she'd found anything out yet. She replied, somewhat tersely, that she would find it a hell of a lot easier to investigate people if she knew who they were. Didn't Angel have any suspicions?

But Angel didn't. I asked her repeatedly if she might have known who it was, but she shrugged and said she'd no idea. She was always getting weird fan-mail.

We started on Ace flights, familiar territory, both of us on check-in, within easy sight of each other. I didn't expect the stalker to turn up at the airport, but then you never knew.

Things quietened down and the sun faded through the windows (Question: who thought it would be a good idea to build a south-facing terminal completely out of glass? It's like working in a giant bloody greenhouse), and Tem, my favourite supervisor, wandered over with the floorwalker's clipboard for a chat.

"You working nights now then, baby?"

I shrugged and nodded. I've got pretty good at this move. "Just for a while. See how I go."

"That's nice of them. Letting you try it out."

"Yeah, well. I'm keeping this company going."

"Thought you'd gone down to part-time?"

"For a while. Had, you know, family things to sort out." A complete lie, but Tem was never going to meet my family. He nodded understandingly.

"Are you coming out to Sheila's leaving thing next week?"

I blinked. I didn't even know who Sheila was.

"Dispatch, darlin'," Tem smiled. "She's buggering off to Stansted Fuel."

"So not really leaving, then?" I glanced over at Angel, who was checking in a businessman for the last flight to Belfast. Normal man, normal suit, normal, normal, normal. Even the way he blatantly checked Angel out was normal. "Tem, do you think Angel's pretty?"

"Angel?" He glanced at her. "She's stunning, babe. Not like you."

"Oh, cheers."

"No, I mean not stunning like you. You've got the build, you know?"

Yeah. I knew. I mean, I'm tall and everything, but would it kill a man to drag his eyes up to my face?

"People are always watching Angel."

"She looks like that film-star. The, er," he clicked his fingers, "you know. Sixties. Bond girl."

If I said IC's name out loud, he'd make the connection. Angel doesn't tell many people who her parents were.

"I'm not big on Bond films," I lied, because I'd watched them all when I was trying to figure this spy thing out.

"Yeah. Well. She does the cute and helpless thing. You're all kind of..."

I raised my eyebrows at him. Statuesque? Amazonian. Nice words, but they usually meant only one thing: I'm too polite to say I think you're fat.

But listen, I'm not. Well, mostly not. I have natural curves. I'm rounded. I have big bone structure.

I *hate* tiny girls like Angel.

"Anyway," Tem tried to recover the conversation, "your boyfriend's a lucky bugger."

"Don't have one," I said automatically.

"What about that blond guy I saw you with?"

"When?"

"Oh, I don't know. Last week. Picked you up. Outside Enterprise House."

I almost asked what car, but I didn't want to highlight the fact that I was sleeping with someone who drove a Vectra. So I said, "Oh, yeah, that was my brother."

"So you're single?" Tem shook his head. "Jesus."

How sweet.

As check-in closed down, Angel and I made out way over to the gate to meet the inbound charter flights full of sleepy tanned tourists fresh from Ayia Napa and the Costa Del Sol. Bastards. I never damn well tan.

We got to VP9 and Angel automatically swung her bag up onto the scanner, walked through without bleeping and handed her pass to the BAA official. I rummaged in my bag for my red pass and warrant card, and they let me through without being scanned. The validation point—or VP as we call it—is there to act like security for staff in exactly the way that passengers go through main security. They scan your bag and you, and if either bleep then they get searched.

Except for me. And Luke. I have things in my bag that don't bear scrutiny. And right now, with a pair of handcuffs tucked down my bra, I could have done without a full body search, too.

Angel was impressed. "So is this part of the—" she began, and my eyes widened in alarm. "The thing you were telling me about?" she finished, mouthing, "Sorry."

"Yes," I said. "It's hell trying to get through there normally. I have to pick my moment so there's no one else there. Most of the BAA guys recognise me, but the other day I went through with Vallie and had to pretend I'd forgotten something so she could go on ahead."

Angel nodded. "Sophie..." she said.

"Yes?"

"That thing with the crutches. Was that real?"

I nodded. "Very real. Very painful. You saw the scar. But I—I can't tell you about it."

She nodded mournfully. "That's what my dad always used to say."

Jesus. Poor Angel, having to live with the knowledge that her parents were doing something so horribly dangerous and that one day, they might just simply not come back.

A thought occurred to me and I got out my Nokia. *How did Greg Winter die?* I texted Maria.

She replied in seconds. *Motorbike accident. Cut & dried. Found him in a ditch. Why?*

I wasn't sure why. Just a suspicion. *Can you access the report?*

Bugger all else to do, she replied, and Angel asked, "Who're you texting?"

"Luke," I said.

"Oh," she said, and we boarded the transit train in silence. Then, just as the doors opened and we stepped out onto the little platform in a swirl of passengers, my phone bleeped again. Several passengers glared at me, and Angel grinned. We're supposed to have our phones switched off at work. But then we're also supposed to have a neat and tidy appearance, and that's not likely to happen any time soon, either.

I opened the message, thinking Maria was working fast, but instead it was from Harvey. *Did you get my message? Who is that girl?*

I smiled. *A client. Why?*

She's amazing. I saw you with her at Lakeside. PS you were right the other girl was awful.

"Now what?" Angel asked.

"How do you feel about polite, burly Americans?" I asked.

"In what kind of context?"

"I don't know."

Are your intentions honourable? I asked Harvey, but I didn't wait for a reply, because we'd got to the top of the escalator and people were already starting to ask us things, all anxious that their plane wasn't outside and waiting for them.

We went over to the gate and did all the official things we have to do. Well, Angel did them, because it was a different flight system to the one I was used to, and I didn't know how the computer programme worked. She went down to meet the inbound flight, and I sat there in the strangely bright satellite, looking around at the lounge where there was only one planeful of people left, their flight boarding in ten minutes, far away. I watched them all file through the gate and disappear down the escalator, then I looked out of the window and saw them all climbing up the steps to the little door in the plane, then the plane pushed back and trundled off to the runway.

Still Angel hadn't come back. I'd seen the passengers swarming past on their way to the transit and the terminal, to argue with customs and complain about their baggage, but Angel hadn't come back up yet.

Panic started to seep in. What if the stalker had been one of the passengers? What if he'd got her down there right now?

I closed the little door on the gate, picked up my bag with my hand ready to whip out my gun, and crept down the still escalator. The hall at the bottom was empty. I looked out of both doors—the exit to the tarmac and the exit to the transit, where the inbound passengers would have gone—but Angel wasn't in either direction.

I made my choice, swiped through the door to the tarmac and crept down the tunnel.

Well, tried to creep. The floor was hollow and really, really noisy. I have got to get some softer shoes.

I made it all the way down outside where the steps were being pulled away from the aircraft and the doors were being snapped shut. No Angel.

"Have you seen Angel?" I asked one of the ramp guys, who shook his head.

"Followed 'em all in. Should've gone back up by now."

Panic was thumping in my chest now. Where the hell was she? I raced back up the tunnel and paused at the door to the transit station. Should I try that or...

No. I swiped open the door back up to the gate station and nearly fainted with relief when I saw Angel standing there, looking puzzled.

"Where did you go?" she asked. "I couldn't see you."

I pressed my hand to my heart, which was just beginning to slow down a little.

"I could ask you the same thing," I said, releasing my hold on the SIG in my bag. "I thought—"

"I was helping someone with a pushchair," Angel said, as I climbed back up the escalator. "Lady all on her own with twins."

"She went to Majorca on her own with twins?"

"I didn't ask."

I dropped my bag on the floor. "You scared the life out of me. From now on, we go down to meet planes together, and screw Air International guidelines."

It was a sentiment often expressed.

There were two more planes to meet, one landing at ten and one at eleven, so we lounged around waiting for them. Angel tried to drag some more out of me about Luke, but I wasn't biting. Instead I sat and thought about him.

So, he wasn't my boyfriend. But why not?

Well, we hadn't met each other's parents or friends. I didn't even know if Luke had any. The only friends of mine he'd ever met were Angel and Tom, the singer in my brother's band who helped us out once with someone who tried to drug me. We told Tom it was date rape and I haven't seen him since.

But not meeting friends and family wasn't a very good reason. Romeo and Juliet never met each other's mates, but they still got married and became fiction's most famous and romantic lovers. Not that I wanted to marry Luke. God, the thought terrified me.

So what was it? The total and utter lack of emotional commitment?

Yeah. That was it. We had sex, and we had fun. There wasn't even the thought of "I love you" hanging around to frighten us. I didn't know where the relationship was going. Should I? Would that spoil it?

We wandered over to the domestic satellite where everything was utterly silent. There are no overnight domestic flights, in or outbound, and Angel said to me, "This is naptime."

"It's what?"

"You didn't think we were going to stay up all night, did you?"

The thought had crossed my mind. "I hadn't really thought about it."

"Pick a seat," she gestured to the rows of hard blue chairs, "and take a nap. The Fuerteventura is delayed so it'll be in around three. Jo's going to ring me when it's approaching." She held up her phone. Jo was in Ops and very helpful. "Sweet dreams."

I lay awake on the uncomfortable chairs for what felt like hours after Angel had dropped off into instant, picturesque sleep. I thought about Angel and her parents, about the person who had flashed a camera through the window last night, about Karen Hanson and her new steel rule, and about Luke.

And then I must have fallen off to sleep, because I was suddenly woken up by a voice in my ear, "So this is what you get paid for."

My eyes jolted open and I found myself staring at a pair of very amused baby blues.

"Luke?" I croaked. "What are you doing here?"

"I've been thinking." He was hunkered down in front of the row of chairs, his face level with mine.

"About?"

He brushed a strand of hair back from my face. "This isn't going to work."

Now I was fully awake. "What?" I said in alarm. Was he breaking up with me?

"This. You working nights. Me working days."

Oh God, he was breaking up with me. Except that you had to have a relationship to break up. He was *cutting me off.*

"What are you saying?" I squeaked, trying to keep my voice down so Angel wouldn't wake up. It was still only just past one in the morning.

"That something has to change. Either you stop shadowing Angel, or I do."

I stared. He wasn't breaking up with me. He was mutinying for me!

"But we can't," I said. "We can't let her out of our sight."

"I spoke to Karen," Luke said. "She's willing to employ outside agents."

I frowned. "Meaning?"

"Meaning, sweetheart," Luke smiled, "we can get someone else in. And I know someone."

Harvey! He already had a thing for Angel. He'd stick to her like Bostick. I opened my mouth to suggest it, but Luke had other ideas. He cupped my face in his hands and kissed me.

"Mmm," I said. "So who's this 'outside agent'?"

"Just someone I know. Very trustworthy. I'll call him in the morning."

I nodded. That sounded like a plan to me. "Have you found out any more about—" I began, but Luke put a finger over my lips, and then he slipped it into my mouth, and then he was kissing me again and then somehow my shirt came undone and I pushed Luke away.

"Not here," I gasped, "not now."

"Why not?"

"Angel," I jerked my head at her. She was still sleeping peacefully.

"She won't—"

"She might," I said firmly. "And I'm not big on discovery fantasies."

Luke sighed and looked around for inspiration. "The bathroom," he said, and before I could protest, he dragged me to my cramped feet and pulled me into the ladies. He pushed me back against the bank of sinks and started kissing me again, working on getting more than my shirt undone. And I, uncomplaining, happily joined in, popping all the buttons on his shirt and running my hands over all those lovely muscles. And then running my hands over—never mind. Luke found the handcuffs and got pretty excited, locking my wrists behind his neck.

We were getting along very well, in fact, until we heard the scream.

"*Angel*," I said, and Luke pulled his jeans back up, grabbed the gun he'd left in one of the sinks and dashed out. I followed, limping on one shoe, terrified because I'd left my bag and my gun and everything out there with Angel, all unguarded, and anything could have happened.

Angel was sitting huddled up on the hard blue chairs, a large envelope in her hands, staring at some large, glossy photos. And Luke was crouched in front of her, trying to wipe away the tears that were falling down her face.

"I didn't know what they were but now I know," she mumbled. "Now I know."

"Know what?" I asked Luke quietly, but he shook his head. I held out my wrists and he unlocked the cuffs.

"Angel, where did you find these?"

She rubbed the seat beside her as I hastily rearranged my clothing. "When I woke up. You weren't here but these were..."

She was sucking in deep breaths and I thought she was going to hyperventilate. I quickly sat down beside her and put my arms around her.

"We're here now," I said, shaking myself, horrified that she'd been left alone long enough for someone to plant these things beside her. Or had they been there before? Had Luke and I just not noticed?

Angel cried against my shoulder and Luke gently took the photos from her. I looked up at him, but he was concentrating on the pictures, flicking through them fast.

"Jesus," he said, and when he looked at me, his face was pale. I'd never seen him like that before. I'd never seen him look so shaken.

"What?" I held my hands out for them, and Luke handed them over, taking Angel into his arms while I tried not to mind that his shirt was undone and she was cuddling up to that fine naked torso.

And then I looked at the photos, slowly at first but then quicker like Luke had done, making a moving sequence out of them. And what I saw was this: a man on a motorbike, moorland around him, the sun just about to come up over the horizon. The pictures were from behind, but getting closer, and then they came to a little bridge over a crack in the moor, and suddenly the biker slewed off the road, through the dry stone wall, and down into the hollow, which was deeper than it looked. I knew this because there were pictures taken looking down at the body as it lay crumpled in the ditch, then pictures taken close up. Of the head in its helmet, the white neck stubbled and dirty, and then suddenly twisted at an unnatural angle, and then there was a close-up of the face.

I'd know that face anywhere.

It was Greg Winter.

Chapter Four

Luke fastened his shirt up and took Angel home and I waited around, nervous and guilty, to meet the Fuerteventura flight. And when I'd seen them all off, I grabbed my bag, which had been no more than six inches from me at all times, and raced down to the car park. So my shift wasn't over yet, so what? There wasn't anything else to do. Angel's Mini was where she'd left it, and I'd got the keys that Luke had remembered to take off her. I drove the little car home, not appreciating it at all.

I got home and threw my clothes on the floor and cuddled Tammy to me, but I couldn't sleep at all. The sky got lighter and I lay there thinking about Greg Winter. He hadn't died in a motorbike accident. He'd been forced off that bike, but I couldn't tell how.

And someone had documented the whole thing. And that someone had been in the domestic satellite, waiting for me to leave Angel.

By five o'clock I couldn't stand it any more. I threw on jeans, T-shirt and fleece and stomped out to the Mini. I'd been meaning to take it back in the morning—but hey, it was morning now, right?

Nearly.

The sky was lightening, just like it had been when Greg was killed, as I drove up to Angel's chapel and parked the Mini next to Ted. Luke's Vectra was there, too, and I felt a surge of relief. I picked up my phone and called his number.

"I'm outside," I said when he picked up, not waiting for him to say anything. "Let me in."

Many keys turned in the locks on the big, thick oak doors, there was a bleep from one of the gargoyles, and then the door opened and Luke stood there, his face sharp with tiredness, his clothes crumpled, and I fell into his arms.

I woke alone in the guest bed where I'd fallen asleep as the sky got light. Luke was gone, and for a moment I panicked, until I heard his voice through the thick velvet curtain that cut off the gallery from the rest of the church.

I got up, my body protesting as I stretched my muscles, and then smiled as I remembered how Luke had sent me to sleep. I peeked through the gap in the curtains and saw Luke sitting at the computer in the south transept, frowning at the screen, looking as sexy this morning as he had last night.

Or maybe, earlier this morning. I looked at my watch. It was now late afternoon. I'd slept through most of the day.

I pulled my clothes on and padded downstairs, and was just about to step out of the tiny stone stairwell when I heard Luke say, "Seriously, not even one?"

"Nope," Angel replied. "Not since I've known her."

I ducked back behind the pillar at the corner of the stairwell. Were they talking about me? What were they saying? What hadn't I had or done since Angel knew me?

"Well," Angel went on, "she sort of had a thing going with Sven—you remember him? But then he went back to Norway and..."

She trailed off, and I imagined Luke shaking his head. Sven had been a plant, an impostor, not Norwegian at all, and he hadn't left. He'd been shot. By me.

"Oh," Angel was saying. "Oh."

"And before the thing with Sven there was nothing?"

"I don't even think she went on a date."

"Jesus," Luke said. "I'm sleeping with a nun."

I blinked. Sleeping with. Not dating, not going out with. Just sleeping with. That put me in my place.

"I'm not a nun," I said, stepping out of my hiding place and walking up the nave to where Angel was washing tomatoes in the font.

"Thought you were asleep," Luke said, no trace of embarrassment or contrition in his voice.

"I was. I woke up." I went to the computer. "Whatcha doin'?"

"Trying to get into the MI5 file on Greg Winter. Having no luck. There's a fucking encryption on it and I can't get through."

"Well," I glanced over at Angel, "it's a wild idea, but maybe Angel could tell you about him? Being his daughter and all."

"Smartarse," Luke said.

"Yes, my arse is very smart."

"She's told me everything she knows. What I really want to know is where those pictures came from and how the hell he fell off his bike."

"He was a great biker," Angel said, slicing up mozzarella in the kitchen. "He knew what he was doing. Could ride for hours without his concentration fading. It wouldn't have been like him to just come off like that."

"I don't know," I said. "Those moors looked pretty empty. Middle of nowhere stuff. Could have been riding for hours. Maybe he did just get tired."

"And maybe there just happened to be someone following him who had a full film in his camera and just didn't feel like reporting it to the coppers," Luke stretched back in his chair and glared up at me lazily.

I made a face and looked around for my bag, which I'd thrown in the direction of the sofa last night—damn, I mean this morning. It was on the coffee table, and I checked my phone for messages from Maria. None.

"Listen, Sophie." Angel came over, looking nervous. "I'm not going to be going into work tonight. Maybe not tomorrow, either. I've called it in. Family emergency."

I nodded. Just because it had happened fifteen years ago didn't make it any less of an emergency.

"Can you access the files on IC?" I asked Luke, and he shook his head. "Why are they blocking them? Shouldn't you have, you know, access?"

"Yep," he said. "But not to these. You need certain levels of clearance."

"And you don't have them?" I was both amazed and cheered that there was something Luke couldn't do.

He scowled at me. "Angel," he said, "look, there's something we need to talk to you about."

She looked wary. In fact, ever since she'd come to SO17 yesterday she'd looked wary.

"It's just that we're not sure this set-up is going to work. All this handing over and shadowing at work—especially if you're not going to be at work. It's not that you're any trouble to guard," he added, and Angel gave him a small smile for it. "But Sophie is still sort of learning the ropes and I need to keep an eye on her too. I just think our time could be better spent investigating things."

"Like each other?" Angel said, and Luke grinned.

"Well, on our off-hours," he said, and I thought, *Liar.* We'd "investigated" all over the office in the weeks before Karen Hanson's arrival. "We need to try and trace those e-mails you've been getting, analyse the handwriting on all these letters—" he waved at a pile that I hadn't even noticed, "—we need to find out the truth about how your father died and what it is this person wants. So what we're going to do is get someone in who's more experienced at this bodyguarding thing. Twenty-four-seven."

"Who?" Angel asked nervously, and I didn't blame her. God only knew who Luke had in his address book.

"A friend of mine. We trained together. He's very trustworthy." Luke looked up at me. "I got a call from Maria this morning," he said. "She wanted me to tell you she hadn't been able to access the report you wanted."

Well, duh.

"Also that she's going down to MI5 to try and get something on it. If we can't reason with the computer—and who bloody can," he slammed the screen with his palm, "then maybe we can reason with them."

Fat chance.

It was dark when I left Luke with Angel so I could go home and get some clean clothes and feed Tammy, who was crying out with hunger. Poor baby. I made a mental note to buy her one of those automated feeders so she wouldn't starve when I got stuck at work.

I'd promised to go straight back and wait with Luke and Angel until this person Luke knew turned up, but I wanted to take a shower first. As I was leaving Luke had said to me, "Angel's single, right?", and I'd glowered at him until he laughed and said, "I'm not interested, I'm just checking. Docherty has been accused of home-wrecking before now."

"Docherty?" I repeated, liking the way the hard H clicked at the back of my throat.

"Yeah. Her new bodyguard. I gave him a call earlier. He's on his way over."

Over from where? I wanted to ask, but didn't, and rushed to Ted to drive home and make myself prettier. Poor Ted was absolutely baking, and he'd only just cooled down by the time we got home. I left his windows open a crack for some air and went in.

There was a time when I'd have walked straight into my flat without looking around at all, but I knew differently now. It was roasting and I ran around opening all the shutters and windows and chugging cold water. Then I got in the shower, turning the water to cold, washing the sweat and the tension away, or at least trying. At the back of my mind and in the knots on my shoulders I felt horribly guilty for leaving Angel like that. And for what? A man who defined our relationship as "sleeping with" not "being with" or even "going out with".

"He's a bastard," I said to myself as I switched the water off and pushed back the shower curtain. "He's a sexy, irresistible bastard."

Then I nearly had a heart attack, because a voice replied, "That's very nice of you to say, but you don't really know me all that well yet."

There was a man in my bathroom—a dark-haired, dark-eyed, dark-clothed brooding man, a Heathcliff template—eyeing me with an expression that really could only be described as sardonic.

I stared at him for about a full minute before his eyes flickered downwards, and I remembered I was naked and pulled the shower curtain across me.

"Here," he said, and his voice was accented heavily. Irish, although I couldn't clearly tell what part of Ireland. Could have been Boston for how clearly I was thinking. He held out the towel I'd left on the rail, and I grabbed it and held it against myself while I looked for my voice. I'd had it a minute ago, where had it gone?

"Who the hell are you?" I managed eventually.

"Docherty."

Of course he was. He held out a hand, which I declined to shake for reasons of modesty.

"What are you doing in my bathroom?"

"Your door was open," he said, and I blinked.

"No, it wasn't." Was it?

"Well," Docherty gave me a slow wolf-grin, "maybe I helped it a little."

I nodded. This was insane. This was the man Luke thought could guard Angel? Was he mad?

"Why are you here?" I asked, trying to wrap the towel around me without flashing him.

"Thought I'd come and see the girl who's keeping Luke from personally protecting IC Winter's daughter."

The way he said it made me sound like one of those uptight girlfriends who get the screaming hab-dabs if their bloke so much as looks at another woman.

"Hey, this was Luke's choice—" I began, and Docherty smiled again.

"I'm not surprised."

I narrowed my eyes. I felt like he could see right through my towel.

"Could you just leave the room for a sec while I slip into something less comfortable?" I asked as politely as I could, and he smiled and walked out. I crept into the bedroom, pulled on my bathrobe and got dressed under it, just in case Docherty decided to come back in. I tied back my wet hair—very attractive, Sophie—and went out into the living room.

And nearly had another heart attack. Docherty had my SIG in his hands and was sighting at Tammy, who was looking curiously at the strange man with the strange metal thing, probably hoping it was going to dispense food.

"Jesus fucking Christ." I leapt at him before I realised the gun was half-cocked. "Don't bloody do that. Jesus." My heart was hammering. Who sent this maniac? "Don't shoot at my cat."

"I wasn't going to shoot her." Docherty calmly handed the gun back. "I was checking the sights. That's a nice piece you've got there."

"Thank you." I put it back in my bag, yanked out the Nokia and called Luke, my eyes on Docherty.

"I'm getting old here," he said.

"So am I. I think I just lost ten years. Luke, can you just tell me what this Docherty guy looks like, please?"

There was a pause, then, sounding confused, Luke said, "About my height but heavier built, dark hair, very Irish and brooding. Strong accent. Why?"

"No reason," I said. "I'm on my way." I ended the call, still looking at Docherty. "Why are you here?"

He shrugged. "IC Winter was a real catch. I've seen the pictures of her daughter. She's even better. If I was Luke I'd never let her out of my sight. Unless I had something better."

He regarded me with his head on one side, and I felt like a piece of meat. "Can we go now?"

"Where?"

"Erm, Angel's?"

"Grand plan. We'll take my car. No offence, but yours is a rust bucket."

Rule number one: you don't insult my car.

"And what do you drive?" I asked archly. Another undercover car like Luke's Vectra? Maria had an old Peugeot 205 and Macbeth usually drove whatever fell off the back of the lorry. All quiet, invisible cars.

"You'll see," he said, showing me a hint of a smile, and opened the door for me. "Ladies first."

I took my time pulling down all the shutters and locking the door and saying goodbye to Tammy, who looked heartbroken that I was leaving her all alone without even the consolation of a big heap of food, and eventually turned to Docherty, who was looking around the small courtyard that came between my flat and the car park.

"Your flowers are dying," he said without looking at me, and swung through the gate. Arrogant bastard. My flowers were fine.

I opened my mouth to tell him that I'd changed my mind and I would be going in my car, fuck whatever he'd got, when I walked around the corner and saw him opening the passenger door of an Aston Martin Vanquish.

A fucking *Vanquish*.

An Aston. A Bond car. A machine so beautiful I'd have given Luke up for it. I wanted that car. I lusted after it. I wanted to have its babies.

"You're shitting me," I said, and my mouth went on temporary strike in disgust.

"Would you like a ride?" Docherty asked, standing there looking cool in black, unaffected by the dying heat of the day, his eyes inviting, the devil asking for my soul.

And I said, "Yes," and got in.

The car—well, it was hardly a car, they should sell this thing as a marital aid. I have never ever been turned on by something as much as I was by this car. The seats were red leather and there were big sexy switches and dials all over. Docherty turned the key, flicked the F1-style gear paddles and pressed the great big red starter button and I nearly had an orgasm. The car roared and purred and shuddered, and I was right there with it.

Docherty lowered the hand brake—thankfully out of my view on his right side, because I think a great big phallic lever like that might have been too much for me—and we were off, slipping out of the car park recklessly fast, sliding to a halt at the end of the drive.

"Left or right?" Docherty asked, and I stared at him, eyes glazed. "Left or right?"

I blinked. I had no idea. "Where are we going?"

"Angel's."

"Oh." I had to think about it, but I couldn't remember which word was which direction. Eventually I pointed, and Docherty, smiling, took off.

God, it was fantastic. When I eventually recovered from the jolt and thrill of the start-up, I began to notice that people were starting to walk into lamp posts at the sight of us. When we stopped at the traffic lights, I saw one of my old schoolteachers standing at the crossing, and gave him a little wave. He waved back, stunned.

"You like the car?" Docherty asked, glancing over at me. His accent was very strong, Oirish more than Irish, slow and measured, his voice deep and smooth. I felt myself go liquid again.

"I *love* the car."

"How far is this chapel?"

I blinked. *Chapel?* "What?"

He grinned. "The chapel where your friend lives."

Oh. Calm down, girl. Save it for Luke. Next time I'm not in the mood, all I'll have to do is think of this car. Luke will never be able to keep up with me.

"A couple of miles."

"Sure you don't want to go further?"

God, yes. I wanted to go all the way.

"No," I said, my voice coming out very breathy. "Just go straight there."

It seemed to take about thirty seconds to get there, and as we rumbled up the wobbly drive, the church doors opened and Luke and Angel came out. Angel looked impressed. Luke looked stunned.

"Fuck me," he said in amazement when I opened the door and got out.

"Later," I said, then I glanced back at the Aston. "Actually, no, not later. Docherty, can we borrow this?"

He got out, grinning. "It's not been Scotchguarded."

"I don't care." Luke ran his hands over the solid curves of the car. "Jesus, where did you get this?"

"Aston factory in Newport Pagnell."

Luke rolled his eyes. "You're not going to tell me, are you?"

"Nope." They met each others' eyes and both gave a little nod in greeting. I don't suppose Alpha males like them are really into hugging. They even seemed too cool for a handshake.

Luke tore his eyes away from the car for a few seconds. "Angel, this is Docherty. He's protected film stars, politicians, big white chiefs on both sides of the Northern Irish conflict. Docherty, this is Angel. She gets about ten phone calls a day from men who are in love with her. Don't add yourself to the list."

"Why would I need to phone her," Docherty asked, looking Angel over speculatively, "when I'll be right here with her?"

Luke rolled his eyes. "Just don't," he said.

"Home-wrecker," I added, watching Docherty watch Angel go inside the church.

"Lifesaver," Luke corrected. He considered it for a second. "Yeah, and home-wrecker too. How'd you find him?"

"He found me. In the shower."

"Yeah, that's Docherty for you." Luke made to follow them inside but I pulled him back by his T-shirt and flicked my eyes at the Aston sitting there looking sexy.

"That's a hot car," I said, and Luke nodded, his eyes on the sculpted air intakes. "Don't you think it's really," I kissed his neck and looked up at him, "hot?"

Luke flicked his eyes down at me suspiciously. "Ye-es..."

"And you haven't even had a ride in it." I looked up again through fluttering lashes. "Would you like a ride?"

Luke frowned and touched my forehead. "Sophie, are you okay?"

Since when did it get so hard to seduce this guy? I rolled my eyes at the car, which gleamed like the huge, throbbing beast I knew it was.

"Don't you think that car is the sexiest thing you've ever seen?"

Luke paused warily. "Is this a test? Am I supposed to say you're sexier?"

I stamped my foot. "No, Luke, you're supposed to shag me. I'm more turned on than I think I've ever been. I'm about to explode here."

At that his eyes gleamed. "Really?" He ran a hand down my back and skimmed his fingers over my buttocks. "How close are you?"

"If you don't help me, I'll explode all by myself."

That did it. Luke grabbed the back of my head and bit my lower lip. "That crypt Angel mentioned..."

"I am not having sex in a crypt!"

He licked my lips and I shuddered. Maybe the crypt wasn't such a bad idea. After all—

"Buffy did," Luke said, and I shuddered again, because he'd read my mind. And then I glanced at the Aston, silent and brooding in the moonlight, and I smiled slowly at Luke. "Up against the car."

Luke blinked. "Seriously?" I nodded. "Where anyone could see us? Thought you didn't—"

"Against the car or nowhere," I said firmly, getting quite desperate now.

Luke looked at the car. Then he looked at Angel's closed door. Then he looked at me.

"You're that desperate?"

I doubted I'd last until he got my knickers off. "Becoming less desperate the more you procrastinate," I said as airily as I could.

Luke grinned and lifted me up against the car's curved flank and flipped my fly undone. "Liar," he breathed into my mouth.

"Luke," I said, playing with the hair at the back of his neck, "you're a spy. I'm a spy. This is an Aston Martin. Fuck me."

He gave me a slow grin. "Love to."

Angel shook her head at us when we went in. "You two are incorrigible," she said.

"You better not have messed up my paint work," Docherty warned, taking in my mussed-up hair and flushed cheeks.

"I don't know what you're talking about," I said.

"We were just," Luke glanced at me, "briefing each other."

"Stop," Angel held up a hand. "Please."

Luke grinned and pulled me over to one of the sofas, slipping his arm around me so I could snuggle up against him. Angel and Docherty exchanged glances.

"I've told him about the letters and the e-mails," Angel said. "About that camera flash we saw the other day, Soph."

Mmm, Luke had a nice chest. All warm and hard. Maybe we could just borrow Angel's bed for a bit—

No! Concentrate, Sophie. "That was, what, two nights ago? And nothing since."

She shook her head. "The photos yesterday." She walked over to her desk and took an envelope out of a drawer. "The real ones went to Karen so she could check them for prints, but we made copies." She gestured to the scanner and photo-quality printer half-hidden by the roll-top of the bureau.

"So they're on your hard drive?" I asked, as Angel handed the pictures to Docherty. "Can you e-mail them to me?"

"If you checked your inbox more often," Luke said, "you'd see I already have."

I made a face at him, but I was still too tingly and relaxed to be in any way mad at him. He'd kept whispering things like, "460 break," and "48-valve, V12," to me. It was when he said, "Top speed 190," that I broke. All that speed, all that power. God. I forced myself to think of bike crashes and murder.

But even that was still disturbingly sexy.

"Have you accessed the autopsy report on it?" Docherty asked, looking at the pictures.

"Tried," Luke said. "It's blocked. Maria's at Thames House now trying to get something out of them."

"Where?" I said.

"MI5," Luke said, shaking his head. Well, it's not my fault I didn't know that. It's his fault for not telling me.

"Maria de Valera?" Docherty asked.

Luke nodded, grinning.

"Christ. Didn't think she'd still be alive."

"Very much so," Luke said, but before I could ask how they all knew each other, when Luke had come to SO17 from the SAS and Maria from the SBS and Docherty didn't look like he'd be allowed past the checkpoint on any military barracks, my Siemens started ringing. I looked at the display. Home.

"I'll just be a sec," I said, reluctantly leaving Luke and going through into the bedroom to talk to my mother.

"Are you coming home for tea tonight?" she asked, and I stared blankly at the Gaudi print above Angel's bed. Hadn't I told her I'd be on nights all this week? Shouldn't I be at work by now?

While I was formulating a reply, my mother went on, "We're having pies. I got you a McCartney one."

Damn. She knows I love them. And she knows I'll feel guilty that she went out of her way to get vegetarian food for me so I'll come to tea.

"We're having Yorkshires," she added, and I sighed.

"What time?"

"About an hour?"

"Sure." I was about to go when my mother asked me something really stupid.

"Aren't you supposed to be at work?"

Gaudi's lovers seemed to be laughing at me. I squinted closer, and realised that it wasn't a print, it was the real deal. "Yes," I said in exasperation, "so why are you calling me?"

"Is Angel working?" My mother managed to completely ignore my question. "Does she want to come too?"

My mother is always inviting my friends over. I barely have to do it anymore. If someone so much as drops me at my parents' house Mum is there offering them coffee or a cold drink or something, there's *Buffy* on TV, show her those shoes you bought, Soph, do you want to stay for tea? We're having pizza with dough balls.

"I—erm, well, she's—I'll ask her and call you back."

I ended the call, scowled at the Gaudi lovers, and went back into the nave. Luke had a can of Director's (how come Angel had beer in her fridge?) and was frowning over the photos. Docherty was reading the e-mails, Angel standing very close behind him.

I opened my mouth to ask Angel if she wanted to come and have dinner at my parents' house, when a thought struck me. So Luke had never really met my parents. Why not now? I think two months is plenty late enough to meet someone's parents. And they were nice people. Not scary or insane or anything. Well, not noticeably.

"Who was that?" Luke asked, looking up.

"My mother. She—er, I'm going over there for tea. In about an hour. Do you want to come?"

"No, thanks," Luke said, and went back to the photos.

No thanks? Not even, "No, I'm too busy" or "No, I'm nervous about meeting them." Or even "No, this relationship is about sex, not meeting parents." Just "No thanks".

I walked back over to the sofa and picked up my bag, intending to calmly replace my phone and go back to looking at the photos. Asking Angel to tea had completely slid out of my mind. But instead, I put the phone away, looked down at Luke, and heard my voice say, "Why not?"

He blinked up at me. "Why not what?"

"Why don't you want to come to tea? You don't even know what we're having. My mum's a great cook."

"I'm sure she is."

"So why don't you—" *Stoppit*, I told myself, *don't mess it up*, "—why don't you want to come?"

He shrugged. "No reason."

I meant to leave it there, I really did, in the same way I meant to put my mobile away and say nothing else on the subject. But my mouth just blabbered on.

"Luke," I said, and I sounded plaintive, and I could hear that Docherty had stopped typing on the computer and I knew he and Angel had front-row seats. "Just give me a reason. In the two months we've been—" oh God, what have we been? A couple? Seeing each other? Enthusiastically shagging? "—in two months you haven't expressed the slightest interest in meeting my family."

"You've never expressed an interest in mine," Luke said, and I felt my blood boil at his reasonable tone. It was true, but then they didn't just live down the road. Mine did. I went there all the time.

"Are they as emotionally unavailable as you?" I asked meanly.

"Fuck off."

"Precisely."

Luke let out a tight sigh and put down the photos. "Sophie, can I talk to you?"

"What are we doing now?"

"Arguing in front of someone I hardly know and someone you don't know at all, even though you've just had sex up against his car."

"I did not need to hear that," Docherty said.

I ignored him and narrowed my eyes at Luke. "Fine," I said, and in the absence of anywhere else to go, stalked—yes, the occasion fully called for stalking—outside, Luke following me closely.

"What the hell is wrong with you?" he asked when we were alone, although I knew if I turned my head I'd see Angel and Docherty watching through the window.

"What's wrong with me?" I stared at him. "What's wrong with you? I am trying to have a conversation about what is wrong with our relationship—"

"What relationship?" Luke said, and I got in the car and drove home.

Chapter Five

My phone kept ringing all the way home, but I ignored it. I thought I saw lights following me, so I pulled off the road into a field and cut my lights, waiting until the car had gone past. Then I realised Luke would go to my flat if he was going to follow me anywhere, so I turned Ted across the field—bugger the farmer—and drove the long way around to my parents'.

When I got there I was vastly relieved to see Luke's Vectra wasn't in the drive. I locked Ted up and let myself in, surprising my mother in the kitchen.

"You're early!"

Nice of her to sound so surprised. I have been known to be early occasionally. Hell, I was born two days early. That sets a pattern, right?

"Yeah. Had nothing else to do. Angel's not coming, she's, er, she's not feeling well."

"What's up with her?"

"Cold," I said. Easiest option. This was England. Everyone had a cold at some point.

"Hope you haven't caught it," said my mother, Florence Nightingale in training.

"No. I'm fine. When's tea ready?"

"Forty-five minutes."

I nodded as my mobile started to ring again, and ran from the room. It was Luke, and I cancelled the call.

What relationship? What fucking relationship? I mean, I never expected it to be a full-blown boyfriend-girlfriend, mini-breaks in the country, holding hands in public, naming our future children sort of thing, but I at least thought that we had some sort of relationship, even if it was based completely on sex and sarcasm. Surely I meant something to him other than a reliable shag?

I stomped up the stairs and started pulling books off their shelves in the spare room, trying to find something about IC and Greg Winter. My dad came in, apparently alerted by the thuds from all the books I was chucking on the floor, and asked what I was doing.

"Walking the bloody dog," I snarled.

"Okay," my dad said cautiously. "Your mum says you were looking for some books on the Winters?"

"Where are they?"

He went into my old room and came out with a box. "They've been in the loft for ages. Bit musty."

I found a smile for him. "Thanks, Dad."

He smiled and went back downstairs. There was football on, which was why I hadn't gone into the sitting room when I arrived. I have a sixth sense for this sort of thing.

I started looking through the biographies and retrospectives. Greg Winter was always my dad's favourite songwriter, he has every album on CD and most on rather valuable vinyl, too. He also had a bit of thing for IC Winter, and there were quite a few glossy coffee table books on her in the box.

I picked one up. It was called *A Winter's Day* and was full of pictures of IC. She'd been beautiful, really beautiful, glowing even in faded black and white pictures. She had one of those smiles that make you want to smile, too. I read the caption. "Despite the froideur her name suggested, Imogen Carmen was a very warm person who always enjoyed spending time with her daughter, Angelique..."

I came across a picture of her and Angel, dressed in identical outfits, taken when Angel was about four, and got a lump in my throat. If my mother died, I don't know what I'd do, and I'm a grown-up now. Angel had been eleven when her mother had finally succumbed to a brain tumour, and twelve when her father had died in that crash.

Been killed in that crash. But the books said nothing about that. No one at all seemed to know anything at all about the MI5 connections. The books all said the same thing about Greg's death—that he'd been found by a passing motorist some ten hours after he'd fallen from the bike, somewhere remote in North Yorkshire. I made a mental note to find out who'd found the body and what state they found it in. There'd been twenty-four pictures in the envelope Angel had been sent. It was entirely possible that the killer had run out of film, not nasty ideas.

My phone started vibrating again: I'd long since turned off the volume because it annoyed me so much. I glanced at the display. Maria.

"Hey," I said, glad that it wasn't Luke, but also kind of wishing it was. I didn't want him to give up so easily.

"Hey yourself. What did you do to Luke? He went mental on me when I asked where you were."

Oh, joy. "I didn't do anything to him. He said we had no relationship. I got in the car and left." Well, actually, I'd had to stomp back inside for my bag first, which slightly ruined the effect, but the principle was there.

"He said you had no relationship?" Maria sucked in her breath. "How dumb is he?"

"I know—" I began, but ran out of steam when I heard Maria's next words.

"You never tell someone there's no relationship, even when there isn't."

"You—you thought there wasn't?"

"You thought there was?"

This could go on.

"Look," Maria said in a kinder tone of voice, "this is Luke we're talking about. He's a commitment-free zone. I'd like to say he has issues, but really he's just a bastard when it comes to women. He doesn't have time for a relationship and even if he did, work would still come a victorious first."

I closed my eyes. Maria had told me all this before.

"Yeah," I said eventually. "I know. I'm just being stupid. I shouldn't have said it, or thought it. I shouldn't have done any of it."

"Now that's just silly," Maria said. "You enjoyed it, no one was hurt—" *I* damn well was, "—so just enjoy the memory. Thank you for the music and all that."

"You think we should end it?"

"I think if you're starting to think in relationship terms about Luke, then yes. Stop shagging him now before it becomes addictive and you can't stop. Dump him before he dumps you."

"How can I dump him?" I said bravely. "We have no relationship. I'm just cutting him off."

Even as I said it I felt my stomach twist. No more Luke. What was I doing to myself? How damn stupid was I being?

"Good girl," Maria said approvingly. "Now, do you want to hear my news?"

"Yes. Please."

"The archivist at Thames House is really cute."

I rolled my eyes. "That's the news?"

"No, that's an extra. The news is I got access to the files on IC and Greg."

"Excellent. Hard copy or disk?"

"Both. With threats of death if I let any details leak…"

"Yada yada yada. What does it say? The Greg one. How did he die?"

"Cause of death—why did you ask me about this yesterday?"

"I had a hunch. Tell me!"

"Cause of death was a broken neck. *But*," Maria paused dramatically, and I drummed my fingers on the picture of IC and Angel, "he was also found to have finger marks on the neck, as though someone had helped his neck to break. No prints, the killer was wearing gloves. Also he had a bullet in his shoulder, a .22, not bad enough to kill him but enough to get him off his bike."

"Ha!" I said, and told her about the photos.

"Luke mentioned them," she said. "He said it was clear it wasn't an accident."

"Not at all." I paused, a horrible thought having occurred to me. "Maria, what about IC? How did she die?"

"Brain tumour," Maria said, as if it was obvious. "Didn't you know?"

"Yes, but then I also knew Greg fell off his bike."

"Good point, well made. No, it was definitely a tumour. There're medical records I'm assuming our supreme commander will understand. They mean bollock-all to me."

It was gratifying to know that there was something Maria didn't excel at.

"So what about Luke?" she said, and I sighed, because for five minutes there my mind had been diverted.

"I suppose I'll have to end it," I said.

"It's for the best."

"Umm. Don't suppose you fancy calling him up to tell him he's dumped?" I asked hopefully.

"You're not twelve any more."

"I thought you'd say that. Wish me luck."

"Good luck. And no goodbye shags."

"Meanie."

I ended the call and stared at the books, but they gave me nothing. Greg and IC had met at an awards ceremony, dated, got engaged then married and had a baby, all in the public eye, all sweet and romantic and lovely. Not sordid and emotionless.

I'd call Luke after tea. It was nearly time to eat anyway. I'd think better on a full stomach.

I went downstairs, trying to think of some way to tell him it was over without creating a huge incriminating void that would taint our working lives, or worse, letting him think he'd won. Of course I knew we had no relationship, I'd always known that, the word slipped out. I just thought it'd be best if we kept our relationship professional. It wouldn't do to get clouded by personal concerns.

Yeah.

The football was just ending and I sat down with a big glass of water, glancing at the wine bottle on the table longingly. No. I had to stay sober. If I had a drink then I'd probably end up chickening out.

Unless I had one for Dutch courage.

No. That would not be smart.

The worst part, I thought as I chewed a carrot and let my parents argue about what to put on telly, was that I'd known this would happen all along. I knew Luke wasn't going to turn to me and say he loved me. I knew there was nothing in it that wasn't work- or sex-related. But I still wanted more. I think. Maybe not with Luke specifically, but I wanted some sort of future with some sort of nice man.

By the time Chalker handed me the tub of ice cream that was as sophisticated as dessert ever got in our house, I had persuaded myself that Luke didn't deserve me, that I should be with a great man who was sweet and kind as well as sexy, and would think about the future of our relationship, instead of just telling me we didn't have one.

In fact, by the time the doorbell rang, I was fully convinced that Luke was a complete rat bag and what he really deserved was a kick up the arse for taking me for granted.

"You look like you're planning to murder someone," Chalker said, as my dad went to answer the door.

"I always look like this," I said, swallowing my ice cream forcefully, and it was a good job, because otherwise I might have choked when my dad walked back in and said in a puzzled voice, "Sophie, do you know anyone called Luke?"

I nearly dropped the ice cream. "Luke?"

"Says he's a friend of yours."

"Oh, no, he's bloody not," I growled, getting up and stomping out of the room as my mother's voice floated after me, "Is he the really cute one who brought you home that time?"

And there he was, standing in the porch because it was raining, looking dishevelled and sexy. Not cute. Luke would have had cute for breakfast.

"Cute, am I?" he said, looking amused.

"No," I said. "What are you doing here?"

"You weren't answering your phone."

"So you followed me?"

"I need to talk to you."

I sighed. "Okay, but not here."

He made to come inside but I blocked him. "What? Thought you wanted me to meet your parents."

"I changed my mind." I glanced out into the rain. It was really chucking it down. Had I been so self-absorbed that I hadn't even noticed that?

I grabbed my bag from the newel post and brandished Ted's keys. "Out here."

Luke looked amazed, but he followed me to the car and, when we got in, leaned over to kiss me.

"Luke, don't."

He pulled back sharply, looking hurt and confused. "You—"

"I didn't want to argue in the house. It's—" how to say it? "—it's over."

He stared at me, and I repeated myself to fill the silence.

Luke tore his gaze away, staring hard at the dash. Not at me. "Over?" he said eventually.

I nodded. "This can't work. You and me," I said, aware I was echoing what he'd said only the night before when we'd made out in the domestic satellite. "I—it's been great," yeah, give him something, "but it can't go on."

"Are you breaking up with me?" Luke said incredulously, and I could well believe it had never happened before.

"Don't you have to have a relationship to break up?"

"Is this because I said—"

"It's not because you said that, but it made me realise that you don't want a relationship and I do," I said, feeling very adult. "I can't separate sex from emotion like you and I don't think it would be very smart to get involved in any kind of relationship outside of our work together," I finished, pleased with myself.

There was a silence, then Luke said flatly, "Sex and emotion."

"Yes."

"I don't tangle one up with the other."

"Good for you," I said, offering a small smile which wasn't returned.

There was another silence. Luke stared at the rainy windscreen.

"No more sex," he said, and something inside me twisted.

"No," I said, meaning to say more but suddenly floored by a double attack of lust and tears. See? Sex and emotion. All together, now.

"So I'll go," Luke said, and I croaked, "Probably best if you do."

He was still a second longer, then he looked at me, then he was gone. I heard his car bumping away over the ruts in the drive, and I put my head on the steering wheel and felt hot tears trickling down my cheeks.

I don't know how long I sat there like that, but it was long enough that I eventually stopped crying and lifted my head, sniffing. It could have been worse. I could have cried in front of him.

I wiped my eyes and put my hand on the door, but as I did the passenger door opened and I turned to tell Luke to go away.

But it wasn't Luke. It was a man with a balaclava and a gun, and he said in a gravely voice, "Drive."

I stared at him for a second, utterly shocked. Through the blurry windscreen I could see the TV in the sitting room. Chalker was sitting there flicking through the music channels. I was sitting here with a gun pointed at my head.

"I don't drive so well with a gun aimed at me," I said, and he shook his head.

"Drive."

I opened my bag, and he waved the gun at me. "No," he said, and his voice was heavily accented, and I realised he probably didn't speak much English. He grabbed my hand. "No. Drive."

I rolled my eyes, trying not to shake. "My keys are in the bag," I said, making what I hoped looked like key motions with my hands, but what were probably filthy things in sign language. "Keys, to start the car?" I pointed at the ignition, and the man grunted.

I took that as assent, fished around in my bag and found my gun.

No. Didn't want to have to clean blood out of the car again.

Illegal stun gun. Excellent.

I manoeuvred the prongs to the outside edge of my bag, letting it fall against his leg, my heart thumping, hoping this would work, and pressed the button.

Nothing.

Damn bloody thing was out of charge. Phones, cameras, tasers, they all run out of juice when you need them.

Balaclava Guy was getting anxious now, waving the gun and going, "Drive! You! Drive! Yes!" He sounded kind of stupid, and there's nothing like a language barrier to get you really pissed off with someone. I pulled out my SIG and aimed it at him.

"No," I said. "I will not drive. I don't know how much you know about guns but this here is a nine millimetre and it will kill you if I pull the trigger. And I've just split up with the best sex I've ever had and am ever likely to have, so I am *not* in a good mood. And I hate to sound like a man but," I ran my eyes over his revolver, "mine's bigger than yours."

For a second we stared at each other while I willed my hands to stop shaking. He didn't lower his gun, so I sucked in a breath and shot his gun arm.

It probably wasn't the cleverest thing to do, and I was pretty sure someone would have heard, but no one came rushing out of my house because, I suspect, they're all too damn lazy. This was the country: it was an old house and there were game shooters and farmers around. If you heard a loud noise, generally you ignored it. Balaclava Guy was shrieking and clutching his arm, where there was a lot of blood that I'd have to clean up later. His gun had fallen into his lap and I picked it up, opened the barrel like Luke had shown me, and emptied the bullets into my hand.

Now what to do? Balaclava Guy was still whinging and mumbling in whatever language he spoke. I couldn't leave him there and go back inside. I didn't want to call Luke.

I fished around for my handcuffs, and when I couldn't find them, flipped open the cubby box between the seats.

Balaclava Guy tried to make an escape, but I waved my gun at him. "I can shoot you again if you want?"

He looked at me with fear in his eyes, and shook his head.

"Good. Glad we understand each other." There was a length of rope in the box, useful when pulling things out of the mud. Ted was very good at pulling things out of the mud. I used the rope to tie Balaclava Guy to the seat, binding his wrists together, ignoring his foreign protests, and sent a text to Chalker.

Going to see Angel. Not back tonight. Then I drove off, out of the village and up towards the office, feeling very pleased with myself.

When I got there, I realised I was probably going to need some kind of help getting Balaclava Guy out of the car. And possibly he might need some medical attention, too. I wanted to find out who he was before he bled to death.

I sat there for a while, Balaclava Guy whimpering annoyingly, and thought. First off, I wasn't going to call Luke. Not only did I need to take a break from him for now, I also didn't want to have to run to him every time I needed help with something. My warrant card said I was a special agent. I could damn well look after myself.

I checked my watch. Half past nine. Maria.

"I need your help," I said when she answered.

"What kind of help?" she asked cautiously. "If this is about Luke, I'm not—"

"It's not about Luke. I have a...a situation here. I need you to help me out."

"What kind of situation?"

"One that requires assistance," I said through gritted teeth, not sure how much Balaclava Guy understood.

She asked where I was, sounding intrigued when I told her, and said she'd be there in fifteen minutes. She turned up in twelve.

"Impressive," I said, running my eyes over her little red 205, which was panting and shuddering.

"Felt like breaking the limit," she said. "Who's this guy?"

"Dunno. He turned up and told me to drive. Not sure how much English he speaks."

"He's injured..."

"Yes." I twirled my gun and nearly dropped it. "He drew on me so I drew on him. And then I shot him."

"Anywhere fatal?"

"Lower arm."

"Oh." She looked disappointed. "You want to put him downstairs?"

"Yep."

"Okay." She went to her car and got a mucky rag out of the door bucket, the sort you use to wipe condensation off windows. "He needs blindfolding."

Good plan. Why hadn't I thought of that?

Balaclava Guy could walk okay, so Maria guided him up the ramp into the office, her own ten millimetre Glock pressed to his head as a reminder. I swiped my red pass on the control panel and unlocked the door, and when we were in, went to the bookshelf on the right hand wall and took off a file. There was another control panel there, and I swiped my card again, keyed in a code and glanced at Maria.

"Can you block his ears? I really should have chosen another thing for my voice recognition."

She grinned and pressed the gun against one balaclava'd ear, and her hand against the other. "Go ahead."

I spoke my name into the microphone, the control panel lit up, and the bookshelf broke in half and slid apart to reveal a little steel elevator.

"Remind me," Maria said, "to change mine as well. Giving your name is not a smart thing to do."

The lift went down one storey—at least I think it's only one storey—and swooshed open onto a small but very expensively decked out lab. At the end of the lab was a small cage, its bars set into thick glass that could be hidden behind steel shutters if we wanted. We pulled Balaclava Guy over and Maria lifted her gun and cracked him on the head with it.

"I should have a heavier gun," she said as he went down. "That took more effort than it used to with my Browning."

"Won't have killed him, will it?"

"Nah. Just keep him quiet." She took off the window rag and pulled the balaclava away with it, and it occurred to me that she could easily have just turned the balaclava around to block his eyes. But then that wouldn't have been as much fun, would it?

He was reasonably good-looking, I was surprised to see, with high, Slavic cheekbones and messy dark hair. Yeah. He could easily have been quite cute, if he hadn't tried to kill me.

You know, I never thought I'd have to say that more than once.

Maria pushed up his shirt sleeve and checked the bullet wound. "Nice job," she said, going over to one of the cupboards, which all required swipe-card entry, and getting a pair of large tweezers out. She extracted my bullet, put it in a metal bowl in the one of the refrigerated cupboards, then cleaned and wrapped a bandage around the wound. While she did this I checked his pockets for ID, and found a Czech passport.

"Interesting," Maria said. "And also incredibly stupid. Who carries their passport around with them?"

I hoped she wouldn't be going through my bag any time soon.

"Staszic, Petr," I read. "Twenty-eight. Occupation: civil servant."

"Doesn't look very civil to me," Maria said. "You want to leave him here?"

"Last time I did that someone escaped."

"That was because of insider treachery," Maria said. "Text everyone there's someone down here. That'll do."

I drove back home with Shawn Colvin on the ghetto blaster to calm me down. It'd been a hell of a day. This time yesterday I was greeting sunburnt holidaymakers with Angel. This time yesterday I knew I'd have Luke to go back to.

He called me a couple of hours after I got in, and he sounded pissed off.

"What did you do this time?"

I felt myself prickle. "I didn't do anything," I sniffed, then added suspiciously, "Why are you asking?"

"The unconscious and bleeding Czech in the lab."

Oh, him. "That wasn't my fault. He got in my car."

"When?"

"Just after you left."

"Christ." He paused. "You okay?"

I picked at a thread on my pyjamas and reached for another Pringle. "I'm fine. He pulled a gun on me but I shot him."

"You're sure he was armed? You didn't shoot an unarmed man?"

I glared at the phone. "I have his gun if you want to see it."

"Any good?"

"How the hell should I know?"

Luke sighed. "Did you knock him out?"

"Maria did."

He sighed again. "Why was Maria there?"

"Because I called her." Idiot.

"Why didn't you call me?"

I was silent for a bit but he didn't seem to be working it out. "Do I really need to answer that?"

"I thought we were having a professional relationship."

"Yes, but not tonight."

Luke sighed a third time. "I'll see you tomorrow?"

"I guess," I said, thinking, *Not if I see you first.*

And then I couldn't sleep.

The first thing that kept me awake was Petr Staszic. Why was he there? Where did he want me to go? Who sent him? I was having trouble believing anyone that incompetent would be acting on their own directions.

Although, look at me.

Why did he want me? He must have been following me to know I was at my parents'— Oh God, the car in my rear mirror!

In the grip of curiosity and insomnia, I pulled a flannel shirt on over the shorts and bra top I slept in, shoved my feet into my trainers and took Ted out for a midnight run. I parked up on the lane outside my parents' house and got out my flashlight, hoping the neighbours wouldn't think I was a burglar.

There was no car anywhere visible. I checked for about half a mile in either direction, then the fields around the house, and

I was about to give in to the cold and go home when I saw something glinting under the hedgerow.

Around here there were very few hedgerows left. Farmers have pulled them all up top make bigger fields that are easier to plough, and then edge their land with fences or rows of regular hedge. There weren't many thick, micro-environment, proper hedgerows left, and I'd bet my last fiver that there was only one with a motorbike under it.

And that hedgerow was right here in front of me.

Now, I know naff-all about bikes, but I could tell this one was cheap and nasty just looking at it. It wasn't very heavy and it was very simple—if rather wet and muddy—to pick up and carry to my car. The very best thing about having a Defender is that you can fit a motorbike in the back. Well, okay, not the very best thing, but a damn useful feature.

I was just shutting up the back of the car when a torch flashed on my face and a voice said, "I don't think that's yours."

I turned, my hand shielding my eyes, and began, "Yes, but—"

Then my ears kick-started my brain, and my eyes got in motion too, and I realised the man with the torch was Harvey.

"What are you doing here?"

He looked confused. "What are you doing here?"

"I live here. Well, used to. That's my parents' house. The owner of this bike ambushed me this evening. So I'm impounding it."

"Impounding?"

"Well, confiscating, really. I could learn to ride a bike."

"More of a scooter, really," Harvey said, peering through the back window. He swung the beam of the torch back on me. "Ambushed, you said? Are you okay?"

"Better than him. What *are* you doing here?"

"Waiting."

"Waiting?"

"I followed a guy on a scooter up here hours ago." He gestured to a car parked in one of the neighbours' drives. How thick was I? How didn't I notice there was actually someone in that car? "He went up the drive but didn't come back down."

"He came with me. Why were you following him?"

"He works for a guy I've been tracking. Dmitri Janulevic."

I shook my head. "What'd he do?"

Harvey made a face. "Nothing yet. But he has before, and he's gonna this time. I've been all over after him."

"All over?"

"China. Russia. Czech Republic. And now here."

Aw. I was touched we'd been included in such an exotic list.

"Well, the biker's name is Petr Staszic," I said. "However you pronounce it. I don't speak Czech."

"I do," Harvey said.

Hello.

Five minutes later, I had him blindfolded in the back of the car—the passenger seat still being a little bloody—and on the way to the office. I took him down to the lab and pulled off the blindfold.

"Ta-da."

"This is the SO17 headquarters?"

"Well, it's sort of just quarters. We're very small."

Harvey gave me a lightning once-over, a slight smile on his face.

"Don't," I warned. "My ego's already had quite a bashing today."

"I wasn't gonna say anything uncomplimentary."

"Hmm." I went over to the cage and unlocked the shutters. They clanged back and Harvey stared at Petr.

"What did you do to him?"

"Nothing! Well, apart from shooting. But he had a gun on me."

"Fair enough." Harvey, from the Land of the Free, shrugged.

"Maria knocked him unconscious. We were planning on coming back in the morning."

"Is this standard hostage procedure?"

"It's standard procedure for people who attack me."

"I'll bear that in mind," Harvey said, and walked over. "Is there an intercom?"

I nodded and switched it on. Then I set up the vid camera I'd brought down with me, and said loudly to Petr, "Wake up."

He did, with a jolt, and babbled something in Czech.

"What did he say?"

"He's not Czech."

"He said that?"

"No, he said, 'What's going on?' But he said it in Russian."

"You speak Russian?"

"Of course." Harvey, old-school CIA, gave me a bewildered look.

"It's on my to-do list," I said. "Ask him where he's from."

The answer came back as, "Russia."

"So why did he have a Czech passport?"

"He's a Czech citizen."

"Dual nationality?"

Harvey paused to remember the word, and when he did there was another pause, this time from Petr.

"*Da*," he said cautiously, and Harvey and I looked at each other and shook our heads.

"Ask him something in Czech," I said. "Something complex."

Harvey rolled out a question and Petr gave a hopeful smile. "*Da?*"

"He doesn't speak a word of it," Harvey said. "I asked him if he was into sado-masochistic sex with foreign lesbians in the basements of Bavarian castles."

I couldn't help laughing. "Well, maybe he is."

We looked at Petr, huddled there looking afraid.

"Maybe not. Okay, ask him why he was following me."

"Orders."

"What orders?"

Harvey frowned as he listened to the reply. "To take you to his boss."

"Who is...?"

I didn't need a translation. "Dmitri Janulevic. Well, you were right. What does Janulevic want with me?"

Petr kept looking up at me like an abused puppy as he explained. Maybe he thought I'd be a soft touch.

Ha!

"Well?" I asked Harvey.

"Janulevic wanted you," he said. "That's pretty much all he'll say."

"Why?" I insisted.

Harvey repeated the question, but Petr shook his head.

"Is it to do with Angel?" I said, and Harvey said, "Who's Angel?"

"The blonde. Lakeside?"

His eyes lit up. "Her name is Angel?"

"Yup. Ask him."

He did, and Petr looked confused. "IC Winter?" I asked. "Greg Winter?"

Petr shook his head, but he did it a fraction too late. I grabbed Harvey's arm. "It's about Angel."

"What? How come? What's going on?"

I shook my head, glancing at Petr. "I still don't trust that he's not listening in. Come on. We can come back later if we think of anything else."

"We?"

"Your case, my case. Is this coincidence or are you following me?"

"Coincidence," Harvey said, but I wasn't sure I believed him.

Back in the car, I let him pull off his blindfold after a couple of miles. "You really don't want me to know where that was, do you?"

"Can't take any chances," I said. "Sorry." Was I like a real secret agent, or what?

Don't answer that.

"Well, yeah, I guess." Harvey looked out of the window. "Isn't that the school where we caught those guys a couple months ago?"

"We? You disappeared and I had to do it all by myself."

"I went for back-up."

"I nearly got killed."

"Hey, we got there in time. Calm down."

I rolled my eyes at him through the rear-view. "I'm calm. I'm just saying."

"Me too. If you hadn't gone off without your partner—"

"He's *not* my partner," I said, perhaps a little more violently than I needed to.

Harvey raised an eyebrow. "From what your friend said at Lakeside—"

"Well, she was wrong. It was wrong. He's not my partner. He's just my colleague. End of."

Harvey had the good sense to keep quiet.

We went back to my house. It was still the middle of the night and, despite my daytime nap, I was knackered. All I wanted to do was go to bed.

"Nice place," Harvey said, looking around my habitat. It was a tip, but then it always was. I was never into the tidy thing. Don't see the point. I have a good memory for where things are. Usually they're just under some other things. "You live here by yourself?"

Loaded question.

"No, I share with Tammy."

He looked surprised. "And who's Tammy?"

"My flatmate."

Harvey looked around. Open-plan living room, bedroom, bathroom. One double bed.

"Erm..."

I grinned. "She's a cat. Very small. Hardly takes up any space."

He looked relieved. "For a second there I thought—but then the thing with Luke..."

"There is no thing with Luke."

Harvey bit his lip. "There was on Sunday."

"No," I kicked off my trainers, "apparently there wasn't. I don't want to talk about it. I want to go to bed." I grabbed my sleeping bag from under the bed and dumped it on the sofa for him. "Have a nice night."

"Sophie, wait."

I turned, but I didn't want to. The Luke thing had upset me more than I'd bargained for. I needed to go somewhere quiet and bawl into my pillow.

"I'm sorry if I upset you. I thought you and Luke were an item."

"Yes, well, so did I. Apparently I was mistaken. But the mistake has been cleared up."

"So…you're not together?"

I don't think we ever were. "No."

"And this is a recent thing?"

I looked at the clock. "About six hours."

"Ah. Okay. Sorry I brought it up." He yawned. "That girl—Angel?"

"Yes?"

"She single?"

I smiled. How cute would that be? "As far as I know."

"Excellent. You can tell me all about her in the morning."

Chapter Six

Morning came all too quickly, and I'd forgotten there was anyone else in the flat until I pounced on Harvey in the kitchen. He looked surprised, then he took my SIG and weighed it in his hands.

"Nice piece. You always greet guests like this?"

"Only when I forget about them."

The thought crossed my mind that he was probably thinking this was exactly why Luke and I had broken up. Which was ironic, because Luke got turned on by me with my gun. He said it was the ultimate danger.

Come to think of it, that's not much of a compliment.

I made a lot of strong coffee and drank most of it myself. Harvey seemed surprised that I was drinking instant, not filter, but I suppose that's Americans for you. He went for orange juice. Purist.

"So what's your plan for today?" he asked. "Apart from telling me all about Angel." He looked off into the distance—or at least, an imaginary distance, the wall being about four feet away.

"Ah, yes, Angel."

"What does she have to do with Janulevic?"

I shrugged. "Beats me." I had another agenda. "What do *you* have to do with Janulevic?"

Harvey drained his orange juice. He looked good in the morning, his shiny hair all tousled, a little bit of stubble humanising the total perfection of his *American Idol* face. He'd been wearing only boxers when I happened upon him nosing through my kitchen cupboards, but he'd quickly got dressed again in his black jeans and T-shirt. I was beginning to realise that people like us (doesn't that sound *cool*?) had a lot of black in their wardrobes. This suited me fine, because black is very slimming and it goes with everything. Except summer.

"Janulevic is after something," Harvey said. "He's an Indiana Jones without the coolness. We don't know what it is, only that he's talked to a lot of ancient historians about it. Archaeologists. Antiques men. Museums—he's broken into a few."

"Anything taken?"

"Archives. Records. He's looking for something specific, but we still can't tell what. He's taken records of ancient Chinese, Egyptian, and Romany artefacts."

"Then how do you know it's something specific?"

"Because he's come across plenty of Chinese, Egyptian and Romany artefacts and left them all alone. Not even touched them."

"You've talked to the people he's talked to?"

Harvey made a face. "Slight problem there."

I knew what it was. "They're all dead?"

"Every last one. And the few we thought we might pre-empt are denying all knowledge of anything ancient at all."

I folded my arms. "I don't get it. Why is the CIA interested in him?"

"A tip-off. Head of Ancient History at Michigan told us there was something coming. He said it was like a plague—like Tutankhamun's curse. Professors dropping dead all over the globe. But we smelled a rat—or more to the point, my boss, who is a buddy of the aforementioned professor, did. Not to mention that if this thing is real... Well, we don't want it in the wrong hands."

I wondered privately who got to decide whose hands were the right ones, but kept my mouth shut. "The Michigan professor?"

"He's under protection—they all are. Oxford and Cambridge too. We spoke to the people at the British Museum—told them not to speak to anyone. But one girl said a few rumours had reached her. She heard a whisper about some Mongol artefact called the Xe La. But no one knows what it is. Just some reference in a book—"

"Which has now disappeared?"

"Right. And the only people who could have told us about it..."

"Are dead."

"You're smart."

"One of my many good qualities." I yawned. "I'm going to go and have a shower." I needed to think about this.

"No," Harvey said, "you're going to play fair and tell me what you know. Why did you think this involved Angel? What does she have to do with the Xe La?"

I raised my palms. "I have no idea."

"Greg and IC Winter? They're both dead."

"Yep."

"You think they knew about the Xe La?"

Ding. I nearly looked up to see if there was, indeed, a light bulb over my head.

"I can ask."

Harvey looked confused. "You're a psychic?"

Ooh, wouldn't that be fun. But he'd never believe me. "No, but I know someone who used to know Greg and IC."

"Who?"

"I'll tell you when I'm clean," I said, and handed him my coffee cup.

So, I said to myself in the shower, *Janulevic is probably after the Xe La. Petr is working for Janulevic. Janulevic sent Petr to get me. Why me? Because I'm a friend of Angel's.*

I hoped it was just because I was her friend. Not because I was her protector. Not because of SO17. Else we were in big trouble.

Why was he after Angel? Because of who her parents were? Because they knew something about the Xe La?

Was that why Greg was killed?

I got out of the shower and dried off thoughtfully, grateful there was no one watching me this time. I needed to see the files on Greg and IC. Maybe if I knew what Greg was working on when he died then I might get another jigsaw piece.

I picked up my Nokia and called Karen Hanson.

"I have a question," I said. "How secret is SO17?"

"You cannot tell your boyfriend."

Clearly she hadn't been paying full attention. "Good, because I don't have one. How about CIA?"

"Keep talking."

I told her about Harvey and Janulevic, and she said she'd been down to see Petr this morning. She spoke a few words of Russian but hadn't understood anything he'd babbled. It was amazing how incoherent people became when they were chained up in a lab. Probably we should think of a new way of detaining people, but there were other things to be done first.

"We can deal with this," Karen said when I'd finished. "We can trade off. Work together. He sounds like he might have something for us."

"Doesn't a trade involve giving him something too?"

"We'll work something out. There must be something."

Angel, I thought, but said nothing. I hung up and got dressed and went out to see Harvey.

"So, do you have a home to go to?" I asked.

"I have a hotel."

"The Hilton?"

"A B&B in the village. You know, I'd like to get my car back."

"Can do. And after that, I have some people for you to meet."

We picked up his car, a dark blue rented Mondeo, and he followed me up to the office. "I know this," he said when we got out. "This is where you tried to catch that guy…"

How does the CIA get anything done when its operatives call everyone "that guy"?

"This is our office," I said. "We came here yesterday."

He didn't look impressed. "It looks kinda normal."

"That's the idea." I swiped us in and we went through to Hanson's office. She smiled when she saw us.

"Karen Hanson, SO17," I said, "James Harvard, CIA."

Harvey held out his hand. "Ma'am."

Suck-up.

"First of all, Four," Hanson said, "tell me about our guest downstairs?"

"He's working for Janulevic."

"Good for him. Who's Janulevic?"

Harvey and I explained about the dead professors and the Xe La. "Have you heard of it?" I asked. Probably she had a degree in Ancient Chinese or something. But she shook her head.

"I'd heard about the missing professors. Ten so far, and five leading archaeologists. Speculation is rife. The tabloid press is calling it an ancient curse, which is absurd as they were all involved in very different fields."

"The most credible theory is some sort of vendetta," Harvey said, and suddenly I remembered the newspaper headline in the Lakeside toilets.

"Revenge of the uneducated," I said, and a voice from behind me said, "You're not that uneducated."

I felt the air in the room thicken and chill rapidly. So SO17 wouldn't have to invest in air-conditioning; just get me, Luke and Harvey in a room together.

"Harvard," Luke said. "What the hell are you doing here?"

"I see you all know each other," Karen said.

"We've met," Harvey said shortly. He and Luke had locked eyes and I was very glad I wasn't standing between them. "Joint initiative," he said. "I have some information that could be useful to you. And I think there's something you could tell me, too."

"Lots of things. Like, you spell 'kidnapped' with two Ps," Luke said.

"Depends on how cheap your dictionary is," Harvey replied, and I rolled my eyes.

"I'll shoot the first one of you to mention Dr. Johnson," I said, and they both stared at me. "Samuel Johnson? The lexicographer? Wrote the first dictionary?"

"I'm impressed," Harvey said.

"You know the word 'lexicographer'?" Luke said, and I scowled at him.

"Don't we have work to do?" I said.

"You know those words too," Luke murmured, still sounding amazed, and I nearly hit him.

Karen Hanson was smiling. "We do indeed have work. Why do you think Janulevic is involved with the Winters?"

"Because he sent Petr to kidnap me," I said, daring Luke to make a comment about the spelling. "And when I asked if it had to do with Angel or her parents, he— Well, he said no, but I'm pretty sure he was lying."

"Angel's parents—wait, Angel's parents are IC and Greg Winter?" Harvey said, his hazel eyes nearly rolling out of his head.

"He's smart," Luke said, and I wondered if he'd always been this sarcastic, or if it was me bringing it out in him.

"Smarter than you," I said. "Yes, Harvey. That's what I was going to tell you. That's the connection."

"You know, there was always a rumour at the Agency that IC was a secret agent for the British government," Harvey said, smiling, apparently trying to break the tension.

"No rumour," I said, and for the second time in a minute Harvey's eyes nearly popped out. "IC and Greg were both agents."

"Recently we discovered that Greg's death was not the accident it seemed," Karen said. "It appears he was murdered."

"And no one knew until now? He died fifteen years ago!"

"The files were sealed," I said. "We had to do a lot of begging to get access. Well, Maria did."

"Who's Maria?"

"Another agent. You'd like her."

Karen Hanson was frowning. "I'm still not sure what any of this has to do with anything. I don't understand how this artefact and the Winters are connected."

"Angel's stalker said she had something he wanted," I said. "Maybe that's it. Maybe he thinks she has this Xe La thing."

Eyes met all around the room and we all piled into Karen's Saab and rushed to Angel's chapel. I found myself sitting in the back with Luke. The air was thick here too, but not so cold. It was like the air before a summer storm—hot, heavy, charged and crackling.

I kept my eyes on the door trim and my legs turned away from him, but I was aware of him with every cell I had.

"This is awesome," Harvey said as we pulled up at the church. I winced, knowing Luke would be sending Harvey a scathing look. "She lives in a church?"

"IC bought it a couple of years before she died and had it renovated," I said. "Angel inherited it when she was eighteen." I got out of the car, grateful to be away from Luke because I could hardly breathe when he was so close, but as Harvey and Karen went up to the church doors, Luke dashed round the car and grabbed my arm.

"We need to talk," he said.

"No, I don't think we do." I wrenched my arm away from him, glaring at the finger marks.

"What the hell is Harvard doing here?"

I relaxed a little. "I ran into him last night. He was after Petr."

"Who?"

"In the cells. The Russian."

"Thought he was Czech?"

"No."

"I wish you'd said something, Sophie, I speak Russian."

Of course he did.

"Well, you won't get anything out of him. Harvey speaks Russian too. All he'd say was that this Janulevic guy sent him to get me. He wouldn't say why."

"Did it occur to you that Harvard could be in league with him?"

"You said that last time, and Harvey ended up saving my life—"

"Hey, I had a hand in that too—"

"Only because he went to get you."

"Because he couldn't handle it on his own. Because," Luke took a step closer, so we were nearly touching, "he knew you needed me."

God, it was tempting. He was so close, and I knew just how good he'd feel. My eyes flickered over to Docherty's Vanquish and closed in memory. Luke skimmed his hands up my bare arms, a millimetre from the skin, and his lips brushed mine.

"Stop it," I whispered, floundering for self-control.

"Come on, Soph, this is stupid," Luke said, running a finger up my jawline, making me shiver.

"You're right," I stepped back, away from temptation. "It's really stupid. Over means over, Luke. Don't make me get my gun out."

His eyes darkened sexily, and I took another step back.

"If I scream, Harvey will come running," I said. "And if he sees you attacking me, he'll shoot you."

Luke looked appalled. "I wasn't going to attack you. Jesus, Sophie, did you think—?"

"I don't know," I stamped my foot, frustrated. "Just—just stop it. We have work to do."

"Just work?" Luke said.

"Yes, just work. Forget everything else. It was fun," I said firmly, "but this is more important."

I strode over to the door, feeling very assertive, and knocked, feeling Luke standing there on the gravel, ten feet behind me. He radiated heat and I pulsed, hot and helpless, praying Angel would open the door before my resolve broke and I ripped all my clothes off and threw myself at Luke's feet.

The hidden camera in the gargoyle flashed and the door opened and Docherty stood there, looking mysterious, running his gaze over me. My cheeks were flaming and my breath was coming fast.

"Are you okay?" he asked.

"I'm fine," I lied transparently.

"Luke's not been harassing you?"

Yes, and I want him to carry on harassing me. "No. We just needed to talk about something."

Since talking was all we'd had time for, Docherty accepted this for the semi-truth it was and opened the door to let me in. Luke followed silently, precisely three and a half feet behind me. I felt his proximity like I had parking sensors. Hot man at five o'clock.

Luke went over to Angel and Karen, and Docherty touched my shoulder, holding me back.

"What's going on?"

"Someone tried to kidnap me last night and he's working for a Czech guy who's been killing academics because he doesn't want anyone to know he's after some Mongol artefact which he thinks Angel has. I think."

Docherty nodded. "I didn't mean that."

"What did you—?"

"You. Luke. Last night you were messing with the suspension on my car, and today you're not looking at each other."

I didn't have to look at him. My Luke radar told me exactly where he was.

"Change of plan," I said. "Your car is safe."

Docherty gave me an indecipherable look, his eyes dark. "Is that so?"

"Absolutely. And it will be safe for a long time."

"Right," Docherty said softly. He glanced at Harvey. "Who's he?"

"CIA. He's after the Czech guy who's after the Mongol thing."

"What's the Mongol thing called?"

"The Xe La."

"Spell it."

I did, and Docherty frowned. "Never heard of it."

I wasn't going to ask how many Mongol artefacts he'd heard of. I wouldn't really be surprised at all if it turned out that he was an authority on ancient Mongol artefacts.

"He's not the reason my car is safe?"

"Harvey? No," I smiled. "He's got a thing for Angel. Only he's never met her."

"Did it occur to you that he could be her stalker?"

Why does everyone have it in for Harvey? "No. You sound just like Luke."

"Do I now?" Docherty said, sounding amused, watching Angel as she detached herself from the group and came over to us.

"You're involved with the CIA now?"

"We're helping each other out," I said. "Angel, do you possess a Mongol artefact called the Xe La?"

She shrugged and shook her head. "I don't possess any Mongol artefacts."

"Have you had any more letters or e-mails lately?"

She shook her head again. "Nothing. I think Docherty scared them off."

Docherty raised an eyebrow, but said nothing. Angel took my arm and tugged me away towards the bedroom. When the door was shut, she lowered her voice and said, "What's going on with you and Luke?"

Argh, did I have a beacon up or something? *Talk to me about my boyfriend problems!*

I threw myself at the bed. "You know how I said he's not my boyfriend?"

"Yes..."

"Well, he's not."

The best thing about a best friend is her ability to be endlessly changeable and utterly supportive when it comes to your love life. When you're going out with someone she's happy for you, jealous of you, thinks he's fab, wants one just like him. When you break up she's right there to tell you he's a bastard, she never liked him anyway, you can do so much better.

She even got me some chocolate. Bless.

Eventually Luke knocked on the screen and opened the door.

"We need to talk to this Petr guy," he said, while Angel glowered loyally at him. "See if we can get a handle on who he's working for."

"It's Janulevic," I said. "Harvey—"

"I need to hear it myself," Luke said evenly. "Are you coming?"

I looked at Angel. She bit her lip. "I think you should go and find out what you can," she said, and I nodded reluctantly and heaved myself off the bed.

Karen drove us all back up to the airport business park and went back into her pot-planted office while Harvey, Luke and I went down to the lab. I was standing between them and I felt like the Christians in the Colosseum must have done when the lions came out for lunch.

Luke rolled back the shutters and switched on the intercom to talk to Petr, who was huddled in a corner, sweating and shaking. Luke said a few things to him, and he sweated and shook even more.

"Are you terrorising him?" I said.

"I'm confirming things." He rolled off another question and the answer came back, a miserable "Dmitri Janulevic".

"See?" Harvey muttered under his breath, and Luke ignored him. He asked Petr another question, but Petr shrugged nervously.

"What?" I asked.

"He doesn't know why Janulevic wanted you."

"Because I'm friends with Angel?"

"Don't feed him anything," Luke said. "Let him answer." He asked Petr again what Janulevic wanted, but got no reply.

I sighed. I'd seen enough films to know how this worked.

"Luke, will you open the door, please?" I said.

"The cell door? Why?"

"I want to show him something."

Luke and Harvey exchanged glances, then Luke swiped the cell door open and I got out my gun and pressed it against Petr's temple.

"Sophie, what the hell—" Luke started, but I cut him off.

"Ask him again."

Luke paused, then repeated the question. Petr trembled up at me, then he mumbled something very quietly.

"What did he say?" I asked.

"He said it's because of who you're friends with."

"Does he have a name?"

The answer came back. "No, but he's seen her. A little blonde girl."

Angel. "What was he trying to do? Threaten her by taking me? Ransom me? Did he want information?"

Luke asked, and Petr shook his head, looking terrified.

"He doesn't know, Soph. He's just a henchman."

"He knows," I said, pressing the gun harder against Petr's temple, and he started genuflecting.

"Sophie," Luke said quietly, but his tone was firm. "He doesn't know. Put the gun away."

I felt patronised, and I hated that. But more than anything I knew Luke was right, and I hated that too.

I lowered the gun, and Petr started breathing again. He mumbled something that made Luke scowl and Harvey laugh.

"What?" I said, stepping out of the cage.

"He said Luke's boss is scary." Harvey pointed at me. "I think that might have been a compliment."

"Just a statement of fact," Luke said, swiping the door shut again and stepping away as Harvey took over the intercom. He and Petr spoke rapidly in Russian for a few minutes, and then he and Luke nodded at each other.

"Sophie's car," Luke said. "It's best off-road."

"Damn straight," I said. "Where are we going?"

"Where Petr was supposed to have taken you yesterday."

We locked Petr away in the dark again and went back upstairs. Karen was browsing through some files in the outer office. "I'm trying to find what Greg Winter was working on when he died," she said. "The record says he was off duty, but I'm not sure I believe that. Did you get anything?"

"An address," Luke said.

"For Janulevic? Do you all have body armour?"

Luke and Harvey nodded and looked at me.

"In my wardrobe," I said meekly, and they both rolled their eyes. Harvey went back to his B&B to shower and change from yesterday's clothes, and Luke followed me back to my flat and stood there looking moody while I tried to remember what I'd done with my Kevlar vest. He inspected the scooter Harvey and I had brought inside last night, but apparently found nothing of interest on it, so went back to watching me as I got hotter and more flustered trying to find my damned vest.

Tammy appeared through the electronic cat flap Luke insisted I had put in for security, and rubbed up against his legs. Poor Tammy was just like me—saw the face and not what was inside.

No, that was mean. Luke was a good guy. He just wasn't someone I needed to be personally involved with.

I finally found the Kevlar, loaded up my gun and we went off to pick Harvey up. His little hotel was on the road where I used to live with my parents. I lived there for ten years. Now I hardly recognised it.

"Okay, where're we going?"

Harvey frowned. "Well, he said something about an ugly place..."

"He said 'Go to Ugley'." Luke rolled his eyes, and I put the car in gear, smiling.

"What's Ugley?" Harvey asked, confused.

"Next village over. Where Angel lives— Well, officially. She's right on the outskirts."

"She lives in a place called *Ugley*?"

"Yep."

"Jesus. You English are insane."

Luke flicked his eyes at me, and I knew he was going to start an argument.

"Don't."

"What, I was just going to say that last time I went to America I drove through the towns of Eighty-Eight, Kentucky; Nameless, Tennessee; and Scratch Ankle, Alabama."

"Now I know you're making that up," I told him.

"No, it's true," he protested.

"I once met a girl from a town called Maggie's Nipples in Wyoming," Harvey volunteered, and I gave in.

"There's a village not far from here called Matching Tye," I said. "I always wanted to have a house there called 'Shirt'."

"All the villages around here have names like PG Wodehouse characters," Luke said. "Chipping Ongar, Biggleswade, Wendens Ambo."

"Saffron Walden, Wimblington, Trumpington," I said. "I think there's a place up by Peterborough called Eye."

"Just north of Cambridge there's a place called Waterbeach," Luke volunteered.

"What's funny about that?" Harvey asked.

"It's a hundred miles inland."

By the time we pulled up the farm track Petr had described, Luke and Harvey had my road atlas out and were picking up on stupid names. Blo Norton, Hellions Bumpstead, Devil's Dyke, Shellow Bowells. Hatfield Peverell. Stocking Pelham. We wondered if there was a castle at Castle Acre in Norfolk, or what kind of calendar confusion they had in March. Harvey wanted to know what made Great Chesterford quite so great and for the life of me, I couldn't remember.

"How do these places get their names?" he asked in bewilderment.

"Corruptions of Old English, Celtic and Norman words," I said.

"I'm impressed," Luke said.

"Stansted Mountfitchet is Anglo Saxon and Norman," I said. "The ground is full of stones, we're at the edge of where the Ice Age glacier came to, so Stansted means 'stony ground', and Mountfitchet is a corruption of the Norman Baron de Montfichet who was awarded the land by William the Conqueror."

There was a silence (well, as much silence as you can get with a diesel engine wobbling over dried ruts of mud) from the back of the car.

Then, "I'm very impressed," Luke said.

"Not just a pretty face," Harvey agreed, and I blushed.

We came to a gate in the hedge at the edge of the field and I backed up a few feet, put Ted into first and patted the dash. "This will only hurt for a second," I said, and rammed him at the gate.

Harvey and Luke ducked, but Ted rolled on majestically, bits of wood falling gracefully back to earth. I patted the dash again. "Good boy."

"You talk to your car a lot?" Harvey asked.

"She talks to it more than me," Luke said.

"That's because I like it more than you," I replied, and instantly felt horrible for being so mean.

Luke was silent the rest of the journey.

Harvey pointed out a crumbling concrete pillbox in the corner of the barley field, half-hidden by the trees of a small wood, and we decided to park up out of sight and make our way through the trees. I personally doubted that Janulevic would still be there—Ted's a wonderful car but he's not what you'd call subtle—but I drew my SIG and checked the fastenings on my Kevlar and crept after Harvey, Luke following behind me.

I'm not afraid. That is to say, I'm not afraid to say that I was absolutely bloody terrified. My hands were shaking and I knew if I had to shoot anything I'd be more likely to hit my foot than any target. I jumped every time a tree branch brushed my shoulder or my ankle. I was wearing chunky DMs and shorts and a sleeveless top under the Kevlar, and figured the Lara Croft look ought to make me feel braver. But it just made me feel really conspicuous.

We gathered ten feet from the pillbox, behind a fat oak tree, and Luke and Harvey made motions with their hands, nodded at each other and started to move.

"Wait," I mouthed, grabbing Luke. "What about me?"

"Stay here," he mouthed, pointing firmly at the ground, and I wanted to protest, but the coward in me—i.e., all of me— nodded and stayed very still, or at least as still as my shaking body would let me.

Harvey peeled off to the left and Luke to the right, moving so there was the least amount of field between them and the pillbox, before starting forwards through the barley.

I watched the synchronised ripples converging on the crumbling concrete shelter, and was pretty sure there was no one in it. I was hot, the Kevlar was heavy and there was something tickling my ankle. I could feel the sweat trickling down my back and pooling behind my knees. Time ticked on, the boys were moving very slowly. I was bored.

And then a shot rang out, and I froze, seeing the barley ripples end abruptly. I stared through sweat-prickled eyes at the pillbox, blinking furiously, trying to see what was going on. Another shot, and then the Harvey ripple darted towards the pillbox, but slightly too late, because someone emerged from the far side, into the other field, and shot across the packed earth.

Harvey launched after him, and I raised my gun, but I couldn't see and my hands were shaking and if I fired a round I'd probably shoot Harvey instead. Or Luke.

Where the hell was Luke?

Horrible fear gripped me, freezing the sweat all over my body, and I pulled myself to my feet, my knees creaking so loudly I was amazed no one shot at me. But it appeared that Janulevic had been alone, because the coast was clear as I stumbled out through the barley to where I'd last seen Luke moving around.

And there he was, sprawled gracelessly on the ground, blood on his body and his head, his eyes closed, lying very still.

I dropped my gun and stared trying to pull his Kevlar off. "Luke! Luke, you bastard arsewipe, say something."

He said nothing.

"Don't you *dare* be dead. I'm not over you yet. Don't—"

And then his fingers closed over mine, and I looked down to see his eyes open and his mouth smiling, and he said, "Not over me?"

I was relieved for about half a second, and then rage took over and I thumped him. "Don't make me bloody worry like that!"

"You were worried?"

"Thought I'd have to get a new partner," I said, and that shut him up. I looked around. "Someone came out of that pillbox and Harvey went after him, but I can't see anything from here." I kneeled up and cautiously raised my head above the waving barley stems. I still couldn't see anything.

"Did you see which direction they took?" Luke asked, and I shrugged.

"Those woods the other side of the next field. Could be anywhere now."

He nodded and sat up, but then his eyes unfocused and he flopped back down again. "Maybe I'll just stay here."

I touched his temple where the blood was thick. "Probably you should get that x-rayed. Are you hurt anywhere else?"

Luke's eyes darkened, and I knew what he was thinking. "Try anything and you'll be a lot more hurt," I warned, and he made a face.

"When I think of things I did for you when you were hurt..."

This was true. A couple of months ago I was in a building site that fell down on me, and when I came to, Luke was there, kissing me and pulling off my clothes. And then when I got back from the hospital after the splintered wood incident, he made a housecall and we barely left the bed for the next day and a half.

"And look how that all turned out," I said, getting the shoulder strap of his Kevlar undone and tearing through the bloody sleeve of his T-shirt. "You were hit," I said, staring at the bullet wound.

"You think? I hate these fucking things." He pulled at the Kevlar. "No one ever shoots at your body when you're wearing one. They go for the head or the arms or the legs or anything."

I was only half listening. The bullet had gone in cleanly, slipping through the muscle of his bicep, and from the hole at the side of his arm I'd guess it had come back out again.

I found it in the hard earth between barley stalks and held it up. "Souvenir."

Luke didn't look so impressed. Figuring Janulevic was out of the picture for now, I helped him to his feet and back to Ted, putting him in the passenger seat which still had bits of Petr's blood on it, and pulled a small first-aid kit out of the cubby box.

And then I heard another shot and ducked into the cab, reaching for my gun again. Luke and I stared around, but all we could see was open field on one side and trees on the other.

And then someone banged on the back door and yanked it open, and I nearly shot at him before I realised it was Harvey, and he was breathless and pointing off to the left. From the trees on the other side of the field, a car burst out and bounced away over the mud.

I dropped my gun, started Ted up and floored it.

Janulevic was in a Subaru Impreza, a goddamn rally car. It was bouncing and rolling, and had the earth been wetter he'd probably have got stuck. But yesterday's rain had steamed away instantly, and the Scoobie roared off in a cloud of dust. Ted couldn't keep up.

"Can't you go any faster?" Harvey said anxiously, and Luke and I both snapped, "No."

"How the hell has he got himself one of those?" Luke muttered, feeling the wound on his head where he'd hit one of those Ice Age rocks on the way down.

"And why?" I added. "Not what you might call a stealth car."

"Neither's yours."

"He has other uses," I said, and demonstrated by rolling down a steep bank onto a little back lane and swerving up the hill after the Impreza. But after a couple of near misses rattling round sharp corners, it became pretty obvious that we were way behind. We came to a junction, and I nearly cried.

"Tyre marks," Luke pointed with his good arm, and we set off, following a trail of skid marks, battered hedges and even a smattering of headlamp glass. But I knew we'd never catch up. I hadn't seen clearly what spec the Scoobie was, but even the basic model could go a good 20 MPH faster than Ted, and had so much horsepower it really should be in the Grand National.

I skidded round a corner that would have made a hairpin look straight, and the last thing I saw was the Subaru skewed across the road, before Luke started yelling. I slammed on the brakes and we spun up and over, crashing and bleeding, and then everything went black.

Chapter Seven

Ted was on his side and I lay there looking at his undercarriage, mud-spattered and complex, like a dead beetle. My head was bleeding but I didn't think anything was broken—which was more than I could say for Harvey, who had dispensed with a seat belt and had been chucked around like a Lotto ball in the big back of the car.

I pulled myself to my feet. I'd been the first to wake up, tangled in my seat belt, sure we were all dead, but I'd found a pulse on Luke's wrist and Harvey's neck, and managed to scramble out through the shattered windscreen before I threw up.

The Subaru was totalled, thrashed right into the bank, but I couldn't see anyone inside it. Janulevic had left it there as a trap. All I could say was that it was a damn good job it had been us who came across it first, not a mad kid in his mum's Fiesta.

Although it'd serve him right. And maybe it would have been slightly better if a tractor had found the car first.

Head reeling, I wobbled back to Ted, reached in through the hole where the windscreen used to be, and touched Luke's bloody shoulder. The Kevlar had once again stopped any serious damage, and he woke up after a few light slaps.

"What the hell happened?"

I unfastened his seat belt. "Janulevic is gone. But he left his car for us to find."

Luke gazed unsteadily out at the wrecked Scoobie. "It's upside down."

"No. We're on our side. Can you move?"

He rolled his shoulders and moved his legs, and I hauled him out through the windscreen.

"Jesus." He looked Ted over. "This is why I told you not to get emotionally attached to your car."

"He'll be fine." I patted a balding tyre. "He's resilient."

"Sophie, nothing's that resilient."

"Ted is," I said stubbornly, and limped around to the back of the car to open it up and get to Harvey. He wouldn't wake up, but I pulled off one of his trainers and tickled his foot, and his body jerked.

"Back not broken," I said to Luke, who was leaning outside, looking pale. "Help me get him out and we'll see if we can get Ted back on his feet."

Luke looked at me like I was mad, but he helped me drag Harvey out of the car and tie my very useful rope to the roof rack, and then he helped—not much, because he was sweating blood, but he tried—to pull Ted back onto his wheels.

Ted rocked and swayed, then righted himself with a thud and sat there, looking a little more battered and a little less capable than before. I got in and turned the key, and he started up.

I looked out at Luke triumphantly.

"Fuck me," he muttered.

"Really not a good time," I replied. "Help me get Harvey back in."

It wasn't the first time Ted had driven the bloodwagon route, and I had a sort of suspicion it wouldn't be the last. His steering was a bit soggy and he was wheezing more than usual, but he'd taken a hell of a lot more body damage than Harvey and he was moving a damn sight more.

I emerged from the hospital with sixteen stitches in my calf and two butterfly clips on my forehead, rattling a bottle of painkillers. Luke insisted on coming home with me and threatened the nurse with his gun if she made him stay overnight, and we left Harvey with a pretty young Asian doctor who assured us that he would be absolutely fine.

We came out into the sunlight, surrounded by curious glances, and stood and stared a bit at Ted, who had massive crumples and scratches all down the passenger side.

"Gives him character," I said, and had to wrench the bent door open for Luke.

I took him home to his place and watched him key in the codes to open his front door, then disable the alarm inside. His arm was in a sling, shoulder heavily bandaged, he had stitches on his forehead and a splint immobilising his knee. He looked exhausted, and as always when tired and in a bad mood, irresistible. I pulled off his shirt and the jeans that had been cut open, watched him swallow some painkillers and fall asleep.

I sat on the edge of the bed, looking at him and thinking how unfair it was that even in such a state he just took on the air of a wounded masterpiece, elegantly wrecked, like a film star on heroin. And finally, shock and exhaustion overwhelming me, I put my head on his warm, hard chest and fell asleep.

It was my phone that woke me, hammering out a happy tune from *Moulin Rouge!*, swelling my brain to exploding point. I forced my eyes open and heaved my bag up onto the bed.

"Hello?" I tried, but it came out as "Mmellow?"

"Sophie? Am I keeping you up?"

It was my mother.

"No, no, I'm fine. I was just, erm, eating."

"So you'll not want to come to tea tonight?"

"Erm." I thought about it, the warm comfort of the kitchen, the cosy bickering, the soft glare of the TV, and sighed. I couldn't face the questions about me and Ted. "No. I'm on my way out." I held my wrist above my head and peered through the darkness at my watch. Three-fifteen. "It's early."

"It's half past eight."

I frowned at the darkness. I hadn't thought three-fifteen was quite right. "My watch stopped. I'm going out with Angel, Mum. Sorry."

"Anywhere nice?"

"Erm. Just drinks in town. People from work."

"Is she better, then?"

What was she on about? "Uh, yeah." That's right, I'd said she was ill, that's why we weren't working... "Much better. Needs to get out."

"Well, tell her to take it easy. Lots of fluids. No alcohol. Will you be coming for tea tomorrow?" my mother added hopefully.

"I, er, I don't know. I'll text you. Text Chalker," I added, remembering that my mother thought her phone was broken when it displayed the message "text". "Bye, Mum." I ended the call and dropped the phone on the floor where it thudded and lay still.

"Drinks?" Luke asked, and I jolted. I'd forgotten he was there. In fact, I'd forgotten I was there. The room was dark and it hadn't occurred to me that I might be anywhere but in my own bed.

"Had to tell her something," I mumbled, and sat up, every muscle in my body aching. "Why do I always seem to be beaten up?"

"You get in the way of collapsing buildings and abandoned rally cars."

"Hey, *it* got in *my* way."

"Sure." Luke had an arm over his face, but then he lifted it, and I winced at the sight of him.

"That bad?"

"I've seen worse."

"On who?"

"Rocky."

He closed his eyes. "I haven't felt this bad since my abseiling rope broke when I was training."

"Ah, youthful memories." I pushed myself to my feet and shoved my hair out of my eyes. I'd managed to kick off the DMs and lose the Kevlar, but I was still mostly dressed, unlike Luke who was down to snug-fitting boxers.

I swung away from the bed before I started getting inappropriate. Luke was patterned with bruises and cuts—a lot of the windscreen glass had apparently gone his way, but I'd escaped the worst of it—he had a bullet wound and a sprained knee and a dozen stitches in the cut on his forehead. Besides which he was an emotional disaster. Getting naked with him would not be a good idea.

I stumbled into the kitchen, needing coffee. Luke's flat is a big loft with one bedroom sectioned off, and the rest open to the old oak rafters. His kitchen is modern, his media equipment expensive, and his furniture classic lived-in leather and oak. He's a security freak and has laser sensors on his windows, double locks on his door and double keypads too.

I made a two-spoon cup of coffee for me, another for Luke, and carried them back in. He was sitting up, the waffle-weave duvet pulled to his waist, and he looked grateful for the coffee.

"So is this how you felt when the building fell down?"

I shrugged. "Probably. Like someone's taken a giant meat hammer to you and you've been tenderised?"

He nodded painfully.

"Yep. That's what it felt like. At least you weren't concussed."

"And at least I didn't ruin an expensive dress."

Ahem. The dress was borrowed and I still haven't told the owner what happened to it. Mainly because she's my friend Ella's boss, and she doesn't even know I took it.

I sipped at my coffee and looked Luke over. God, even under those bruises he had a fabulous body. Was it stupid of me to give that up just because of a romantic dream about a "proper' relationship"? Which could never live up to my expectations anyway. He'd hate my family, my dad wouldn't trust him, Chalker would think he was a loser (but then Chalker thinks everyone's a loser), my mum would probably terrify him. If I went and fell for him, he'd break my heart. If I slept with him again, I'd fall for him.

Luke was looking at me like he was thinking similar things. Maybe not relationshippy, future things, but like this would be a good chance to jump me.

"No," I said.

"No what?"

"No sex. You're—"

"I had sex with you when you were hurt."

I stared at him. He winced.

"Yeah, I heard that too. Sorry."

"So you should be." I looked at my watch again before remembering that it had stopped. "I should go. Tammy'll be starving."

Luke looked reluctant. "Don't," he said.

"She'll start eating the furniture."

"Come back. Please."

I hesitated. Oh, hell, who was I fooling?

"We can watch *Buffy*," Luke offered.

"Do you have ice cream?"

"Well, no, but you could take a fiver from my wallet and get some on the way…"

I rolled my eyes.

"I have Pringles," Luke coaxed.

Sold.

I went home and fed Tammy, showered and changed out of my sweaty, dusty, bloody Lara outfit into joggers and a T-shirt, all clean and soft and smelling like fabric conditioner, checked my cavernous bag for overnight things—I started carrying these after about a week on the job, I hardly ever sleep at my own place—chucked my sleeping bag on Ted's torn and bloody passenger seat, and clunked back to Luke's.

He was sitting on the sofa when I came back in, showered and clean and wearing a similar outfit to mine.

"How'd you manage a shower?" I asked, impressed, thinking of all his stitches and dressings.

He grinned and pointed to the kitchen. "Clingfilm. Remember? You taught me that."

Oh, yes. Clever me.

I sat down on the big leather chesterfield and unzipped my sleeping bag to make a blanket. Luke piled up cushions and poured the Pringles onto a plate, and I opened up the ice cream I'd got on the way. Do we know how to have a night in, or what?

"What series are we looking at?" Luke asked, gesturing to the DVD boxed sets on the table. It was quite sweet, actually, he was an even bigger *Buffy* freak than me. And I have the soundtrack and everything.

"I'm thinking early stuff," I said. "Pre-death."

"Which death?"

"Well, the proper one, obviously. The first time was only for, like, a minute or two."

"Series three?"

"Sounds good to me."

It wasn't long before I found myself curled against him under the sleeping bag, and then I was snuggled under his good arm, and then my head was on his shoulder, and then Buffy was kissing Angel and I was falling asleep, curled up with Luke, feeling safe.

My phone woke me again, but this time it was my Nokia, and I didn't recognise the number.

"Hello?"

"Sophie?" A deep, dark, familiar voice. "Docherty. Where are you?"

"Erm. Home." I blinked at Luke, who was playing sleepily with my hair. "What—how did you get this number?"

"Luke. I need you to come over to Angel's. We have a problem."

"What sort of problem?"

"You'll see. Is Luke with you?"

"Erm, no," I said guiltily. "But I can call him...?"

There was a very slight pause, and I could hear a smile in Docherty's voice when he replied, "Sure. See you in ten."

Ten was optimistic. It'd take us that long to get there, and that was without getting dressed and making ourselves look presentable.

"Docherty." I yawned. "He says they have a problem. Wants us to go straight over."

"What's the time?"

I looked at my watch. "Three fifteen." No. It was light. I looked at my phone. "Nearly ten. In the morning."

Luke looked surprised. "How many episodes did we watch?"

"Half a dozen. Ish." I stretched, feeling stiff, and stood up. "Coffee."

We inhaled a couple of pints each and left the house. Luke's flat is above a roofer's yard and they all stopped to watch him limping down the steps without his crutches, which he said were stupid and he wasn't going to use them. Men.

A bare twenty minutes after Docherty called me, we were outside Angel's church, being scanned by the gargoyle.

"Mary, mother of God," Docherty opened the door, "what happened to you?"

"Had a little run in with Janulevic," I said.

"Almost had a run *into* Janulevic," Luke qualified. "Sophie killed his car."

"But not him?"

"Nowhere to be seen," I said. "Well, maybe he was, but we were all unconscious at the time."

"We all?" Angel appeared behind Docherty, looking pale and fragile. She was of the same mould as Luke: somehow adversity seems to make them even more beautiful. If I was crying or hurt or ill, I just looked white and stupid. "Who else was with you?"

"Harvey."

"Harvey from yesterday?" Angel looked like she might cry. "Is he all right?"

"I think so. Actually if you'll give me a minute, I'll go and call the hospital—"

"Hospital?"

Docherty gave me a warning look. "I think you should come and look at these first," he said, beckoning me over to the coffee table where a manilla envelope was lying with some glossy photos peeping out.

Uh-oh.

I leafed through them. They were pictures from Sunday night—the camera flash I thought I'd seen. Pictures of me and Angel watching *Pretty Woman*, pictures of us making enchiladas in the kitchen, all covered in tomatoes and vege-mince, pictures of us sitting in our pyjamas, talking. Pictures of us sleeping.

"Jesus," I said, and glanced up at Luke, who was looking over my shoulder. "I told you I saw someone."

"And he saw you, too." Luke peered at the top shot, of me curled up in my sleeping bag. "That's a close zoom from the bedroom window. These guys aren't messing around."

"Well, he knows about cars, he knows about cameras, and he's not a bad shot," I said. "Boy, this is going to be fun."

We left a trembling Angel with Docherty, and I suspected his comforting might be slightly more than a pat on the back. I called the hospital and they said Harvey was awake and asking after me and Luke, so I said we'd go to see him as soon as we'd been in to the office to make our report.

"What's with the 'we'?" Luke said.

"You're not coming?"

"Not unless I have to."

"You're a miserable bugger," I said, last night's kind thoughts about him evaporating.

"I don't like the guy."

No kidding, I thought, and put the car in gear.

Maria was scrolling through files on the computer when we walked in. She looked up, blinked, and got to her feet. "This should be good," she said, following us into Karen's office.

Karen was talking on the phone—a lot of yeses, mm-hmms, frowns and a final, "Well, find out. Bye." She looked up. "I take it you didn't find Janulevic? I was waiting for a call yesterday."

"We had more urgent things to do," I said. "Like make sure Harvey wasn't bleeding internally."

"Where is he?"

"Princess Alexandra. He's going to be okay."

"What happened?"

We told her about the shoot-out and the car chase, and I felt really, really cool. This was spy film stuff. I was on my way. Look out, Bond.

Only, Bond doesn't limp quite so much.

Karen sighed when we'd finished. "You don't know where he went?"

"Or even if it was really him," Luke said. "We don't have a description. Really, he could have any number of people working for him."

"We haven't heard of anyone else. But then, how would we? Everyone he's come into contact with has disappeared."

I read the description of Dmitri Janulevic. Average height, average build. Brown hair. Brown eyes. Age unknown—maybe thirties or forties.

"Well, that narrows it down," I said.

"Who did you see yesterday?"

I shrugged. "I had my head down. I couldn't see."

"Luke?"

He shook his head. "I was unconscious at the time."

"No excuse," Maria chided.

"He was wearing a blue shirt," I volunteered, and got three deadpan looks for it. "And he knows cars. And he has a good camera." I told her about the pictures and sent a text to Docherty's number, asking him to scan and e-mail them to the office.

"Do you have anything else on this Xe La?" Karen asked, and we shook our heads.

"I've been Googling all day," Maria said. "Ancient shrines, encyclopaedias, the lot. Not a damn thing."

"Keep trying," Karen said. "I have a contact at the British Museum, I'll see if I can get to him. Agent Four, find out what you can from our American friend. The CIA don't always share everything. Three..."

Luke looked hopeful.

"Go home. Rest."

He scowled, and Maria punched his arm. "Fun, huh? Want to help me Google?"

"Oh, joy."

I followed them out. Maria sat down at the computer and Luke went over to the bookshelf.

"On second thoughts, I'm going to go and see our Russian friend. See if he has anything else for us."

"Have fun," I said. "I'm going to see Harvey."

I found him in a private room, surrounded by adoring nurses and little girls with plaster casts. Everyone loves Harvey. Even lying there with a brace around his neck and a needle in his hand, he looked heroic. Maybe the bandages made him more heroic.

He smiled when he saw me. "The girl herself," he said. "I was just telling Nurse Robson—"

A plump nurse beamed. "I said, call me Glenda."

"I was telling Glenda here about your driving skills."

"Oh God."

"There's a rumour there was an old battered Land Rover outside yesterday..."

"That would be Ted."

"Ted is your car?" I nodded. *I* think it's normal to name a car. Harvey shook his head. "And it still works?"

"Yep. It'd take more than a Scoobie to bring him down."

"A what?" Harvey asked, but he didn't look really interested. I let it drop. "Could we have a bit of time alone?" he asked the nurses, who trailed away, looking disconsolate. The little girls went too, promising to come back and see their Uncle Harvey later.

"Do you have like a magnet or something?" I asked, sitting on the edge of the bed. "Something only females feel? 'Cos none of the men I've met trust you."

"That's because of the chick magnet the CIA implanted in me. Sophie. What the hell happened yesterday? The last thing I remember is seeing Janulevic stopped in the road—"

"You saw him?"

"Wasn't that his car?"

"Yes, but he wasn't in it when I came to."

"You were knocked out too?"

"We all were. The Subaru is totalled—" which reminded me, someone should really tell the police about that, "—and Ted was on his side. Me and Luke pulled him upright and brought you up here."

"Luke's okay? I asked about him but they said he wasn't here."

"They wanted to keep him in but he's too stubborn. He's okay."

"What about you?"

"I'm okay too."

We were quiet a bit, then Harvey said, "You really drove us up here after that crash?"

"Not the first time. Ted makes a good bloodwagon."

"But you're hurt."

I shrugged heroically. "What was I supposed to do? Stay there and wait for someone else to come and crash into us?"

Harvey smiled. "You're brave, Sophie. I admire that."

I blushed. I don't get called brave very often. In fact, "I think it's called bravado," I told him. "I'm really an absolute coward."

He grinned. "So what about Janulevic? He escaped?"

"The car was mashed, but there really wasn't anyone in it. The only thing I can think of was that he got out and left the car there for us to go into."

"So he can't have been far?"

I frowned. "No. Dammit, we should have stayed."

"Hey, if we'd stayed—"

"I know, you or Luke could have died. I didn't know how severe his injuries were."

"Luke could have died?" Harvey clicked his fingers in mock-annoyance. "Damn." At least I think it was mock. "You win some, lose some."

"Why don't you like him?"

"He's a suspicious bastard. And he doesn't like me."

"He's just jealous."

"Because you like me?"

That wasn't what I was going to say, but it was a lot more flattering than "because you have proper secret agent back-up".

"Janulevic," I said firmly. "I need to know what you know."

"You already do."

"Have you met him? Do you have file photos?"

"One, very grainy. And we're not even sure it's him. He just looks...normal. Dark hair. Can't see his eyes."

"Height?"

"Can't tell that either."

"So you've never met him?"

He shook his head. "Sorry. Everyone who's met him is dead. Apart from Petr."

"Petr who is as thick as shit." I thumped my hand on the bed, making Harvey wince. "And no one's ever been able to catch him?"

"We never know where he's going until he's already left."

"No airline records? Or does he have a private plane?" Strictly speaking, he'd still need to register flight plans and go through immigration whenever he went from one country to another, but that was frighteningly easy to escape.

"He travels by regular plane, by the time we've found the records..."

"He's already gone." I nodded. "We could alert the airlines to tell us if he books a flight."

And then I had a brilliant idea.

"Or we could *make* him book a flight."

"What do you mean?"

"Get out some sort of rumour that the Xe La is somewhere else. Or that someone who knows about it is there. Then when he books a flight, we'll be waiting for him."

Harvey stared at me, and I wondered if perhaps I'd been very stupid. Then he shook his head. "You're a bloody genius," he said, and I preened.

Chapter Eight

Karen was impressed with my idea too, and decided we should hack into the Louvre database to plant the idea there. Then she added it as a news item to a couple of websites.

"What if he doesn't check online?" I asked.

"He will."

"If he's on the lam, he might—"

"Newspapers?" Maria suggested.

"Would a newspaper run a story about a Mongol artefact?"

"They'd run a story about academics being killed," Luke said. "Call them up and say you're a professor of somewhere and you've heard the Xe La is in France somewhere."

I had a sudden attack of conscience. "What if he actually breaks into the Louvre?"

"He won't," Karen said, "because you'll be there to catch him at the airport."

I deliberately kept my eyes away from Luke. Last time I was supposed to have caught someone I ended up on a flight to Rome by mistake. "Will I get back-up?"

"Of course," said Karen. "Myself and Macbeth will be there."

Two of them. Great. "No police?"

"No police, Sophie," Luke said. "They don't even know about SO17. Karen, what about Petr?"

"What about him?"

"He could give Janulevic the information."

"You mean we should release him?"

He shrugged. "It's a thought. I think we've got everything out of him anyway."

Karen frowned. "Sophie, did he see where you were bringing him?"

"I don't think so," I said, realising that he probably had. "It was night, anyway."

"We blindfolded him when we brought him in," Maria said helpfully.

"Take him away. Drive about ten miles and let him go. Tell him you're going to France to check out a lead but don't tell him what."

We looked at each other.

"Now," Karen prompted, and I stood up.

"Alone?"

They all smiled, and Karen said, "You're armed, and he's tied up. I think you'll be all right."

I wasn't so sure, but I went and got Petr, put his balaclava on backwards, and lobbed him in the back of my car. Luke stood watching.

"You sure you don't want a hand?"

No. I can't do this by myself. I'm too scared. "I'm fine," I said. "I can handle this."

"Be careful," Luke said, and watched me drive away.

I went up towards the terminal, then turned off onto the little back lanes and drove until I was fairly sure we were in the middle of nowhere. Then I stopped, opened up the back, and had a sudden panic attack.

"Quickly," I called Luke, "what's Russian for 'I have to let you go because I'm going to Paris to check out a lead?'"

He laughed. "Wondered when you'd get to that." He rolled and spat out a long, complex sentence. Then he waited.

"I can't say that," I sulked, and Luke laughed again. He shortened it, and I repeated it to Petr, loudly, knowing this was the worst con ever.

Then I got back in Ted and drove away, leaving Petr on the edge of a field, several miles from anywhere. I got back to the office, and Luke shook his head at me. "Told you you needed someone with you," he said, and I scowled.

My phone rang and it was Angel. I went outside to answer it, glad for the excuse to escape.

"What's up?"

"Cabin fever. I need to get out. I need to go shopping."

"I'm sure Docherty would love to—"

"Don't you get the feeling Docherty might combust in sunlight?"

I laughed. "Glad it's not just me. Well, look. I could maybe meet you in town for an hour..."

"More than that," Angel said, "and you have to pick me up. Can't go anywhere alone."

I arranged to pick her up in half an hour and we'd go to Cambridge. It's hard to feel unsafe in Cambridge. With all the big brains around, it's easy to feel quite plebeian, but not unsafe.

I went back in, and Karen looked up enquiringly. "Problem?"

"Angel. She wants to go out," I said. "I'm picking her up in half an hour."

"What's wrong with her escort?"

"Have you ever met Docherty?"

Karen shook her head. "He came highly recommended—"

"Oh, he's a great bodyguard," Maria smiled, "but not what you might call inconspicuous. Or a great shopping partner."

Luke stared. "You're going shopping?"

"What's wrong with that?"

"You went on Sunday."

Maria, Karen and I gave him blank looks.

"How much can you shop? Do you have a secret trust fund or something? Where do you get all your money?"

"The credit card fairy," I said. "And I need a new watch. Mine's stuck at three-fifteen."

Luke was still looking incredulous as I left. Men just don't understand shopping. They don't understand how wandering around, buying expensive and undrinkable coffee, looking at clothes you're never going to buy and torturing your feet in pretty shoes can possibly be considered recreational. But then I don't understand football, either.

Docherty gave me a dark look when I picked Angel up.

"You're not supposed to be encouraging her," he said.

"I did no encouraging at all."

"You could have said no."

"And miss a shopping trip? You don't understand women, do you, Docherty?"

He scowled at me and I smiled happily. I don't know why I was in such a good mood. I'd trashed my car, lost a suspect and my calf was killing me where the stitches were holding it together. But on the other hand, I'd come up with fantastic felon-bait, had impressed my boss and was going shopping. And—

And, okay, it's shameful, but whenever I thought about falling asleep with Luke yesterday, just curled under his arm so comfortably, watching *Buffy* while my eyelids succumbed to gravity, I felt all warm and glowy inside. It had felt good, really good. Companionable. And I didn't know where it was going, but I liked it.

Angel perked up a bit in the car—her car, since mine had no CD player and was looking like Homer Simpson had just driven it in a demolition derby. "Those photos," she said, "they just freaked me out."

"Well, photos of us sleeping are scary."

"No, you know what I mean."

I did, and whenever I thought about it my warm glow dimmed a little.

"But you have Docherty now," I said, and watched her carefully. But there was no reaction.

"It's very comforting to have someone like that around," she said carefully. "But he's a little scary."

"He is?"

"Well, yes. He never seems to even sleep. Or eat. Or anything. Sophie, I'm not sure I've even seen him outside in the daylight. Maybe he is a vampire."

I rolled my eyes. "Angel, you live in a church."

"A religious vampire. I don't know."

We parked up and headed for coffee. Angel started making lists of all the pointless things she wanted to buy—something sweet for the bath, candles, yellow shoes since she didn't have any that colour, new underwear...

"Angel," I put down my Americano, "are you aware you're buying fuck-me things?"

She looked offended, or at least tried to. "Coincidence."

"Candles, scented bath oil, pretty underwear? Are you going to try it on for Docherty?"

"Don't be ridiculous."

I didn't think I was being ridiculous. "You don't find him the littlest bit sexy?"

"No," she said. "Not at all."

I sighed and shook my head. "Angel, Angel, Angel," I said. "You should have admitted to a little bit. Even Tammy would find him a little bit sexy. Now I *know* you've got the hots for him."

"Does anyone even say 'got the hots' any more?" Angel side-tracked. "It's kind of an Eighties thing..."

I raised my eyebrows and shook my head. "Admit it."

"No."

"That's practically an admission anyway. You fancy Docherty."

Angel sniffed and licked up some of the cream on her white chocolate mocha (How does she stay so thin? *How?*). "Well, you said yourself, he's very sexy."

I was pretty sure I hadn't said that, but I let it go.

"Have you been in his car yet?"

"No..."

"Ask him for a ride. Go on, ask him."

"Just like that? Those words?"

I had a blinding flash of asking Luke the same thing, and shuddered. "It'll work," I promised her, and she smiled a little feline smile.

Feline? Oh, shit, Tammy! I hadn't been back to feed her. She'd be starving!

"Oh, my poor baby," I said, grabbing my phone and dialling Luke while Angel looked on, mystified. "Where are you?" I asked when he picked up.

"Office. Why?"

"I need you to do me a favour. I didn't feed Tammy this morning and she'll be absolutely starving. Can you just go over and—"

"Sophie," Luke cut me off, "were you not present yesterday? Arm in sling. Knee in splint. I can hardly bloody walk, let alone drive."

I made a face. "But she'll be really hungry..."

"And I really can't drive with one arm and one leg. Can't you ask your mum to do it?"

"No, 'cos then she'll want to know why I wasn't there this morning."

"Tell her you were working."

"I always feed Tammy before I go." I drummed my fingers on the table. Angel sipped her drink.

"What's up?" she mouthed.

"I didn't feed Tammy this morning," I said, "and Luke can't do it because he can't drive."

"Ask Docherty," Angel said, and I beamed at her.

"Genius."

"Me?" Luke asked.

"No. Not you. Bye," I said, and called up Docherty's number.

He answered on the first ring. "Sophie?"

"I need a favour."

"What kind of favour?"

"I need you to feed my cat."

There was a long pause. I glanced at Angel, and she suddenly started laughing. I was about to ask her why, when I realised.

"Are we talking four legs and a tail here?" Docherty asked. "Or something kinkier?"

"Four legs," I said, colouring, and Angel laughed even harder. "My actual cat," I said. "In my flat. I didn't feed her this morning and she'll be starving and you're the only person I can think of who could get in and feed her without scaring the shit out of her." Macbeth could have broken in, but Tammy wouldn't have accepted so much as a compliment from him. She didn't like men, especially big men.

Apart from Luke. Traitor.

"Okay," Docherty sighed. "I might have to call in the favour from you another time, though."

Whatever. I couldn't believe I'd neglected my baby that much. I was a bad mother. Poor Tammy had been a rescue kitten. She'd think I didn't love her.

"Okay," I said to Angel when I put the phone down. "I'm traumatised now. I need to go and buy something to take the guilt away."

"She's a cat, Soph," Angel said. "The most vicious little cat since Jerry's Tom. She'll have eaten something."

"Something very un-nutritious," I grumbled, draining my coffee and standing up. "Come on."

I went to a pet shop and bought Tammy one of those automated feeders so I wouldn't have to go through this again. Then I bought her a wind-up mouse to apologise. And a tin of fancy, hideously expensive cat food.

"Better now?" Angel asked, as we were leaving the shop.

"Slightly," I said, and picked up my phone, which was ringing. Docherty. "Is she okay?"

"The cat? I can't see her."

"She'll be outside. Shake the biscuit tin and call her name—"

"Is she a vicious cat?" Docherty interrupted, and I smiled.

"You're not scared of her? Docherty, she's smaller than your foot."

"Does she kill a lot?" he wanted to know.

"Well, only recreationally."

"Big things?"

I knew what was coming. "What has she left on the floor?" She'd brought down squirrels twice her size before. Pigeons. Giant rats. She'd even had a go at the neighbour's small yappy dog but I'd called her off, fearing the worst from said neighbour.

"It's not on the floor. It's on the sofa."

Ew. "What is it?"

"Petr Staszic."

Luke was already there when I pulled up, having left Angel in Docherty's custody back at her own place.

"So *now* you can get a lift here?" I said, slightly shakily.

"Docherty picked me up. Sophie, I'm not sure you'll want to go in there."

"Is he really dead?"

"Pretty much, yeah."

"How dead? I mean, how long?"

He shrugged. "Can't have been that long because he was alive two hours ago. But he's cold."

I started to shudder and Luke put his good arm around me. "You want to come back to mine?"

Probably that would not be a good idea. "I need to see," I said, and pushed the door open. Petr Staszic was lying on the sofa, his eyes open, a small bullet wound in his temple. There was a knife stuck in his chest, pinning a note there. I stood and stared for quite a while before getting the courage to go closer and read the note.

There were letters, and they were grouped together in a way which suggested words. Other than that, it could have been in Martian for all the sense it made.

"What does it mean?"

"I don't know," Luke said. "I think it's in Czech. You got a notepad?"

I crossed to the desk and gave him the pad of paper there. Luke gave me a heavy look and waggled the fingers coming out of his sling. "Could you possibly write it down?"

Numbly, I did, hoping I'd got all the accents right, not wanting to get too close to check.

"I've called Karen," Luke said. "She's going to come and pick him up, do an autopsy. But I guess the cause of death is pretty obvious..."

I nodded.

"Sophie, are you all right?"

Jesus, stupid question time.

"I'm okay," I said. "I need a new sofa."

"Yep."

"I'll get my things," I said, and walked past the body into my bedroom, pushing the door to so Luke couldn't see how much I was shaking when I let my guard down.

A couple of months ago someone started sending me the fingers of someone who'd been killed for helping me. I'd pick up the post and there would be a fat envelope with a smelly, decaying finger inside. The first one had been bleeding, all over the doormat.

Then, after we'd found out who the bad guys were, I went after them. Well, we all went after them, but it was me and Macbeth who fired the shots that killed two of them. The other is in jail for a very long time.

I've killed a man. I've seen one mangled by the baggage belt system. I've picked up dead fingers. But I've never had a dead body just turn up in my apartment. Not the body of someone I was talking to a couple of hours ago.

I packed my bag and went back out to Luke. He was talking on his phone.

"...pretty cut and dried. Bullet in his head caused by someone who thought he'd been betrayed, maybe? Someone who wanted to warn Sophie off? Well, it didn't work last time." He glanced over at me. "Yeah, I think she'll be okay. Kinda shocked. She's going to come over to mine. Okay. See you in five."

He ended the call. "Karen. She's nearly here."

"Talking while driving?"

He smiled. "Hands free. We'd better wait 'til she gets here."

I nodded and looked around for somewhere to sit. Apart from the sofa there was my beanbag, which was right next to the sofa. And there was the floor. Which had blood on it.

"I need air," I said, and stumbled outside. I couldn't look at Petr's bloody face and staring eyes anymore.

Karen turned up a few minutes later in a 3-Series Coupe. "Do you mind if I take your car?" she asked me. "Can't really fit a body in this one."

I nodded vaguely and handed her the keys.

"Sophie, are you all right?"

Why were people asking me that? Did I look all right? Did they think I'd be fine after finding a body in my flat?

"I'll be okay," I said, as Luke came out. "The keys," I showed her which one worked which lock. "For the flat. Lock up. Luke, how did he get in?"

Luke shrugged. "Docherty said he found the door open."

"I thought those locks were secure."

"Yep, me too. Come on," he took my arm, "my car's still here. Unless you'd rather walk? The air'll do you good."

We started down the drive. "Has that ever, ever been true?"

He smiled. "They told you that at school, too?"

"Yeah, the fresh air'll do you good. When of course all it did was give me a cold. And once a black eye, too."

He raised his eyebrows as we got into his car.

"At a party. I was really drunk so they told me to go outside and get some air, and this girl came up and started accusing me of..." I frowned. I was never quite sure. Something to do with her boyfriend. "We got into a bitch fight. I got a black eye."

"Bet that made you popular."

I checked for sarcasm, found none, then remembered that to a bloke, black eyes were cool. "Pariah would be a more accurate word," I said. "I think people were scared of me."

"Still are."

"Well, that's what I want to hear." I rubbed my arms. "Janulevic wasn't scared of me."

"Yeah," Luke said, "he was."

"How'd you figure that?"

"If he wasn't scared of you, he'd have come after you. He wouldn't have warned you. I think he's been re-evaluating ever since you chased after him yesterday."

It was very sweet of him, but I wasn't sure I believed a word. If he was scared of me, he wouldn't have warned me. He'd have run away. I run away from things I'm scared of.

But then I'm not a psycho obsessed with a billion-year-old Mongol artefact.

Luke's flat wasn't far, about half a mile maybe, on the road out towards my parents'. I thought longingly for a second about going home for the night, but I was all out of excuses. It'd have to be Luke's. And I'd have to be strong. I was feeling pathetic, and despite the limp and the sling and the stitches, he was still looking really sexy.

Damn him.

He let me in and I paused for a second before dumping my bag by the sofa. I shook out my sleeping bag, just to make things really clear. I wasn't going to sleep with him.

"You hungry?" Luke went into the kitchen and started flipping lights on. "I have food, but you might have to help me." He gestured to the sling.

"I'm not hungry."

"Let me put it another way: I am and I can't cook with one hand."

I stared at him.

"Okay," Luke unfastened the sling and rolled his shoulders. "It was annoying me anyway." He flexed his arm and winced. "Remind me not to use that too much."

I nodded vaguely.

"Sophie?"

I blinked. "Do you have a dictionary?"

Luke frowned and crossed to the bookshelves lining one wall of the loft. "I have lots."

"A Czech one."

"Ah. That would be no. But," he switched on the computer, "I have something even better."

I went and stood behind him as he dialled up and searched for a translation website. He found one, and after a lot of swearing over the stupid accented letters, typed in the message Janulevic had left. The translation came up.

Do not try to trick me.

Oh, Jesus.

I started to feel lightheaded. He'd known it was a trap so he killed Petr to warn me?

"*Sophie,*" Luke said, jumping up and catching me as my knees buckled.

"Still think he's scared of me?" I mumbled, as Luke pulled me over to the sofa, pushed my head between my knees, and then left.

He left. I needed him there and he left. I sucked in a couple of deep breaths, telling myself Janulevic was obviously a few pennies short of a pound, he'd have killed Petr anyway, it wasn't my fault. But I didn't believe me.

Eventually Luke said something, my name I think, and I looked up, and he turned my head to the TV where Spike was standing there all naked and lovely, being sarcastic to Buffy. I focused on the screen for a few minutes until the scene played out and the other Scoobies came on screen, and then I looked up at Luke.

"Better?"

And then I smiled, because he knew nothing cheered me up more than seeing James Marsters with his shirt off. Well, Luke with his shirt off cheered me up too, but this wasn't really the time.

"Better," I said. "Thank you."

"When in doubt, turn to *Buffy* and the woefully underrated sixth season." He sat down beside me. "Want to watch some more?"

I shook my head. "I'm kinda Buffied out."

He stared. He felt my forehead. "Now I know you're in shock."

"Cut that out. I'm okay. It just got me for a second."

Okay, so I'm the worst spy ever. I get scared by a dead body in my flat. But can you honestly tell me you could take all this and not get freaked? Well, can you?

There you go.

Luke was looking at me with hot eyes. "I can think of something else that might make you feel better..."

I rolled my eyes. "What part of 'traumatised' don't you understand? Or maybe it's 'bullet wound' you're having trouble with," I punched his bandaged arm, and he flinched. "If that's the case, I could give you another, refresh your memory?"

Luke sighed. "You know, this might be easier if I knew why you keep blowing me off."

"You know why."

"No, Sophie, I don't. You just changed your mind—"

"I didn't change anything," I said, getting up and moving away from his heat because it was distracting me. "I just realised a few things."

"Such as...?"

"We want different things."

"I want *Buffy*, you want...?"

I closed my eyes. This wasn't going to get me anywhere. "*Back To The Future* trilogy?"

Luke smiled. "We can do that."

We watched all three films, all six and half hours, and then went on to the DVD special features. It was way past dark when Luke switched the DVD player off, kissed my forehead and went to bed, leaving me there on the chesterfield, curled up in my sleeping bag, wondering why he hadn't pushed it any further, why I'd got such a platonic kiss goodnight, why he hadn't asked me to share his bed and why I wanted it so damn much.

Well, obviously, I wanted it so damn much because I knew what it was like. But that wasn't the point.

My phone rang, and it was Docherty.

"You okay?"

"I'm fine," I said. "Karen took the body away for an autopsy."

"Bet you a hundred it was the bullet that killed him."

"Aw, and there was me going for Tammy scaring him to death."

Dammit, Tammy! I resolved to set my alarm, get up super-early and drive up to Tesco for a massive tin of tuna for her. No, smoked salmon. And some cream. Guilt food.

"Where are you?"

"Luke's. On the sofa," I added, and Docherty laughed gently.

"Where's he?"

"Not on the sofa," I said miserably.

"How come?"

Fucking principles. "Was there something you wanted?"

"This Xe La thing. I think I might know someone who could tell us about it."

"Someone who's still alive?"

"Well, I spoke to him ten minutes ago. I'm guessing he's still alive."

"Great, well, then, give me his phone number or something and I'll call him tomorrow."

"I can do better than that. I can take you to see him."

"Great!" Maybe it wasn't such a bad day after all. "Where does he live?"

"Ireland. I'll meet you at the airport at five-thirty tomorrow," Docherty said, and cut the call.

I lay there, staring at the phone for quite a while. Ireland? Five-thirty in the morning? I looked at the clock. It was gone midnight.

"Who was that?" Luke asked, and I looked up to see him standing in the bedroom doorway. He was wearing boxers and a couple of bandages, and I wanted to ravish him.

"Docherty. I'm going to Ireland tomorrow."

Luke blinked. "I'm sorry, I thought you just said—"

"He knows someone out there who can tell us about this Xe La thing."

"Do you have to go there?"

"Apparently."

Luke nodded tiredly. "What about Angel?"

Bollocks. Angel. I dialled Docherty. "What about Angel?"

"Your friend Macbeth is coming over."

I relayed this information to Luke, who nodded, got his phone and called Macbeth to check.

"Do I really have to come with you tomorrow?" I asked Docherty.

"Well, no, you don't have to. But it is SO17 business. And Professor Kennedy likes blondes."

"Can't Luke go?" I grumbled.

"Not that kind of blond. I'll see you tomorrow," Docherty said. "Pack for an overnight," and then he was gone.

I looked up at Luke, who was finishing his call. "Macbeth's going over there for five tomorrow," he said. "He's going to drop your car off in a bit."

"I don't want to get up early. I got up yesterday."

"How have you survived shift work for two years?" Luke asked, stretching and yawning. Damn, I wished he hadn't done that.

"By telling myself to get a new job."

"Well, now you have one."

"And I'm getting less sleep."

Luke grinned. "I can take a hint. 'Night."

And then he was gone, too, leaving me to mumble a sad little "goodnight" to his closed door, and lie there all night getting very hot and twitchy thinking about him lying there in his boxers, all fit and toned and hot and gorgeous.

By the time morning came, I'd slept about half an hour, trying to put thoughts of the dead man on my sofa out of my head by thinking about Luke, and thoughts of Luke out of my head by thinking about the dead man. Probably I should have come up with something else to take my mind off things, but my head was full of confusion.

I'd been dreaming about Luke all night, about the things we used to do and the things I wanted to do, and when I woke up to the sound of his voice whispering my name, his fingers brushing the hair away from my face, his skin hot against mine, I smiled.

Chapter Nine

He was inches from my skin. "Luke..."

"Are you awake?"

"Mmm." I stretched happily.

"Good. You have to be at the airport in twenty minutes."

My eyes slammed open and I stared at him. "Shit!"

I shoved him away and leapt off the sofa, forgetting that I was still tangled up in my sleeping bag and crashing down on the floor in a very unsexy heap. Luke laughed. I rubbed my throbbing calf, scowling at him.

"Why didn't you wake me up earlier?"

"I was asleep too. Didn't you set your alarm?"

Damn. I knew there was something I should have done. I crawled out of my sleeping bag and grabbed my bag, heading for the bathroom. I just about had time for a shower, as long as I made it really, really quick.

It was while I was in the shower that I realised I'd have to go home and get some more clothes. All I had were the shorts and T-shirt I'd been wearing last night. I didn't have anything warm, or my phone charger or my wallet or anything. Just moisturiser and deodorant.

I threw myself into my clothes and hurtled for the door, Luke sitting on the bed, watching me with lazy amusement.

"Have you ever been on time for anything?" he asked.

"I was born early. Since then, no." I snatched up my sleeping bag and made for the front door. "Dammit, Luke, what's your code?"

"I'm not that stupid," he said, coming through into the living room. "I already unlocked it."

I yanked at the door handle. Smartarse. "I'll see you tomorrow. Apparently I'm staying overnight. Can you feed Tammy for me? Give her lots of nice things and tell her I'm sorry."

"I'm sure she'll understand."

I dashed out to Ted, who was sitting there looking heroic, and realised I couldn't get in. "Keys," I yelled up to Luke, who was standing in the doorway. He looked in the letterbox and chucked them down to me. I threw up the bag of things I'd bought for Tammy, got in the car, and screeched back to my flat.

Five minutes to go. Not impossible, in the same way that telekinesis was not impossible. I hauled out my little hostess suitcase, slammed a few things into it, tied a fleece sweater around my waist, put my gun into its little travelling case and checked I'd got my licence.

Then I got into Ted and drove a lot faster than is advisable with a battered car, making it to the staff car park just in time to realise I'd left my pass at home and so couldn't get into said car park.

Fuck it, I thought, *I am not paying for airport parking,* and I rammed Ted at the barrier. We went through, parked in the carpool only area, and I raced up to the terminal, only remembering when I got to the top of the undercroft stairs that I had no idea where I was supposed to be meeting Docherty, or even where exactly we were going. I hadn't even managed to find out what airline we were with.

I stared praying it wasn't Ace. I couldn't cope with colleagues when I was in this state.

My phone started ringing and I knew it was Docherty even before I looked at it.

"I know, I'm late, I overslept," I said.

"Where are you?"

"Just coming past Boots."

"I'm at the Ace desks. Do you know where that is?"

Patronising git. "I'm sure I can find it," I said, and when I spotted him, tried to sneak up behind and scare him.

He turned and grabbed my wrists. "Got you."

"Where are we even going?"

"Kerry." He gestured to the desk. "Check in."

I heaved my suitcase onto the belt, handed over my passport, and waved the gun case at the (thankfully unknown) check-in chick. "I have a firearm."

She nodded, totally unconcerned. The first time anyone told me they had a gun, I nearly fainted. Now I just do exactly what she did—called the police and the security people, weighed and tagged it, and waved it off with a very nice man in a hi-vis.

The policeman who checked my licence gave me a once-over. "Do I know you?"

"I work here."

"Why are you taking a gun with you?"

I sighed and got out my military ID. "I take it everywhere."

He nodded and let me go. My heart was still thumping: I have a good-girl's fear of the police, even when I know that, strictly speaking, I'm sort of above them.

Ooh, get me. Above the police. Not the law, just the police.

When the policeman had gone, I looked around for Docherty and found him talking to the check-in girl.

"Do you have an ETA?"

"I'm afraid not," she said. "The problem is the plane is grounded in France, and so until we can find a replacement your flight is delayed indefinitely. I'm sorry, I've only just been told."

I looked at Docherty. Did this mean we wouldn't have to go? I could go back to bed? Mmm, bed.

"When's the next flight?" Docherty asked.

She looked something up on the computer. "To Kerry? 1420," she said.

Docherty looked up at the Ace map. "How about Shannon?"

"There's an 0850 flight," she said.

"How do I book that?"

She looked at the customer service desk where the queue nearly reached to Ireland itself. "Best if you phone up."

Docherty got out his phone and dialled. But apparently the 0850 Shannon flight was full, and there wasn't another until this afternoon. He tried a Cork flight, but the next available one was even later.

"We could get a Knock flight at 1130," he said.

"Is that good?"

"Well, the Shannon would be better, but that's full now, too. What the hell is going on?"

I got out my own mobile and called Kelly in Ops. "Do you know anything about a lot of delays to Ireland?"

"ATC strike in France," Kelly told me. "Nothing going in or out. Lot of planes stuck there since yesterday, you know how many flights we have terminating there. Massive delays for everyone. Even cancelling some flights."

"Fantastic."

"Why? Are you at the gate?"

"No, I'm flying to Ireland. I should be boarding in ten minutes, but instead I'm getting an eleven-thirty flight. Do you know where Knock is?"

"I don't even know *what* Knock is."

I smiled. Airports make you very insular. "Okay, cheers, Kelly."

"Bye."

I looked over at Docherty. "Could have had an extra couple of hours in bed," he said, and I gave him a death look.

"I'm going to get a magazine," I said. "Actually, fuck it, I'm getting a whole bloody novel."

We spent about an hour reorganising my luggage and gun—Docherty didn't seem to have either—and went through to Starbucks where I threw caution to the wind and got Angel's favourite, a white chocolate mocha. And you know what? It was disgusting.

"I need pure caffeine," I said, leaving the white froth and cream and ordering a venti Americano with an extra shot of espresso. And then I started to feel slightly dizzy, so I got a chocolate and strawberry muffin to soak up the caffeine.

Docherty was watching me in amazement. "How can you eat that stuff?"

"I open my mouth, bite, then chew. And after that, I swallow."

"Don't you find it full of sugar?"

"That's precisely what I like about it."

The flight was delayed a further hour, but by then we were already through into airside so Docherty couldn't change it again. I sat there and read my book, and he sat there staring into the distance. Docherty was weird.

And I got to spend my weekend with him. Yippedee doo dah.

By the time we boarded the flight, I had nearly finished my book, and it was a boring book, too. Docherty had somehow got us exit seats—I suspect by intimidating the PSA behind my back—and I sat down to read the last few boring pages.

The flight wasn't long, and we got to Knock airport just after two in the afternoon. Not bad to say we should have arrived about five hours earlier, and over a hundred miles away. We went to baggage reclaim and waited for hours for my bag. No bag. I went to the desk and enquired after the whereabouts of my firearm. No firearm.

"It's a SIG-Sauer nine millimetre," I said. "It's a dangerous weapon. And you don't know where it is?"

She shook her head apologetically. "Did you change your flight?"

"Erm, yes, we were going to go to Kerry..."

"Then there's a possibility it's in Kerry."

How do these planes not get hijacked more often?

The woman promised to track down my gun and have it couriered to Kerry airport for me, since Docherty was reluctant to give out our address in Ireland, and we went out to the car hire desk.

I didn't realise until I looked at the map in the hire car that we were so far away from where we should be. I took History at school, okay, not Geography. Knock is up in the top bit of Ireland, and Kerry is down at the bottom left. "Where exactly are we going?" I asked Docherty.

"It's not likely to be on the map."

What a surprise.

"Whereabouts? Do you need directions?"

For the first time since I'd met him, Docherty looked slightly fearful. "I know the way."

The roads in Ireland seemed to meander a lot, and we passed through a million adorable little villages, all painted in bright festival colours, topped off with thatch roofs and flowers in the windows.

"It's so pretty," I said, and Docherty cut his eyes at me.

"You've never been to Ireland before?"

"I went to Dublin about five years ago. With my mum. Her grandfather's Irish."

This didn't elicit any kind of response.

"Which part of Ireland are you from?"

"Kilkenny."

"Like in *South Park*?"

Docherty looked at me like I'd just announced I wanted a threesome with him and a duck.

"You know, 'Oh my God, they killed Kenny'?"

He was still staring at me.

"Never mind," I said, just so he'd get his eyes back on the road. He didn't seem to be missing his Aston, but then he never seemed to show very much emotion at all. He brooded a lot. He was good at brooding.

It started to rain in the early afternoon, just as we passed Galway and saw the grey sea in the distance. I'd thought Irish rain might be softer and prettier, but it was just as depressing as the rain back home. At least the scenery was good here. I love Essex, but if you're not into oil seed rape in a big way, the scenery can be a little uninspiring. This was poetry land. This was Yeats and Keats—wait, are they both Irish? George Bernard Shaw and, erm, Enya. Hmm.

The car started juddering somewhere in County Clare and passed out just after Limerick. I say just after; on the map it was about a thumbnail's width. To us it represented the middle of nowhere.

Docherty sighed and got out the breakdown leaflet from the glovebox. His hand brushed my knee and sent a jolt through me. This was ridiculous. I needed to get some, but not from him.

"They'll be about an hour," he said when he'd finished speaking to the breakdown people.

"An hour?"

"Busy day. People break down more in the rain."

I wasn't sure if he was joking or not. Sometimes it was hard to tell.

So we sat there the car in a lay-by, watching other cars whistle by to their destinations, splattering us with mud as they went. Rain tapped and danced on the windows. I started my book again, but got bored and switched to the magazine. But the magazine was all about clothes I couldn't afford, celebrities I didn't like and orgasms I didn't need to think about.

I got the map out.

"There's a place here called Two Mile Borris," I said. Docherty was unmoved. "And somewhere in Limerick called Hospital. Imagine living there. People'd think you were a permanent invalid."

Docherty flicked his eyebrows, but said nothing. I checked my watch, then remembered it didn't work and wondered why I was still wearing it. I looked at the clock on my phone. We'd been here more than an hour.

"When did they say they'd be here?"

"Now."

"Oh."

We waited another half hour. Docherty called the breakdown people again and was told someone was on their way but they were very busy today. The rain stopped, then it started again. My stomach started rumbling loudly.

"Have you eaten anything but that muffin today?" Docherty asked.

"Oh, yes, I had a three-course meal on the plane," I said. "What do you think? You've been with me all the time."

He looked out of the window at a blurry sign. "There's a place called Kilgarry three kilometres away. They might have somewhere to eat."

Three kilometres was about two miles. About the distance from my flat to my parents' house. "I could walk three kilometres." I'd walked ten, for charity, a couple of times. It took a little over two hours. Three should be easy. Forty-five minutes.

"You have anything waterproof?"

"Yes, but it's in Kerry."

The rain was lighter, but still enough to soak me thoroughly, not to mention chill my bare legs, making me shiver. It took us over an hour to walk to Kilgarry—I no longer have any faith in Irish road signs. Or my own mathematics. Docherty strode ahead at about a million miles an hour, leaving me to straggle unglamorously after him.

But when we got there it was worth it. I swear, we'd just walked straight into Ballykissangel. Everything was pretty. The rain stopped and the sun came out for a while to shine on the perfect little cobbled streets and bright buildings.

We found a pub called Murphy's—of course—and there was a sign outside promising food all day long.

My stomach let out a louder rumble and Docherty smiled, pushing the door open.

Inside the pub was as unlike every fake paddy pub I've ever been in, and exactly like all the old pubs in my village and beyond. There was the deep-down smell of ingrained smoke and old beer, but slightly different, tainted by the peat fire on the far wall. There were the leathery regulars who never, ever seem to leave, no matter what the time or the day. There were wonderfully familiar fonts advertising beers I'd never drunk but seen in pubs all over the place. Proper beers. This place looked like it wouldn't know an alcopop if it minced up and smashed itself on the old, scarred tables.

It smelled like cigarette smoke and crisps and beer, like old wood and rain and even a slight tint of faded perfume. It smelled like the pubs of my childhood, and I smiled as I looked around.

Docherty had Guinness—what else?—and I ordered a half of Bulmers. I had a cheese sandwich and chips, and it tasted *good.*

By the time the chatty landlady came to take our plates away, I was a pint and a half of strong cider up, tired and pretty happy. I didn't want to have to walk back through the rain, which had just started, to the car, which probably wouldn't. The Day From Hell seemed to be getting marginally better.

"Do you reckon anyone will have come to the car?" I asked Docherty. He was looking damn fine in the low light of the pub.

He looked at his watch. "We've been gone two hours," he said. "Quite probably the car will have been nicked by now."

I wasn't really alarmed—after all, it wasn't our car. Surely the hire people had insurance for that sort of thing?

"Do we have to go back and check?" I asked dubiously, and Docherty looked me over.

"I think you'd better stay here," he said. "I'll see if I can get a ride out there."

He went to speak to the landlady, who picked up a phone and made a call, and ten minutes later a tractor trundled up outside the pub.

No one flinched, not even me, because I've been getting stuck in tractor-induced traffic jams since I was old enough to say, "Bloody things". This was quite a young age.

To my surprise, Docherty got back to his feet and went outside. Minutes later, the tractor rumbled off down the street, endangering elderly buildings as it went.

"Where did he go?" I asked my cider.

"Flaherty's giving him a lift to your car," the landlady said in a delightfully Oirish accent you could have cut with something sharp. "If it's broken, he'll tow it back."

"That's nice of Flaherty," I said, hiccupping over the name so it came out like 'flirty.'

"What is it you're doing in Kilgarry?" the landlady wanted to know.

"We're going somewhere. I'm not sure where. Docherty knows where."

"Docherty? Does he not have a first name?"

I blinked at her. "I'm not sure he does."

The landlady laughed and took a seat at my table, lighting up a cigarette and blowing out a happy cloud of smoke. It was then I knew I was drunk, because I wanted to ask her for a cigarette, and I've never smoked. Well, once or twice, but I never really saw the point.

"So is it a dirty weekend you're on?" she asked, sounding— and looking—like Marty's great-great-whatever-grandmother in *Back To The Future III*. Big, strong accent. Big, strong red hair. Both probably fake, but do you think I cared?

"Well, it's sort of wet and muddy," I said, "but so far not too dirty. It's hard to get excited in a Mark V Fiesta, you know?"

Clearly she didn't, but she nodded anyway. "Do you have a name, then?"

I extended my hand, beaming. It's true, you know, about Ireland, that strangers are just friends you haven't met yet. "Sophie."

"Well, I'm Sheelagh. And aren't you just the English Rose? Isn't she pretty, fellas?"

I blushed drunkenly to a chorus of appreciation from the leathery regulars.

"And why is it you've come all the way to the Old Country with such a grand fella if you're not a wee bit naughty?"

Hmm, naughty with Docherty. That idea held definite potential. "We've come to meet someone. We're colleagues."

"Sure, and I'm Catherine Zeta Jones! I've seen the way you're lookin' at each other. Sure, you could light a fire."

It was so charming the way every "I" became an "Oi". Loight a foire. Very Cranberries. Dolores thingummy.

"Will I bring you another drink?" Sheelagh asked, and I thought about the rich, cool, sweet cider, and nodded. She got up to fetch it for me, and as she did my phone started ringing, and everyone in the pub regarded me with great interest.

"Docherty? Is the car okay?"

"There's a note," he said, sounding pissed off. "They came to fix the car but we weren't there, so could we call them at our earliest convenience."

"Kind of playing it fast and loose with their use of the word 'convenience'," I said, and looked around to see if anyone had heard me be so funny.

"Flaherty's going to tow it back to the pub for us and maybe we can get a taxi or something."

"Right. Taxi." I could ask my new best friend Sheelagh about that.

"I'll see you in fifteen," he said, and the line went dead. How cool is that? Very *X-files*. Just a dead line. No "bye-bye, see you later". Just cut the line...

Sheelagh brought my drink over. "Will you be wanting a room?" she asked.

"A room?"

"Sure, we've got a couple. Unless," she twinkled at me, "you'll be after one between you...?"

I blushed again. "We really are just colleagues."

"But you'd like to be...?"

I thought about Docherty. Man, he was fine. Flawless and sultry and dark and brooding. Mmm.

Sheelagh was watching me. "I'll get you a room," she said.

When Docherty came back he asked her if there was a taxi firm nearby. She shook her head.

"There's one out in Ballycrag," she added doubtfully, not looking at me. "But they're not so good in the afternoons. What I'd suggest is you get a room here and maybe try them tomorrow. That motor of yours doesn't look like it's going anywhere."

"I think I'll call them anyway," Docherty said, reaching for his mobile.

"No!" Sheelagh grabbed her phone. "I'll call them for you. Sit down and have another drink. On the house for all your troubles."

Docherty, whatever else he might be, was also patently Irish, and accepted the free Guinness while Sheelagh pretended to call the taxi firm in Ballycrag (had to be a made-up name) and looked disappointed.

"They can't get a taxi out tonight," she said, looking at us mournfully, and Docherty sighed.

"I've spent too long living in cities," he muttered. "Do you have a couple of rooms?"

"We've just the one."

Docherty looked at me, and I shrugged as nonchalantly as I could. "I don't mind sharing," I said. "We're both grown-ups."

"We'll take it then," he said to Sheelagh, who gave me an outrageous wink when Docherty had turned his back to her.

"Do you have any luggage?"

"No. The airline lost it." Bloody stupid Ace. Can't trust a low-cost airline with anything.

We sat in the pub for another couple of hours as the rain continued to patter down outside, watching the bar fill up, listening to the happy banter of proper Irish people, breathing in the rich earthy smell of the peat fire, drinking a lot more...

Okay, so I'm a lightweight. I shouldn't be, because I'm five foot ten and built like Norma Jean Baker.

Come to think of it, wasn't her maiden name Docherty?

I looked up at the man sitting beside me, as silent now as he had been in the car, and felt a wave of lust. Sod Luke and his stupid casual sex philosophy. That only worked with people you weren't going to see again. I wanted a hot night with a sexy, brooding man. A man like Docherty.

I reached out and touched his arm. "Docherty..."

He looked at me, then his watch. "I think I'll go to bed."

"I think I'll join you." I stood up and wobbled slightly. Docherty caught me before I fell.

"I think that's a good idea."

Sheelagh gave me a thumbs-up as we passed the bar and made our way up the little staircase to the room Docherty had the key for. It was small and charming, with a patchwork bedspread and flowers in the window. There was one bed, and it was a double.

"Which side do you want?" Docherty looked at the bed, not at me.

"Which one do you want?" I batted my eyelashes.

He gave me a look. "Sophie, how much have you had to drink?"

I frowned. "I can't remember. Maybe a little bit too much. But I feel fine," I assured him, and pulled off my sweater.

"You don't look fine," Docherty said, and I glanced at the mirror. I thought I looked great—dishevelled and flushed, like a nineteenth century heroine. Shame my bodice wasn't ripped, but there's not much you can do with a jersey top.

I pulled said top off, and Docherty narrowed his eyes at me.

"What are you doing?"

I tried to make my voice go all Kathleen Turner seductive, but ended up sounding more like Marge Simpson. "I can't sleep in my clothes. And besides," I walked boldly over and aimed my DD-cups at him, "I'm not sure I'll have much use for them tonight anyway."

Docherty looked me over slowly. I pulled in my stomach.

"Sophie," he said in a low voice, and I looked up eagerly. "Without wanting to go all Dustin Hoffman—" God, even the way he said that was sexy: Dosstin. Mmm... "—are you trying to seduce me?"

I pouted. "Would you like me to seduce you?"

There was a long silence, during which I started to feel ever so slightly foolish.

"I thought you had something going on with Luke."

I stamped my foot. "No," I said in frustration. "I have nothing going on with Luke."

"So why were you staying at his place last night?"

"I told you, I was on the sofa. Nothing happened. I was traumatised."

"Are you still traumatised?"

"No." Just drunk and really horny.

Docherty looked at me for a long time, and I was just about to admit to a crushing defeat and step away when he cupped my face in his hands and kissed me, long and hard.

And when I say hard, I mean *hard*.

"I thought I was supposed to be seducing you," I said breathlessly when he let me go, hot and flushed and very excited.

"Change of plan," Docherty said, and kissed me again, pressing me down onto the patchwork throw, doing interesting things in the area of my bra. "Just tell me one thing."

"Mmm?"

"This is not about Luke."

I blinked, the heat receding slightly. "Why would it be about Luke?"

"You've just got out of a relationship with him—"

"There was no relationship."

Docherty rolled his eyes. "Right, and I'm David Beckham."

Actually, there was a sort of resemblance. If Becks had dark hair and a brooding expression and bigger shoulders and a totally different face. And was Irish.

"That was the problem," I clarified. "He didn't want any kind of relationship."

Docherty moved back a few inches. "You want a relationship with me?"

"No! No, I just want to have sex."

He frowned. "I don't get it."

What's not to get? Was he simple?

"You do know what sex is?"

"I defined it," Docherty said, and one look at his dark, liquid eyes told me he wasn't joking. "But I don't understand the relationship part. Spell it out for me."

"I can't sleep with Luke because I want a proper relationship with him. But I don't want a relationship with you, so it's okay to sleep with you." It was perfectly obvious to me.

Docherty frowned. "So you just want to sleep with me because you can't sleep with Luke, for fear of getting involved?"

"Yes!" I was glad he'd got it. I pulled him back down to me. "Where were we?"

But Docherty seemed less eager. "I'm not sure I like being a substitute," he said. "This is all about Luke, isn't it? You want him more than me, don't you?"

Well, duh.

Docherty is sexy. Really, really sexy. And I was incredibly flattered that he wanted me. Believe me, I was appreciating this a whole lot. *But,* and it's a big but, he wasn't Luke. And Luke was who I wanted.

Not Docherty.

"Oh, bollocks." I flopped back on the bed. "See, that just spoiled the mood."

Docherty moved away. "Thought it might."

I glared up at him, trying to figure out if the squishy feeling in my stomach was some kind of kindly emotion for Luke, or just good old-fashioned nausea. "You did that on purpose."

"You'd have regretted it when you were sober."

"Duh. Isn't that the point of a one-night stand?"

Docherty gave a faint smile. "Do you want to use the bathroom first?"

I shook my head. "You go."

I watched him leave the room, still dark and sexy, and sighed in annoyance. The really stupid thing was that he was right. Damn him. Right about me, right about Luke. Right, right, right, as a one-legged drill sergeant might have said.

God, I am drunk.

Chapter Ten

When I next opened my eyes, it was morning, and I was crashed out in my underwear. I didn't remember taking my jeans off, but then I had been really plastered. My mouth was dry and my head was thumping. The sunlight stabbed my eyes.

I managed to drag myself onto my back and look around. Docherty was nowhere to be seen.

The bathroom was across the hall, and I threw my fleece pullover over my underwear to stumble out there and try and make myself slightly more presentable. I had no shampoo so a shower would have done more harm than good. There was a deodorant in my bag and a little bottle of moisturiser, and I managed to smudge on a little bit of makeup to make myself feel more human. I filled up my water bottle and drained it about ten times, plugged my phones into their battery-powered chargers, and went back to the bedroom.

I met Docherty in the corridor. He looked over the low-zipped fleece and my bare legs, and raised his eyebrows.

"Morning," I croaked.

"Morning. Did you sleep well?"

I yawned and nodded and pushed open the door to the bedroom. Docherty stood and watched me pull on my jeans and T-shirt, then he said, "There's breakfast downstairs if you're hungry."

I thought about it. "Will it be greasy?"

"I should think so."

"Lead on."

Sheelagh kept giving me saucy looks and winking as she served me fried eggs and tomatoes and waffles and toast. She was very surprised to hear I was a vegetarian, and offered me kippers instead of sausages. I politely declined.

"Flaherty fixed the car," Docherty said. He was drinking white coffee. No food. "We can be on our way when you've done."

I nodded. More hours in a car. Just what my hangover needed.

We said goodbye to Sheelagh, promised to come back and see her some time (or at least I did) and were on our way in the newly fixed Fiesta. I opened the window for air and tried to sleep, but the roads were too bumpy. Obviously Flaherty hadn't touched the suspension.

"Docherty," I said after a couple of dozen miles.

"Yes?"

"Last night." I felt my colour rise. "Did I...?"

"Yes."

I checked his face carefully for emotion. Nothing.

"Did we...?"

"No."

Still nothing.

"You talked me out of it."

"Yes."

I sighed. "How come you're so talkative?"

This earned a sideways glance. "Just naturally blabby, I guess."

Butch Cassidy and the Sundance Kid. At least I knew he had good taste in films, even if he never watched *South Park.*

"Do we have far to go?"

"Not far now."

Not helpful.

About an hour later, my Nokia rang. It was Luke, and I answered with mixed feelings.

"Why the hell weren't you answering yesterday?"

And there it was, my usual mixture of lust and irritation. No squishy feelings at all.

"No signal. And my battery's low anyway."

"You have your charger, right?"

"I have an emergency charger. My proper mains charger is in my suitcase. My suitcase is somewhere in the region of Kerry airport. I don't know where the hell we are, but it isn't Kerry."

"Actually..." Doherty murmured, and I ignored him.

"Ace lost your luggage?" Luke asked.

"Bingo."

"What about your gun?"

"Lost that too."

"Fantastic."

"My thoughts exactly. Well, actually, my thoughts are a hundred percent unrepeatable, but there you go."

"Did you get anything from this Kennedy guy?"

"Haven't got there yet."

"What?"

I relayed the story of the Day From Hell, carefully talking round the bit where I'd tried to seduce Docherty. "So it might be another night."

"Marvellous."

"Why do you sound so cheerful?"

Luke sighed. "Because your friend Angel feels guilty about the crash on Wednesday, so she's been dragging me up to the hospital to go and see your friend Harvey."

I smiled. "Isn't Macbeth supposed to be watching her?"

"Macbeth has managed to be very busy whenever Angel wants to do anything remotely girlie. As has Maria. I am going *nuts* here."

"*Poverino*," I said, without much sympathy. I'm not exactly sure what that means, Luke used to say it when he was being Italian and I was being pathetic at the airport. But it sounds very sympathetic, even in a sarcastic tone of voice.

It's probably obscene.

"Anyway," he said. "We went up to the crash site. Still a big mess."

"If you find a hubcap, that's Ted's."

"I'll bear that in mind. The Scoobie is still there with a big old Police Aware sticker on it. We asked the neighbours—"

"What neighbours?"

"About a mile up the road."

Of course.

"They called the police on it because it was blocking the road. So now it's in a lay-by instead. I wouldn't count on anyone retrieving it, either, because you know what?"

I think I could guess. "It was stolen?"

"Clever bunny. They have another couple of performance cars on their list—not Porsches or anything like that, but someone nicked an Evo VII on Wednesday night and it hasn't been seen since."

"He knows his cars."

"About as well as you do."

I wasn't sure if that was a compliment or not.

"It *could* be coincidence..."

"I don't believe in them and I know you don't, either."

"Great. Has Maria got anywhere with those files? Greg Winter's last mission?"

"His last mission was before IC died. He was on leave when he was shot."

"Do you believe that?"

"Nope. Oh, and one more thing..."

"Surprise me."

"Greg was killed with a .22, right?"

"Right."

"I was shot with a .22. And so was Petr. Same gun."

I whistled. "Can Karen tell if it's the same gun that got Greg?"

"Doubtful. But you know, I wouldn't really be that surprised."

Fantastic. I ended the call and looked over at Docherty. "The gun that shot Luke is the same gun that killed Petr."

"What a surprise."

"Same calibre as the gun that shot Greg Winter."

"Lots of people have .22s."

"Well, yeah. But I still think there's something icky about it."

Docherty nearly smiled at that. "Icky? Is that a professional term?"

I prickled. "It is now."

He turned off the little road onto a very narrow boreen. "Not far now."

He said that an hour ago.

But this time he meant it. At the end of the little track was a gate, and through the gate was a courtyard with chickens and a couple of collies scratching about. The buildings on three sides were neat and clean. Flowers in the windows. Clean steps. Nice.

"Is this it?" I asked Docherty.

"This is it."

We got out of the car and I stretched, feeling horribly scruffy. And then we went up the steps and into a big scrubbed kitchen where a beautiful black-haired girl was kneading bread, and I felt even scruffier.

Docherty said something to her in Irish, and she nodded and smiled and made a reply. I don't understand Irish at all. They have the same alphabet as us, but they seem to approach it sort of sideways.

"This is Sophie," Docherty said, and I smiled nervously. "Sophie, this is Éibhlís Kennedy."

I blinked. Did he just call her Eyelash?

"That's an unusual name," I ventured. "How are you spelling that?"

She paused, as if she couldn't remember, then spelled it out. See? Sideways. "The 'E' and the second 'I' have acute accents. It's quite complicated. They were going to call me Mary."

Irish. Different species.

"I'm sorry," I said. "I just thought the professor would be older. And, you know, a guy."

Docherty and Éibhlís smiled.

"He is." Éibhlís said. "I'm his daughter."

Ah. I felt my face flush.

"Would you be wanting anything to eat?" she asked, and I closed my eyes and thought about barmbrack and Irish butter and natural cider. When I opened them again, Éibhlís was taking biscuits out of a packet and putting them on a plate. She opened up a large fridge and offered me mineral water, Diet Coke, Budweiser, Guinness or wine. There was English Breakfast tea or Costa Rican coffee on offer, both to be made with organic milk.

I felt Docherty's gaze on me and said I'd just have water. Coffee would have been good, but I was so dehydrated I felt as if my body was slowly shrivelling.

"Is the old man around?" Docherty asked, and Éibhlís shrugged.

"He's out with the horses. You're a little bit late, so..."

A whole day. It didn't seem to be bothering her. She poured herself a Guinness, then one for Docherty, and we followed her through to a stone-floored living room, lined with books and papers and CDs and a lot of PlayStation games.

"Do you not have any luggage?"

I shook my head. "The airline lost it."

"Ah, well. Travelling light's always a better option anyway."

Hmm.

"I've cleared you out a room upstairs," she said, waving her hand at a precarious staircase. "Will you be staying tonight?"

"I think so," Docherty said. "I'll call the airline and re-book for tomorrow."

"So, Sophie," Éibhlís said, "tell me about this SO17 you're working for," and I sprayed water all over myself.

"It's supposed to be a secret organisation," I said, glaring at Docherty.

"Éibhlís won't tell anyone."

"That's not really the point," I said. "Even the British police don't know about it."

"The British police couldn't find their arses with both hands," Éibhlís said dismissively. "Do you have a gun?"

"Somewhere," I said.

"Airline lost that too," Docherty explained.

"Some airline."

"Well, they gave Sophie a job."

"Hey!"

They both smiled at me. "Sure, we're joking," Éibhlís said. "Haven't you heard Michael's sense of humour?"

I stared. Michael?

Now, that just spoiled the illusion. It was such a normal name. Docherty on its own sounded so much more brooding and mysterious.

There was the sound of clattering hooves outside and I looked out of the little window to see a fit man in his sixties swinging off a large chestnut horse. Éibhlís got up and went outside to him, and Docherty followed her, and I sat there for a few seconds before following, too. I wasn't sure I totally got this. I'd been expecting— Well, I don't know what I was expecting. A musty old man in a college library, maybe? An ancient geezer in a wheelchair? Not a robust man with a tan, handing the reins of the horse to his daughter and clapping Docherty on the back. They exchanged a rapid stream of Irish that sounded impressive but could really have been a shopping list for all I knew. I don't do languages. Especially not ones that need you to learn the alphabet all over again.

Professor Kennedy—for I assumed that was who he was— looked me over and said something in Irish.

I blinked politely. "I'm afraid I don't understand."

"*Sasanach*," Docherty said, and I frowned suspiciously.

"What did you just call me?"

"English," Docherty said, and Kennedy laughed.

"And sure you're an English Rose," the professor said, lifting my chin. "Even if you are hungover."

I blushed bright pink.

"Éibhlís," Kennedy yelled. "Is there any lunch to be had?"

She yelled back something and Kennedy nodded. "How's chicken soup for you?"

I winced. "Er, I don't eat meat," I said, and felt like the *Big Fat Greek Wedding* girl. *"What do you mean, he don't eat no meat?"*

"None at all?" Kennedy was staring.

"Erm, no. I eat fish," I volunteered.

"Why?"

"Well, because I could kill a fish," I said, wanting to curl up and die.

Kennedy looked at me for a long while, then he laughed. "Sure, that's good reasoning," he said. "Are you sure you're not Irish?"

"I think my mother's grandfather was. But that might be wishful thinking."

"Everyone wants a bit of Irish in them," Docherty said, with a meaningfully penetrating stare at me that made—I swear—even my hair blush.

I ended up having bread and cheese for lunch, but since the bread had been made that morning and the cheese was fresh Irish cheddar, I was more than happy. I sat there at the big oak table in the kitchen, feet tapping the slate floor, listening to a burble of Irish voices. Éibhlís came back in and got some soup, and was soon arguing with her father about the Internet. Her position was that it was a great tool for communication and information, not to mention shopping, and he maintained that it was a ploy for global domination by the Yanks. I wasn't sure who I agreed with most, because they were both so bloody entertaining. Docherty kept out of the discussion, and I got to wondering if he even knew what the Internet was. He didn't really seem like one for technology.

Éibhlís cleared away our plates and stacked them in the dishwasher next to the huge old-fashioned farmhouse sink. So much for bucolic Oirishness.

"Now then." Kennedy got to his feet and patted his flat belly. "What is it you've come all the way out here for?"

I glanced at Docherty but he wasn't forthcoming.

"*Michael* said you might be able to tell me something about this artefact we're trying to trace," I said, ignoring Docherty's glare. "It's Mongolian, called the Xe La."

Kennedy frowned and went through the living room into a very crowded study. It might have been a large room, were it not for the shelves and shelves of cascading books and files, cases of stony things, three computers and 3D map of Ireland spread out on a large table.

"Mongolian," he said. "I don't know of anything... What era?"

I blinked. "I don't know. Nobody knows. We're not even totally sure it's Mongolian."

Kennedy raised his palms. "Not even sure it's Mongolian," he muttered. "Do you know what it looks like?"

I shook my head.

"What it does?"

"Does?"

"All artefacts do something. Even if it's only in legend. The best ones earn you money while they're doing it," he said, and I understood from this where the horses had come from.

"Why is it you want to know about it?"

I sighed. "Well, it's a bit of a long story." I told him about the threats Angel had been getting, the photos and the stalking, about how we were sure the stalker was after something he thought Angel had. I explained about Janulevic sending Petr after me, and how we'd connected them both to this artefact and concluded that Janulevic thought Angel had it.

"Why would Angel have it?"

"I don't know. But it's all connected with her father's death. We think. Someone sent her photos of her father being shot from his bike and killed. MI5 say he wasn't working for them at the time. But if that's so, why did someone kill him and make it look like an accident, and document the whole thing?"

Kennedy frowned. "You think he had the artefact?"

"I think that was why he was killed. I think someone thought he was transporting the Xe La and that's why he was killed. But he didn't have it, so they're still looking, and they reckon his daughter must have it."

"But why wait fifteen years?"

I raised my hands. "I don't know."

Kennedy crossed to a box of files on the far wall. "Greg Winter," he said. "He came to me once about a—"

He looked up at me suddenly. "Spell Xe La," he said, and I did.

"Have you seen it written down? Who told you it was spelled like that?"

I tried to think. Had anyone told me?

Kennedy grabbed a pad and a pen and wrote "Séala". "Not Xe La. It's Irish. You pronounce it the same way, more or less."

He suddenly looked very excited.

"What does it mean? In Irish?"

"It means seal or mark. Like you might have on a letter, for instance. In terms of what you're looking at, it's a seal ring. Believed to have been forged for a king of Ulster, it fell into the possession of the evil elf Cluricaune, who hid it for centuries. The stories don't have much interest in it other than saying it will grant the bearer his or her heart's desire."

Blimey.

"Do you know what it looks like?"

Kennedy shook his head. "I've a few books if you want to look through them...?"

I nodded, but my eagerness soon faded when I realised that the Irish "few" didn't just apply to miles. It applied to books, too. There weren't a few. There were bloody dozens.

I spent the rest of the day looking through all these fabulous old books—some of them texts on parchment—feeling very privileged. I learnt all sorts of great things about Celtic myths and legends—so much better than Greek ones! I kept having to get out Kennedy's big fat Irish-English dictionary to translate things, and learnt a lot about Irish pronunciation. It's quite simple when you get the hang of it. At least, I assume it would be. I didn't quite get the hang of it, myself.

I hardy noticed it get dark, until Éibhlís came in and asked if I wanted anything to eat.

"I've made you a vegetable stew," she said. "It's a Delia recipe..."

I smiled. "Can't go wrong with that." I slipped a bookmark into the text and followed her out into the kitchen. I hadn't seen Docherty since lunchtime, or Kennedy since he'd told me about the Séala. I hadn't even thought to call anyone about it. I'd call Luke later, after tea.

But tea turned out to go on for hours, with Éibhlís and her father sparking off another debate, about the Euro this time, which I tried and failed to not get involved in.

"What do you mean, easier?" Kennedy roared.

"Well, you know, if I have to go to a lot of different countries, it's a lot easier to have one currency in my wallet..."

"Exactly, but it's not losing cultural identity," Éibhlís said, and Kennedy looked mutinous.

"Well, no, not really..."

"Sophie," Kennedy said, "did you not think the Irish Punt was a charming currency?"

I have to say it hardly crossed my mind and when it did, it was just that Punt was a funny word.

"Erm, well, yes, I suppose so..."

"And speaking as an English girl, you must have found it easier to use, what with being nearly the same as your own..."

"But what if she was French, Da?" Éibhlís asked. "Would she have found it easier then?"

"Ach, the French," Kennedy said dismissively. "Stop your jawing, girl, and fetch me me dessert."

Dessert was homemade cheesecake. Éibhlís appeared to not only be beautiful, but a fabulous cook. The vegetable stew had been gorgeous.

We were sitting outside in the courtyard, under a gas heater that played gentle light on the candlelit table. While Éibhlís and Kennedy argued happily all through dessert, Docherty turned to me and asked quietly, "Did you find anything useful?"

"Yes. It's not Mongolian, it's Irish, and it's a seal ring. Said to give the bearer his heart's desire."

Docherty whistled. "So I guess we have to hope that Janulevic wants world peace."

"Maybe his heart's desire is for better hair," I said. "To lose weight. Learn English."

"Maybe he wants the love of a good woman."

"Maybe."

But honestly? This was a man who'd killed every person who'd ever heard of the Séala. Somehow I didn't think his heart's desire involved hugs and puppies.

Éibhlís didn't even bother to clear the plates away before she fetched a little round flat drum, a bodhrán I think she called it, and a penny whistle, and a fiddle and a guitar, and handed them round and started playing and singing. Kennedy was on the guitar and his daughter alternated the whistle and violin. To my surprise, Docherty picked up the bodhrán and played along.

It was fabulous. Actually, what it was like was when I still lived with my parents, and my dad would insist we'd all sit out in the garden for tea when it was summer, even when it was freezing, we'd all be sitting there in jeans and fleeces, shivering and drinking lots of wine to keep the cold out. And after a while Chalker would go and get his guitar, and we'd sit there playing Beatles songs until the wine ran out or the neighbours started getting grumpy. A couple of times last year, when I went home for tea, Chalker might have a few band mates over and we'd have a jam in the back garden under the fairy lights I'd put up years ago for a garden party and never taken down. I love fairy lights.

It got late, and Éibhlís fell silent as her father sang on in Irish. Docherty placed the drum quietly on the table and we all listened as the song, old and beautiful, went on and on.

Before I realised it, Docherty was shaking me awake and telling me it was late, I should go to bed, and I fell asleep beside him under a soft duvet.

Chapter Eleven

I woke alone when it was light and lay there for a while. I'd had some wine last night, but not enough to get me really drunk. Not enough to give me a hangover. I was feeling good. I'd found out something important about the Séala, something that put us ahead of Janulevic. He didn't know it was Irish. And he obviously didn't know Kennedy knew about it, or Kennedy would be dead.

I'd tried to tell him and Éibhlís countless times last night that they might be in danger, but they'd just shrugged it off and said they'd be fine. No harm could come to them here.

Well, yes, I could see their point, but I'd always believed the same thing about my little flat. Right up until the minute when someone threw a flaming bottle through my window three months ago.

I stretched under the covers and wished I'd got some clean clothes to put on. Well, not so much clothes as underwear. Two days was pushing it. Three was just unhealthy.

A knock on the door announced Éibhlís, asking if I wanted coffee or anything else.

"Coffee would be great," I said, "but so would clean underwear."

"What size are you?"

Uh, what size am I really, or what can I tell her? "Twelve. UK." Did they have the same sizes in Ireland?

She nodded and disappeared, coming back a minute later and throwing me a selection of knickers. "Fresh out the laundry," she said. "I'm afraid I can't do much for you in the way of a bra..."

"I can live with this one. Thanks, Éibhlís."

She smiled. "Don't mention it."

"Do you know where Docherty went?"

"Out for a walk. He's a bit of a loner."

"Tell me about it."

She regarded me carefully. "Is there something going on with you two?"

I shook my head quickly.

"Neither of you complained about sharing a bed."

"We shared one the night before." I paused. "I mean, nothing happened—well, pretty much nothing—I mean, I have someone at home," I fabricated.

"Is he a patch on Docherty?"

I thought about Luke. "He's better."

She looked impressed. "Does he have a brother?"

"I—" You know, I had no idea. "I don't think so."

"Ah, well. Will I fetch you some towels for the shower?"

A subtle way of telling me I looked a wreck.

"Thanks," I nodded. "That's kind of you."

"Don't mention it."

She brought the towels and left, and I lay there a while longer before getting up, making my way to the bathroom, and washing all the grime of the last two days off me in the shower. Éibhlís had some coconut shampoo and it smelled divine. I got dressed, put on some makeup, and spotted the car keys lying on the floor. *They'll get lost there*, I thought, and put them in my pocket to give to Docherty later.

By the time I came down to breakfast I was feeling a hell of a lot better than I had the morning before. I ate some cereal and inhaled some coffee, and looked out of the window. The sky was clear and bright, I had sunglasses in my bag, the grass was green and I felt lively. I'd let the sun dry my hair.

"I think I'll go for a walk," I announced to Éibhlís and Kennedy. "See if I can find Docherty."

They nodded and told me that there was a path at the back of the stables that ran in a wide loop, a very pretty walk a couple of kilometres long.

A couple of Irish kilometres, no doubt. I hoped our flight wasn't until the evening.

The walk was indeed very pretty, and I felt pretty happy as I meandered along, saying hello to the horses grazing in the fields, feeding them handfuls of grass and laughing as they tickled my hand, snuffling the grass up. My phone battery was dead from searching for signal all night, and my emergency charger was all out of batteries, but it was okay, I could buy some on the way to the airport. Surely there must be a well-stocked shop around here somewhere—where had Éibhlís got all her groceries from?

I made a mental to-do list as I walked, breathing in great lungfuls of gorgeous clean air. I wanted to bottle that air and take it home with me. First thing, though, was to scan in the pages of some of those documents and e-mail them to myself. That way I could print them out for Luke and Karen and Angel. We could do an Internet search for the Séala when I got back.

I also had to get hold of Docherty and find out what was going on with our return travel arrangements. I assumed we were going home today, but I could be wrong. Everything here moved very slowly. We could be here for weeks.

Shame.

When I knew what was going on, I ought to report back to Karen. I was sure there'd be a house phone I could use, but the thing was I didn't know the number. I could hardly call up

Directory Enquiries and ask them for the SO17 number, could I? And I doubted Luke or Maria would be listed.

I doubted Macbeth even had a house, let alone a house phone.

I could call Angel, I suppose. She could speak to Luke for me. But her number was unlisted, too, and I wasn't entirely sure if I knew it off by heart properly.

I was probably about half a mile from the house when it happened. A huge, booming explosion that shook the ground and sent the horses nearby galloping to the other side of the paddock.

Janulevic, I thought, and set off at a run.

Suddenly the ground seemed muddy, the air too heavy to run in, my lungs were bursting, I couldn't run because my legs were made of lead. Really squidgy lead. I rounded the corner of the hedge that bordered the boreen, and where the house should have been was a great big pile of smouldering rubble.

I stood and stared for quite a while, smoke stinging my eyes, and my only thought was that I was really, really glad I had the car keys, and I could get the hell out of here.

The Fiesta had one side—the driver's side—caved in, but I could get in the passenger side and shuffle over, start the ignition and pray for it to kick over, and then I gunned it down the drive. Janulevic had tried to get me before. He'd be trying to get me now. I shoved thoughts of Docherty and Éibhlís and Kennedy and documents out of my head and rammed pedal to metal.

I drove through the gently drifting clouds of smoke, recklessly twisting down narrow lanes and paying no attention to where I was going. It wasn't until I found myself coming up to a little town that I realised I'd have to get myself an actual direction to go in.

I pulled into a parking space and got the road map out of the glove box, shaking. I was over the county border into Cork now, and according to the map not far from the city itself.

The city which had an airport.

It seemed like hours until I got there, but get there I did, abandoning the car and zombie-walking into the terminal. I found the Ace booking desk and got myself a flight back to Stansted in an hour. Then I wandered over to the pay phones, shoved in a few cents and dialled the emergency services.

"I couldn't see as I drove past," I said, "but I think the house burned down. I heard an explosion. Maybe it was gas. It was very smoky. There might have been people in there. I think there were horses, too. Someone needs to go and help."

They asked for the address and I gave it as well as I could, trying to remember the towns and villages I'd driven through. And then they asked for my name, and I put the phone down and went upstairs to airside and got myself a large Irish whiskey, even thought I hate whiskey and it was the middle of the day, and downed it in one.

Then I cried.

The thought occurred to me as I was boarding.

I was wondering how Janulevic knew where we were. And from there I got to wondering how he knew where I lived. And then, out of nowhere, came the sneaky, perfidious little thought that Docherty had been there both times.

Docherty had found Petr's body. Docherty had left the house an hour before the bomb went off. Docherty had got me to go to Ireland. He'd had access to all the things Angel knew, to everything in her house, looking for the Séala.

And I'd just fed him more information.

I started to feel clammy and shaky. The crewman checking my boarding pass had to catch me as I nearly fell.

"Are you all right?"

I stared at him. "I—I'm fine, I think I'm fine... I just got dizzy." I wandered down to my seat, my mind racing. I couldn't use my phone on board, of course I knew that—and even if the airline had let me I couldn't anyway, because I'd forgotten to get batteries for my charger.

It took quite a while to explain what I needed. I was one of the last ones to board and they wouldn't let me off. I had to take my seat and wait until we were properly airborne before I could get anyone to listen to me, and even then I think they thought I was a terrorist.

I wrote out a message for the trolley dolly. "I need you to radio this to Stansted ATC," I said, "and get them to call it through to the police. Tell them we don't need any police presence, but this person *must* be there."

Looking bewildered, she took my note and went up into the cockpit. A few minutes later, she came back.

"They got the message," she said. "They'll do what they can."

The flight went horribly slow for me and when we landed, everyone was in my way. I raced up the jet bridge, my heart thumping, and when I saw Luke waiting at the top I threw my arms around him.

"What is it?" he said. "What's so urgent?"

"Where's Angel?"

"What? She's with Macbeth."

"At home?"

"Yes—"

"Get her out of there. She needs to go. Go away. Somewhere secret. Don't tell anyone."

"Sophie, are you all right?"

"I'm okay. I'm fine."

He rubbed a thumb across my forehead. "Is that ash? What's going on?"

"We have to go," I said. "We have to go and get Angel out of her house."

Luke started walking. "Is she in danger there?"

"Yes. Very definite danger. From Docherty."

Luke stopped walking.

"Docherty? Soph, did you hit your head?"

"No, but about three hours ago I saw Professor Kennedy's house blown up. He was in it. With his daughter. Docherty was nowhere to be seen. I know, I went out looking for him. Luke, he took me out there to get rid of me. Along with the Kennedys. He did it all together so it'd look like Janulevic did it. And he killed Petr. That's how he found him. Janulevic didn't put him there."

Luke was looking at me like I'd just turned green and vomited lava all over the satellite floor.

"Docherty—" he began, and I held up my hand.

"He knew about the gun," I said.

"What gun?"

"When you called me, yesterday, and said about the gun that shot Petr being the same that shot you? Docherty said a lot of people have .22s."

"...So?"

"So, I never told him it was a .22."

Luke stared at me for a long time. Then he grabbed my hand and started moving. Fast. "We have to move Angel," he said. "Why didn't you call me before?"

"I only realised when I was on the plane. My phone is dead. My suitcase... Dammit, and my gun too, they're still at Kerry airport. At least, I hope they are."

Luke tossed me his mobile. "Call them. Call Angel too. Tell her to get packing. You have any idea where she can go?"

I had no idea at all.

I called Angel and told her to start packing up her essentials, that we'd sort something out when we got there. She sounded alarmed, and I hadn't the composure to reassure her.

"I'll explain when we get there," I said. Then I called the Ace ticket desk and got them to give me the number of Kerry airport. Eventually I got through to their baggage desk, where they said they had a suitcase and a firearm awaiting collection. I told them to send both items to Stansted, ended the call and went up to the baggage desk where I told them to give me a call when my things arrived. Then I followed Luke down to the car park and drove him home.

"How'd you get here?"

"Karen drove me over. She still won't let me drive."

"I notice you lost the splint. And the sling."

"They annoyed me."

Let that be a lesson to me.

I made a quick stop at my house to say hello to Tammy, who wasn't talking to me, and to pick up the revolver I'd half-inched from Petr. It was still loaded, and I tucked it into my handbag. We set off for Angel's and found her throwing things into a case, looking panicked as Macbeth tried and failed to reassure her.

"Where's Docherty?" she asked.

"Hopefully far, far away. He's a bad guy, Angel. He tried to have me killed. We need to get you away—"

"But how can he be bad? He protected me..."

"He was trying to find this Séala thing. Angel, it's Celtic, a seal, maybe a seal ring. Do you have anything like that?"

She shook her head. "My dad's signet ring..."

"Show me."

We followed her into her bedroom and she opened up her little jewellery box. I knew she had a safe upstairs where all her mother's jewels were kept, but all the things in here were personal—a christening spoon, a charm bracelet, a pendant with pictures of her parents in it. And her father's signet ring.

Luke and I looked at it. A normal gold ring. "It still pretty much means nothing to me," I confessed.

"Well, it means something to me," Angel said, tipping out the contents of her makeup bag and replacing them with the things from the jewellery box. "Sophie, could you go and get the Simon & Patrick for me, please?"

I frowned and went upstairs to get it. I don't know the first thing about guitars, but I knew Chalker had saved up for one of these for the sole reason that Greg Winter used to have one. Once he came over and Angel let him play and it was like seeing a holy man at Lourdes. All his dreams had come true.

I brought the guitar down with its hard case, and watched Angel pack it away. "You really can't think of anything that might be a seal?"

She cast her eyes around the room. "I really can't. Mum was never really into Celtic jewellery, she liked her diamonds, you know? And Dad really only wore this and his wedding ring."

"Maybe it's not jewellery," Luke said.

"It could be anything," I said in despair. "Right now we have to think about getting Angel away. If Docherty comes back, I don't want you anywhere near this place."

"Do you maybe have some friends you could stay with?" Luke asked.

Angel shrugged. "I'm guessing this doesn't include you," she said to me, and I shook my head. "Well, Livvy and Charis live in London..."

"Too busy," Luke said.

"Penny lives just up the road..."

"Too close," I said.

"Well, I suppose there's Livvy's dad's house..."

"Where's that?"

"Cornwall."

"You think he'll let you stay?"

"He probably won't even notice. It's huge. Oh—" She put her hand to her mouth.

"What?"

"The Trust Ball. It's supposed to be tomorrow, it's in London..."

"No," Luke said. "No way."

"But it's every year." Angel's voice was firm. "It raises millions for the Trust."

"What trust?" Macbeth asked. I'd forgotten he was there, which is quite a feat.

"The IC Winter Cancer Trust," I said. "Every year they have a huge charity ball to raise money. Totally A-list. Coverage in the glossies and everything."

"But not this year," Luke said.

"Yes," Angel said, "*this year.*"

"It's too high-profile—"

"The security is amazing! Livvy arranges it. Bouncers all over the place, everyone gets scanned as they come in. Even the caterers. He won't get in."

"I don't care. It's not happening."

Angel looked mutinous, and I suggested quickly, "Why don't you give Livvy a ring and see if you can go down and stay at her dad's place? We'll sort something out about the ball."

Angel looked doubtful, but she left the bedroom and went out into the kitchen to call her very posh friend Livvy.

"She's not going to give up about this ball," I said. "Her dad set up the trust and it's happened every year since IC died. It's the closest thing Angel has to a religion."

"Can you say that in a house of God?" Macbeth wondered.

"Whereabouts in Cornwall is this place?" Luke asked me.

"I've never been, but I think it's off to the south somewhere. Off the coast."

"Off the coast? What, is it a yacht?"

"No," I shook my head, "it's on a, what do you call it, like a peninsula or something. Somewhere near Falmouth."

"That's the Lizard peninsular," Macbeth said.

"No, it's not there. It's off the coast. In the sea. On a sort of little island, you can only get across when the tide's out or you have to take a boat."

"Like St Michael's Mount?"

"Do not mention the name Michael," I said darkly.

Luke looked puzzled.

"That's Docherty's name."

"Seriously? I never knew that."

"Can we get back to the issue at hand here?" Macbeth said, but Angel opened the door and walked in before anyone else could speak. She had the cordless phone pressed to her ear.

"We have a proposition," she said, and Luke looked wary.

"We?"

"Me and Livvy. Her PR firm is handling the ball. She says maybe we could hold it at Pela Orso."

"What?"

"Lancelot's castle?" Macbeth frowned, and Angel looked impressed.

"That's what it's named for, yes. It's really remote—out to sea most of the time. We could maybe charter 'copters from Newquay airport, make it an adventure." She listened to something from Livvy, and then said, "We could get all the guests to assemble at City airport and fly them all down in secrecy."

Luke looked sceptical. Macbeth looked thoughtful. I was thinking, *how cool is this?*

"That could work," I said. "No, I think it could. It'd generate huge publicity, everyone'll be trying to figure out where they are..."

"The sea might give it away," Luke said.

"Yes, but by then they'll be there, and anyway, it'll be dark. Afterwards it won't matter so much where everyone was. And I don't think Docherty's the type to read glossies anyway."

It took us ages to persuade Luke, and in the end I called Maria and Karen, who both thought it was an excellent idea and suggested that Luke and I went to the ball to keep an eye on things. Outvoted, Luke gave in, while I wondered idly who Karen had planned on sending to the ball to bodyguard Angel in the first place. Macbeth carried Angel's stuff out to the car and drove her off down to Cornwall, and I was left with Luke, who scowled a lot like everything was my fault.

"Don't look at me like that," I said, "it wasn't my idea."

"I didn't hear you disagreeing."

"I think it will work. It'll be really cool. It'll protect Angel and boost the charity's profile."

Luke glared at me and threw himself at the sofa. He was wearing jeans and a T-shirt and I could see the bandage around his left bicep. Somehow it made him look sexier.

"And look at it this way—you get to go to one of the most exclusive parties of the year."

"Big deal," Luke said. "I go to all the exclusive parties. There's always someone there needs keeping an eye on."

"Well, you're just a bundle of fun today."

He sighed and ran a hand through his hair. "I just can't believe Docherty is in on this."

"Believe it."

"It could have been Janulevic..."

"How did he know where we were? Luke, I didn't know where we were and I was there. Janulevic couldn't have known where I lived, either. He—oh God, Luke!"

"What?"

"It was Docherty who was shooting at us! Who shot you. We just assumed it was Janulevic because we thought we were after him. What if this whole thing is made up?"

"What do you mean?"

"We don't even know if Janulevic exists. Docherty could be masquerading as him to put us off the trail. If you're looking for a Czech you wouldn't suspect an Irishman. If he really is Irish."

"He is. At least, he was when I trained with him."

"SAS?"

Luke nodded and stood up. "Soph, you really think he was trying to kill you?"

I nodded and shivered, and he came over and put his arms around me. "Well, he missed. You're good at escaping that, you know?"

"So far."

"Don't get maudlin on me."

"I trusted him, Luke."

"Me too. I suggested him."

I said nothing. There was nothing I could think of to say.

He stroked back my hair. "You have enough bullets for that gun?"

I shrugged. "Nothing to refill it with. I need to get my SIG back. And my damn phone charger."

"Use mine."

"Where is it?"

"My place." He ran his fingers over the cut on my temple. "Maybe you should come and stay with me until we go down to Cornwall. Docherty knows where you live."

Tempting, very tempting. "He probably knows where you live. He could be tracking my car." I thought about that. He could have put a GPS device on the car when it was crashed. I wouldn't have noticed.

"So leave your car here. We'll take Angel's."

"He's probably tracking that, too."

"You know, you're making a lot of excuses. We could get the bus."

I recoiled. "I don't do buses."

"Me neither." Luke dropped his arms and stepped back, and I felt a rush of cold air. "You might want to sort out a cattery for Tammy."

"What? Why?"

"You're going down to Cornwall."

"I'll take her to my parents'," I said, realising even as I said it that I couldn't, because then I'd have to tell them where I was going. "I'll think of something."

Angel's phone rang and I turned up the volume on the answer machine to listen. To my surprise, a very familiar American voice rang out.

"Angel? It's Harvey. I guess you're not there. Listen, I just got told I can leave tomorrow, so if your offer's still on I'd like to take you up on it. If you could give me a call back, that'd be great. Bye."

I raised my eyebrows at Luke, who was looking moody. "Offer?"

"Call him back."

"No, that sounded personal."

"I don't care. Call him back."

Marvelling at his mood swings (If I didn't know better I'd say he was really a woman. But I do know better. Much, much better), I picked up the phone and dialled 1471 for the number. Then I called Harvey at the hospital.

"Sophie? It's great to hear from you." There was a bleep as Luke turned the speakerphone on and I glared at him. "I was just about to call you to see if you knew where Angel is."

"She's, uh, she had to go away," I said. "It's not safe for her at home. I just heard your message. Whatever the offer is, it's probably going to have to be postponed."

Harvey sighed. "She said I could come and stay with her for a while. Just 'til I'm back on my feet. Do you know where she is?"

I looked at Luke. He shook his head. I deliberated whether or not to tell Harvey, then decided that as he was after the possibly fictional Janulevic, I didn't want to get him on Docherty's hit list.

"I don't," I said. "It's very secret. Karen went over our heads. But listen, why don't you stay at my place? I have to go away tomorrow, I could do with someone picking up the post and feeding the cat."

"That's really great of you, Sophie. I appreciate that," Harvey said, as Luke glowered at me.

I arranged to pick Harvey up tomorrow and put the phone down half a second before Luke snarled, "What the hell was that about?"

"Was what about?"

"Inviting the Yank to stay?"

"He needs a place to stay and I need a house-sitter," I said calmly. Why was it such a problem?

"For all you know he could be involved with Janulevic—"

"Don't you mean Docherty?"

Luke narrowed his eyes at me. "Is this because I hired Docherty?"

"No! Jesus, Luke, stop taking it all so personally."

"I am not—"

"Yes, you are. Harvey is a friend of mine and Angel's—"

"Oh, yeah, I can see what a friend of Angel's he is. You know she's been telling him all about this case?"

"She trusts him. And so do I."

"And look how that worked out with Docherty."

I stared. "You hired him!"

"So it is about me?"

I mean, really. How egotistical was he?

"You have problems," I told him, when my powers of speech had returned. "Real problems."

Then I went outside, ignoring him coming after me, and drove away.

Chapter Twelve

I mean, really, was I being stupid here? Or was Luke being a drama queen? What was wrong with Harvey staying at my house? I wouldn't even be there most of the time and it wasn't as if anything was going to happen—he and Angel were clearly bats about each other.

And besides! Luke and I were over!

I got home and put Shawn Colvin on to calm me down. Then I called Angel. "Harvey called. He said you'd invited him to stay."

"Oh," she said, sounding embarrassed. "Oh, yeah. Well, he didn't have anywhere to go, and I do sort of still feel slightly responsible."

"Plus you fancy him rotten."

She was silent. I smiled.

"That too," she admitted after a long pause. "He said how all his stuff was in a B&B so I just went to pick it up, and he had nowhere to go... He really shouldn't be alone."

"Well, he's going to have to be. I have to come down to Cornwall tomorrow and he can't possibly come. He's too much of a liability as he is, all injured."

"I'd look after him," Angel said wistfully.

"You have this whole ball thing to organise."

"Livvy's coming down tonight," she said. "She's getting the planes and helicopters sorted out. Got to mess around with landing permission or something. She wants to have the 'copters land on the actual island, but there's no helipad and she can't remember how big the lawn is or if it's flat enough..."

"Well, let me know what's going on," I said, sensing a long party rant coming on. "I have to go."

So go I did, then I sat there feeling useless, and rather vulnerable. To be honest I wasn't happy at the thought of leaving an injured man and a cat to guard my flat, but what else could I do? There were locks on the doors and shutters for the windows, Tammy's cat flap was electronically operated, and I guessed Harvey would have a gun with him. He always used to.

It was just that I didn't know where Docherty was or what he was planning. Sure, he probably thought I'd been killed in the blast, and was therefore not likely to come after me again, but what if he realised the car was missing and started checking flight manifests?

I grabbed my bag and left the house. I could get one step ahead of him.

At the office, I logged on to the flight database and started checking all the inbound flights to Stansted for Docherty's name. I hadn't seen his documents when he checked in, but I was reasonably sure he'd used his real name. Just to be sure, I opened up the Knock flight we'd been on and found his seat next to mine. Yes. Michael Docherty.

Originally we'd been booked on a return to Kerry, so there was still a booking on the system for Green, Sophie, and Docherty, Michael, departing on Saturday at 1930 from Kerry airport. But, as we'd still been at the Kennedys' then, neither seat had been taken. I searched all Kerry-Stansted flights from last night until Tuesday for Docherty's name and found nothing. Then I checked Cork and Shannon flights, Dublin and

Knock and Derry, even though that was a long shot. Nothing. He hadn't booked anything so far.

I sat and drummed my fingers for a bit. Then I picked up my mobile, which was charging up from the computer, and dialled one of the emergency contacts Luke had programmed in for me when I first got the phone. I'd never had cause to call the military, but now I figured it was time.

"I have a suspect who is supposed to be in Ireland," I said, once I'd identified myself, "but I'm pretty sure he'll be flying back over soon. Probably to Stansted. I need your back-up to detain him."

Commander Graves asked, "Who is he? What is he suspected of?"

"Trying to kill me."

"Ah."

"I've been checking flights but he's not booked in so far. I'm going to call the airlines for cooperation but if I find out he's flying in, do I get your back-up?"

"You do. I heard about your takedown at the school. That was impressive work."

I preened a little. "Well, thank you." Then I remembered myself and added, "I'll be in touch."

Feeling very professional and efficient, I then called up each of the airlines that flew from Ireland to anywhere, just to be on the safe side, and asked them to alert me if Michael Docherty booked a flight.

By the time I was done, it was mid-afternoon and I was exhausted, not to mention starving. That was a lot of airlines. I picked up my bag and wandered up to the Metro for a sandwich, and when I returned, Maria's little red 205 was outside.

"What the hell did you do to Luke?" she asked as I went in, and added, "Again."

"I didn't do anything," I protested. "He's in a bad mood because I said Harvey could stay at my place. And probably also because Karen said one of us has to watch Angel's house, and I left him there."

"I know. I'm going over in a bit to take over. Why is it such a problem that Harvey stays at yours?"

"Have you met him?"

She shook her head.

"He's really cute. And a complete gentleman. Unlike Luke," I added, throwing my bag on the floor and tearing open my sandwich packet with maybe slightly more violence than was necessary.

Maria watched me. "Uh-oh."

"Uh-oh what?"

"You and Luke." She reached in her bag and started unwrapping a Chupa Chups lolly. Maria has a bigger sweet tooth than anyone I know, yet she's horribly, annoyingly thin. Maybe she has some system where all her body fat ends up on my hips.

"How do you get to eat so much and not get fat?" I complained.

"Good genes. Sit-ups. You and Luke," she repeated, her eyes on me.

I slouched down in the desk chair. "What about me and Luke?" I said sulkily.

"What is going on?"

I did a palms-up. "Beats me. One minute he's all sexy and kissing me, then he gets jealous of Harvey and stops talking to me properly, and sometimes he's all sweet and lets me watch *Buffy* with him, and then sometimes he's just professional and looks completely exasperated with me because, let's face it, I am a crap spy."

"No, you're not."

"Maybe I'm too fat." I pinched my stomach and glared at the sandwich. "I shouldn't be eating this."

"You're not too fat." Maria rolled her beautiful eyes. "You're gorgeous. And you know it, so stop fishing for compliments."

"I'm not," I said, although I was.

"Luke wouldn't have shagged you in the first place if he thought you were too fat," Maria said reasonably. "He has pretty high standards."

"Maybe he's just bored with me."

"Are you kidding? You're like round-the-clock entertainment."

I wasn't sure if that was a compliment or not.

"I just wish I knew why he keeps blowing so hot and cold," I said, and sounded a lot more forlorn than I meant to.

"Because he doesn't know how to deal with you," Maria said wisely, sucking on her lolly. "He caught you because he wanted you, and now he has you and it's never lasted this long before, so he doesn't know what to do with you."

"Oh, great."

"No, I mean, if he didn't give a damn, then he'd have let you know a long time ago. He's not exactly kind when it comes to women."

I thought about him wiping away Angel's tears when she found the photos of her father, and about him putting *Buffy* on for me when I was scared, and about how he'd told me once he was proud of me when I caught a bad guy and was terrified, and about how good it felt to have his arms around me.

He could be kind sometimes.

"But if he gives a damn, why doesn't he say so?" I said. "The whole reason I stopped sleeping with him was because I thought he didn't want me for anything but sex."

"It's more than that. He likes you."

"Damn funny way of showing it."

Maria smiled. Then she smiled a bit wider. You could practically see the idea sparkling in her head.

"What?" I said cautiously.

"I'll ask him," she said.

"No. No no no no no. No asking."

"I'll be subtle. I'm really good at subtle. And," she went through into Karen's office and came back with a little transmitter, "you can listen in."

I thought she was insane, but I didn't say anything. She said she'd put her wire on and then grill Luke when she gave him a lift home from Angel's. The transmitter she'd given me was remote: I could use it here at the office, or at home or wherever I wanted. The sound quality was good and I could talk to her as well as listen.

If I could figure out how to work the damn thing.

Maria left to go home and get some things for an overnight stay at Angel's, and I sat there feeling nervous. What if she talked to him and he said he didn't give a damn about me, actually, he just wanted an occasional shag and he couldn't be arsed to go out and find anyone else? What if he said I was grotesque and pathetic and it was all a bet?

I picked up the phone and almost called Maria, and then it occurred to me that maybe Luke might say something lovely about me.

Damn. Why couldn't I be ego-less, like Angel?

To kill a bit of time and quiet my guilty conscience, I started searching websites for any news about this morning's explosion. I found one reference to it, on a regional Irish news site, reckoning it was a gas explosion. But I was pretty sure they'd been too remote for gas, and besides, I'd have smelled it. Plus a great big fireball like that would have blown up the car, too, not just aimed some masonry at it.

But the site said nothing about any survivors. Feeling sick, I started looking for hospitals in the area and writing down phone numbers. Then I started dialling.

I found them eventually, in a hospital in Tralee. They'd been admitted that morning, after the garda responded to an anonymous phone call that there had been a fire at a remote farmhouse. Professor Kennedy was being kept under observation. He'd escaped most of the blast, having been out in the stables at the time, but Éibhlís was in ICU with severe burns. Her condition was described to me as unstable at best.

I thanked the nurse and put the phone down, head in hands, feeling nauseous. What did they deserve to be blown up for? To be honest it was some sort of miracle they were both still alive, but even if Éibhlís pulled through, what sort of quality of life would she have?

I was sitting there feeling miserable and guilty for escaping and not helping, worrying about the horses, who were almost surely going to be either already dead or so injured they'd be shot, when my mobile trilled.

It was Maria. "I'm just coming up to the church now. I'll turn on the wire when I park."

I switched on the transmitter and, sure enough, could hear her shutting off the car's engine, thunking the door shut and crunching across the gravel to the front door.

"This place is so cool," she said.

"Wait until you see the inside."

"No time now," she replied, and I was sure that if I'd had picture, I'd have seen her winking. "I've got a mission."

My heart was thumping. My palms were wet. I don't think I've been this nervous since I accidentally got onto the motorway on my first driving test. Needless to say, I failed, although I did everything else perfectly. The examiner didn't have much of a sense of humour.

I heard Luke opening the door, setting the alarms and locking it and mentioning to Maria that round-the-clock surveillance meant just that, and he was sure he could drive Angel's Mini back home.

I panicked. Maria replied calmly that there was no way in hell she was letting him drive with a fucked knee and that if he tried, she'd break both his legs.

They got in the car and I heard her chatting to him, but couldn't hear a word over the road noise.

"You need a quieter car," I said, and she seemed to acknowledge that, because the conversation died down. Luke wasn't being talkative. He'd sounded pretty pissed off before.

After what seemed like years—surely she was taking a long way around? Maybe via John O'Groats—they finally pulled up outside Luke's house. One of the roofers was doing something very noisy in the yard and I could hardly hear Maria as she asked Luke if she could borrow his *Pulp Fiction* DVD to watch at Angel's. She followed him up the stairs—I heard the pips of the alarms being disabled—then they were inside and everything was quiet. That loft has good sound insulation.

"You know," Maria said idly, and my heartbeat started speeding up again, "this would have been a lot easier if you'd got Sophie to come and pick you up."

"I don't think Sophie's talking to me."

"Lover's tiff?"

"Don't you have to be lovers to have one of those?"

"I thought you were."

"Yeah, well, that makes two of us." He sounded really pissed off, and I wondered if this was really the best time to get curious about our relationship. Or lack of.

"He doesn't sound happy," I said into the microphone. "Maybe you should—"

"So what happened?" Maria asked, and I realised I might as well not bother. Probably she'd taken out the earpiece.

"With Sophie? I have no fucking idea." Luke moved farther away, and I heard Maria's heels tapping on the floor as she followed him. There were cupboards banging, they were in the kitchen now.

"'Cos she was really upset when you broke up."

Luke laughed, but it wasn't a "gosh, that was funny" laugh. "Really? She told you that? *She* broke up with *me*," he said, his tone bitter at the injustice of it. I could well believe it had never happened before. Probably I was the only woman in the world stupid enough to let him go.

"Because she thought your relationship had no future."

"Well, maybe it doesn't."

I stared at the speaker. I couldn't breathe. I'd suspected it all along, but that didn't mean I wanted to hear it.

"Luke, stop being a fuckwit and listen to me," Maria said, and I sucked in a breath. She was going to kick his arse for me. "You know it has a future. This is Sophie. She's not a silly little girl—"

"Yeah, she is," Luke said, and maybe I was just hearing what I wanted to hear, but he sounded quite fond. Or maybe I was just going mad.

"Well, maybe sometimes she is," Maria conceded, and I felt like crying. "But she's clever and funny and good-looking and I know how you like your girls statuesque."

I *hate* that word.

"And I've seen you two together. You look good together. She likes you, Luke. She really wants you."

Was I that transparent?

Okay, yes, when it came to Luke, I knew I was.

There was a long silence, and then Maria sighed.

"Is this that stupid thing where you're trying to compensate for years of childhood loneliness by making everyone want you? Because, Luke, honey, *get over it.* It's not your fault your parents died. It's not your fault your family was too busy for you. Stop fucking people over just because you're a fuck-up too."

I didn't know his parents had died. I only knew he went to boarding school. Shit, did his family really not want him? How could you not want Luke? Talk about textbook psychology.

"I wasn't trying to make her want me," Luke said, his voice tight and stubborn.

"But you did. Luke, you like her. A lot. You can't lie to me, I know you too well."

"Okay, all right, I like her. But that's all. Don't try and push us together. I don't need this."

"You need her," Maria said quietly. "How long has it been since you had her?"

"Five days."

Four days, twenty hours, thirty-four minutes and about twenty seconds. Not that I was counting.

"Five days and you're flying off the handle."

"So?" Luke sounded angry. "It's just sex. I could go out and find another girl—someone hotter, someone who doesn't talk back all the time, someone who can maybe throw and catch—" Hey! Not my fault I'm clumsy —"and shag her instead. And you know what, maybe I should."

"So go on, then. Go on, right now. Go up to the pub or into town and get a bird and shag her. If Sophie means nothing to you. Come on," I heard her jangling keys, "I'll even give you a lift."

My heart rate was trying to break the Vanquish's top speed record. I clutched the transmitter with palms that were pouring with sweat. No one was saying anything.

And then Luke spoke, quiet and distant, and I had to strain to hear him.

"I thought about her this morning," he said. "When I woke up. Out there in Ireland with that smooth-talking bastard. You reckon she slept with him?"

I blinked. So *that's* what this was about?

"I don't think so," Maria said gently.

"He tried to bloody kill her, Maria. Do you know how many years that girl has taken off my life? I can't go and get another bloody girl because I keep thinking about *her*."

And then, right then, my heart stopped. He really thought about me?

"How many girls do you know who are like her? Who'd get turned on by car statistics? Who'd take on a lunatic job like this? Who'd...who'd take off all her clothes and say 'educate me'?"

"*Really?*" Maria said, and I blushed hard, hoping I wouldn't see her any time soon.

"She's a fucking maniac with a firearm. She brought down a master criminal five minutes after firing her first gun. She— she..." Luke gave an impatient sigh, as if he was really annoyed with himself. "Her hair smells like coconuts."

There was a long silence, which ended when I shoved back my chair, grabbed my bag and jumped into Ted without stopping to check if the door was locked. Without a single glance out of any window or mirror, I drove straight to Luke's where the yard was empty of Maria's car, God bless her, abandoned Ted and raced up the stairs, kicked open Luke's unlocked door and ran through the flat to the bathroom, where water was drumming.

I pulled back the shower curtain and stared at Luke, who froze, naked and soapy and just incredible.

"Did you mean it?" I asked, my voice husking, trying not to tremble.

"Sophie?"

The water splashed on me. It was cold. "What you said to Maria. Did you mean it?"

Another long beat, when I thought my heart was going to break right out of my chest, and then he nodded.

I pulled off my T-shirt, yanked off my shorts and kicked my shoes away. Then I ducked under the cold water, gasping, and looked up at Luke. "Prove it."

Chapter Thirteen

A while ago I said that sleeping with Luke was educational, a fact that he remembered. Well, now I reckon I must have a PhD at least. I have never been so exhausted or completely, bone-deep happy in all my life.

I also never thought I'd enjoy education so bloody much.

I was woken from a well-deserved sleep by my phone trilling and bleeping. I couldn't remember where I'd left it, and I was too knackered to move, but Luke swung out of bed and padded into the bathroom, coming back out and chucking my bag at me.

"Ow."

"I can't believe you have the Bond theme on your phone."

I wasn't going to tell him I'd downloaded the Darth Vadar theme for when he called me. "I thought it was topical."

He got back into bed and snuggled up behind me as I pulled out the phone, glanced at the display, and said a sleepy, "Hello?" to Maria.

"Hey. Are you okay?"

"I'm very okay," I said happily as Luke stroked my hair away from the back of my neck, strand by damp strand.

"Really?" She sounded surprised. "Are you sure?"

"Very sure."

"Did I wake you?"

"Mmm. Yes." I glanced at the clock. Just before midnight. "But it's okay. I've been asleep for a while."

"Speak for yourself," Luke murmured against the back of my neck.

"Is there someone with you?"

"Erm, yes." Now I was surprised. I'd always thought Maria was quite bright. "Luke, remember?"

"Really?" She sounded thoroughly confused. "But— I don't understand. After what he said—"

"I'm never getting out of this bed," I finished happily, and Luke started licking my shoulder.

"But—Sophie—was the transmitter malfunctioning? Did you miss it?"

"Miss what?" I said, a little icy trickle of uneasiness cutting through my warm, happy fug.

"What he said about you."

"No, I heard it. That's why I'm here."

"Heard what?" Luke mumbled against my neck. "Tell her to sod off."

"But if you're there... I mean, Sophie, I thought you wanted..."

I pushed Luke away and sat up, frowning. "Tell me."

Maria paused and gave an uneasy sigh. "He said... Oh God, Soph, he said he didn't love you. He said he could never love you. He said there could never..."

The icy trickle was a big stream now. "What, Maria? What did he say?"

She sniffed. "He said there could never be anything more than just sex between you."

I stared down at Luke, lying there looking so beautiful, the source of all my happiness, and my mind went blank of everything but a hideous, numbing pain.

How could I have been so fucking stupid?

Listen, Sophie, don't go off half-cocked, use your brain and listen.

"I—" I croaked, and Luke frowned.

"What is it? Are you okay? Is Maria—"

"I have to go," I said, and dropped the phone and scrambled out of bed, away from him. My clothes were in the bathroom, my underwear soaked through from the shower, so I left it and just stepped into my shorts and T-shirt, shaking and shivering, no idea of what to say or do in my head.

And when I went back out the bedroom was empty, the sheets crumpled, both Luke and my phone gone and I realised with hot, heavy dread that I had never ended the call to Maria.

Luke was sitting out on the chesterfield, wearing only his jeans, staring at the phone he held in his lovely hands. My phone. He turned to look at me, and I knew Maria had told him the truth.

"You wanted to end it," I said, before he could speak.

"You spied on me," he replied, his voice as flat as mine.

"I'm a spy, Luke."

"Not a very good one."

I stared at him, winded for a few seconds.

Bastard.

And then I found my voice.

"You know, I knew you had no respect for me as an agent," I said. "I always knew that. And I minded, but I didn't mind so much because I thought you had a little bit of respect for me as a person. Just a little," I said, my voice breaking, treacherous tears starting to spill down my face. "But now I can see you don't—"

"Hey," Luke stood up, tall and strong and more than a little scary, "you can't talk about respect when you bugged that whole conversation. You set her up, didn't you? You sent Maria in here to suss me out—"

"Well, you never told me how you felt! And I can't believe you...I can't believe you let me...let me do all that," I waved a distraught hand at the bedroom, choking on my own stupid tears, "when you knew I wanted more, you tricked me..."

Damn, look at me. Standing there crying like a pathetic loser, when what I'd wanted to do was make a dignified exit, some smart quip, get on with my life. I didn't need him.

But he'd made me so bloody happy, just for a few hours, and I thought it might last. Despite all the severe weather warnings, I thought it might last.

God, Sophie Green, you really are so fucking stupid.

I made two steps towards him, took my phone without touching him or looking at him—quite a feat, really—and left. He didn't try to stop me.

What followed should have been the sort of episode you usually get in films, where the heroine, looking wan but beautiful, drives home in the rain, her tears matching the rivers of water falling artistically down her windscreen, lets herself in and watches a mournful black and white film on the telly, eating ice cream *that will never make her fat*, while her faithful pet licks up her salty tears with an expression of adoring sympathy, and the soundtrack plays Sheryl Crow's "No One Said It Would Be Easy", or Chris Isaak's "I Wonder", or anything by the Cranberries.

But what actually happened was that it was dark and chilly and I nearly crashed several times on the way home, because I never stopped to wipe the condensation from the windscreen and anyway, I couldn't see for crying. My nose was running, my throat was aching, and when I got in Tammy just gave me a reproachful look and whined for food. I forked some out, feeling guilty for not feeding her properly, uselessness overwhelming me. I couldn't even look after a cat properly. My face was pink and puffy and my hair was doing strange things because it hadn't dried properly and I was so damn depressed, and you might hardly believe this, but I couldn't even watch *Buffy*.

I just sat there talking to myself over it, trying to find something mournful on the stereo but stopping as soon as I got a sad song, bursting into fresh floods of tears, wailing out conversations I should have had, things I should have said, what I was going to say when I saw him again.

If I could ever bring myself to see him again. Probably I'd just dissolve under a fresh flood of tears. I'd melt away like the Wicked Witch of the North, steaming and screeching, but correcting myself as I went, because it always annoyed me that really, she dissolved, even when she kept yelling out that she was melting. Stupid bint.

Eventually Tammy crawled over, looking worried, and licked my hand helpfully, and I wailed even more, because Tammy's so nervous she never, ever licks anyone, she hardly even purrs, and it was just so sweet of her to worry about me like this.

If I wasn't on the Pill I'd think I was getting my period. I was being truly, record-breakingly pathetic.

"Why doesn't he love me?" I asked Tammy tearfully, and she licked my nose in anxious reply.

"Because he's a shallow and unappreciative bastard," came a dark voice from the little front door lobby, and I nearly had a heart attack, because Docherty was standing there.

"How did you get in?" I croaked.

"Your door was unlocked."

Of course. Somebody please slap the miserable blonde on the sofa.

Docherty stood there in the doorway, looking dark and forbidding. "Where did you go?"

"Go?" When? Jesus, had he been following me?

"I thought you'd been blown up."

I stared at him for a second. So I'd been right.

"No," I said, rather unnecessarily.

"How do you think he knew we were there?"

I paused for a few seconds, my heart thumping madly (at this rate I'd be having a coronary next week), then I lifted Tammy carefully off my lap, stood up and crossed to my bag, which was lying on the kitchen counter.

Then I lifted out Petr's gun and aimed it at Docherty.

"Oh, I don't know," I said. "Could it be because you told him?"

For a long second, we looked at each other. Docherty moved very slightly to the left and I waved the gun.

"No," I said, "no moving. Take your coat off. Slowly."

He didn't move, and I realised the hammer of the revolver was in the uncocked position. Slap me again. I pushed it into place with my thumb and was rewarded with a lovely click. I lifted my chin and levelled my gaze at Docherty. I'd tasted him. He'd had his hand inside my bra. And then he'd tried to kill me.

In deference to his excellent kissing, however, I thought I should be at least a little bit fair to him.

"I think maybe you ought to know that I've been having what is possibly the worst day of my life so far," I said. "So if you do anything to piss me off, I'll put a bullet right between your eyes. Take. Your. Goddamned. Coat. Off."

He did, his eyes on mine. He had a double gun brace with a pistol for each hand and I walked over, my heart threatening to smash right through my breastbone, and took both guns. Matching Heckler Koch pistols. Nice.

I wanted to unload them, but I wasn't exactly sure how to do that, so I just put them both behind me on the unit, my gun still aimed at Docherty.

"Sophie," he began, but I shook my head.

"Was it right from the start?" I said, beyond frightened now, just really pissed off. "You must have been jumping for joy when Luke called you to take care of Angel."

Docherty said nothing and I regarded his dark eyes and impassive face. "No," I amended, "no jumping. Did you really think I was dead?"

He nodded, his eyes on mine. "I thought Janulevic had blown you up."

"No," I said, waving the revolver, "you didn't, because it wasn't Janulevic at all. You blew the house up."

"I—"

"Why did you even bother to take me to Ireland? Just so you could make it look like an accident? Kill us all at the same time? Three birds with one bomb. What were you going to tell Luke?" A cold shiver ran up my back. "Or were you going to kill him, too?"

A really awful thought occurred to me. Maybe Luke was already dead.

"Sophie," Docherty said, his voice low, "listen to me. I didn't kill anyone."

"God, Docherty, I *know* you're lying. You've been lying all the time. It all makes sense. I realised this morning. You didn't find Petr here, you brought him here. You shot at me and Luke and Harvey. You left the Scoobie in the road."

"Why would I drive a piece of Jap crap when I have an Aston Martin?"

"Because you didn't want to trash the Aston." I narrowed my eyes. "Is it outside?"

He gave a very brief nod.

"Mind if I borrow it?"

He stared at me. I stared back, fearless and numb.

"You wouldn't."

"I would," I said, aiming the gun at him. "And you know what? I'm going to, too."

I shot him in the shoulder, then I pulled back the hammer, like they do in Westerns, and shot him again, in the leg this time. And when he was on the floor, curled over and bleeding on my faux-pine boards, I bashed the back of his head with the revolver, watched him go still, then staggered back to the sofa, stunned and crying.

Morning came, and I'd hardly slept. I'd called Karen in the middle of the night and, although she was not happy, she'd come out to my flat and helped me take Docherty to the lockup in the lab. She said he'd probably come through the bullet wounds without any serious complications and told me to get some sleep, because I had to drive down to Cornwall tomorrow. But sleep didn't come. The day had been exhausting, mentally and emotionally exhausting, and all I wanted to do was cry, even when my eyes were dry.

Eventually I dragged myself out of bed and ate a large bar of chocolate for breakfast, washed down with coffee so strong the spoon nearly stood up. I hate those books and films where the heroine gets so depressed she can't eat and gets really thin, but still looks fab. When I get depressed I want to eat the entire Cadbury factory. Nuts and bolts and all.

I called the hospital and told them I'd be coming to pick Harvey up, and then I went out to the car. I started the engine, then remembered about the twin Heckler Koch pistols I'd shoved in a drawer away from Karen's eyes. She'd not said a word about my unorthodox takedown, just that she was impressed I'd caught him before he did any serious damage. I wanted to tell her that Éibhlís Kennedy might have something to say about serious damage, but I was too tired and said nothing.

I retrieved the guns and put them in my big heavy handbag. Now armed with three guns, none of which were mine, I felt slightly better equipped to face the day. *Watch out, world, I'm here and I'm really pissed off.*

But just as I came around the corner back into the little car park, I saw someone standing by Ted's crumpled passenger door. A middle-aged man with brown hair, wearing jeans and a polo shirt.

"Can I help you?" I asked, and he took one look at me, raised a gun and fired.

I ducked, and the bullet buried itself in the wall behind me. I fumbled for one of my bloody millions of guns, but by the time I'd got my finger on the trigger of the revolver, the guy was in my car, over in the driver's seat, and Ted was being reversed out of the slot at a speed I'd never be able to replicate.

"You fucking, fucking bastard," I said, firing off a shot that did nothing but break the driver's window. "Come back!"

Yeah, right. Why did I even say it? I fired another shot, aiming for the wheels, but hit the ground instead. I was so bad at this. And I was running out of bullets, too.

But the shot alarmed Tammy, who'd been in a tree across the car park, and she bolted down to the ground and over to the house. Right in the path of the car. I saw it all in slow motion— the guy saw her, looked right at me and rammed his foot on the pedal.

There was an awful crunch, a sound I'll never, ever forget, and then a screech, and then Ted was gone and Tammy was a bloody mess of bones and fur.

I tried to remember all those RSPCA leaflets I'd had when we got Tammy as a baby kitten, completely tiny and afraid of everything. This was a cat with shadow-phobia. She was a rescue cat, so small and unbelievably adorable, and I could never understand how anyone could be cruel to something so soft and pretty and helpless. Maybe it was because she was so helpless. I don't know. People are sick.

While Tammy's life flashed before my eyes she lay there, completely still, and I was almost sure she was dead until I saw her tail move. Overjoyed, I lifted her head and her eyes flickered. If she could move her tail, I reasoned, then her back wasn't broken. I ran over to the semi-abandoned building site on the far side of the car park and grabbed a hazard sign to put in front of Tammy so no one would drive into her while I ran inside, hardly noticing I was crying some more (*How*? How much fluid did I have in my body?), grabbed her travel box and a couple of old towels from the hall cupboard and dashed back out, fastening the top door lock and forgetting the rest. It was agonising, getting her into the box, but I managed, sending up prayers in all religions that I wasn't damaging her any further. Carless, I had to walk up to the vet's, about half a mile away, and I started up the hill, trying to hold Tammy's box steady.

The Vanquish was parked on the street, a risky thing to do even in a village like this. I briefly contemplated getting in and driving, but then I remembered that it had an F1-style gearbox and I'd never fathom it out in time. Walking would be quicker.

I was halfway up the hill, nearly onto the main road, when I became half aware of a car bleeping and flashing me. A silver Vectra pulled to a halt in front of me, and Luke got out.

Great. You know, I thought that day in Ireland was bad. Now I felt like the Day From Hell was actually a free pass to a luxurious spa.

I ignored Luke and walked on past.

"Sophie? Don't bloody ignore me."

"I don't have time," I said, and Tammy cried helplessly at me, breaking my heart.

"Where are you going?"

"Vet," I said. "She's hurt."

He grabbed me and swung me round to face him, and I cried out, because Tammy was being shaken all over her box. Poor, poor baby. She must think I hate her.

"Let go of me," I sobbed, crying really hard.

"Get in the car."

"No," I tried to break free. He was holding up traffic and people were starting to bleep. "Go away."

"Get in the car, I'll drive you there. It'll be quicker."

I agonised about it for a second or two, then got in the car, settling Tammy's box on my lap. She was bleeding all over, soaking through the towels onto my clothes and my skin. She kept mewing, so frightened and hurt, and I kept crying, and Luke had to haul me out of the car when we got to the vet's, because I'd been so busy promising Tammy she wouldn't die that I hadn't even noticed where we were.

"I need help," I said to the whole waiting room, people with dogs and hamsters and rabbits in boxes, and the receptionist called something through, and a woman in a white coat came out, and Luke followed me into a consulting room, and listened to me bleat about the car hitting her, and all the while the vet was looking Tammy over with a doubtful look on her face.

"We can operate on her," she said, "but I must warn you it will be very, very expensive. Do you have insurance?"

"No," I hiccupped. "I'll find the money."

"I'll lend you—" Luke began, and I held up an arm to silence him, accidentally hitting him on the chin.

"No. I'll manage."

"I also have to tell you it might not be totally successful. It may be kinder to put her to sleep."

I stared at her. Who was this woman and who put her in charge of my baby? "No," I cried, "not that, don't even say that. Help her, she's healthy and really, really strong. She's my baby," I sobbed, totally hysterical now, and Luke tried to put his arms around me but I fought him off.

"We'll do what we can," the vet said, and we were politely evicted from the room. I gave the receptionist all my phone numbers, the office number and my parents', too, ignoring Luke's furious look, and stumbled out into the daylight.

"Sophie," Luke began, and I shook my head.

"Please go away."

"What?"

"Thank you for the lift," I sniffed, "but please go away."

He stood still for a few seconds, then I heard the car door slam, the engine kick over, and he was gone.

I sat down on the pavement, scrolled through my mental *Buffy* catalogue, and brought up an image of Spike being sarcastic. Then I mentally removed his shirt. Then I felt a bit better.

I walked home, gathering strange looks, and saw the Vanquish squatting there on the pavement, looking sexy.

I felt for the keys in my pocket. I needed something strong to distract my mind, and as sex with Luke seemed a remote possibility, the car would have to do.

Besides, and this was high praise indeed, there was a possibility that driving the Aston Martin Vanquish might actually be better than sex.

Not sex with Luke, you understand. I wasn't mad. But still, you know, on an average scale. It could be better. It had already contributed once. It might actually be so sexy I'd be unable to drive it. But in the interests of science, I figured I ought to find out.

First things first, though. One must research. I went and got my Top Gear magazines and read up on the gearbox.

Complicated. But after the weekend I'd had, I could do anything. If the damn box pissed me off, I'd rip it out.

I got in the car, put the key in, and turned it. Quiet. A little too quiet. Then lights came on and things started making noises. The gear display said I was in first, so I put my foot on the brake and pulled both the gear paddles to put it into neutral. So far so good.

You know, I've never even driven an automatic before. I drove my driving school car, and then Mum's little car, and then Ted.

Poor Ted. Where the hell was he?

While I tried to remember what to do next, I called the police station to report my missing car. They were faintly amazed when I told them it had disappeared from under my eyes, but I told them about Tammy and my voice wobbled and they shut up and told me they'd do what they could. I.e., nothing.

I turned my attention back to the car. I should have written this down.

Oh, yes. Starter button. All big and red and shiny. All the best things are. I licked my lips, and pressed it.

There was a huge, magnificent roar, and I shuddered happily. I was feeling better already. I pulled the right paddle to put me into first, checked my mirrors and found the traffic was actually waiting for me. Smiling now, I put my foot on the throttle and shivered with pleasure again. Then I reached for the handbrake, remembered it was on the door side of the seat, and dropped it, and we were off, up the hill so fast I nearly hit the oncoming traffic.

My God, it was fast. But at the same time, it hardly felt fast. It felt natural. I knew I was doing about fifty through the village, and I didn't care. I flew by a policeman, and do you know what he did?

He waved.

I was halfway to Angel's house when I remembered that the hospital was in the other direction. So I took a drive around some of the residential streets, getting the feel of the car, hoping to God I wouldn't stall, falling in love every time I heard it growl or felt it pulse.

I was a little nervous about leaving it outside the hospital at Harlow, and kept looking out of the window to check it was still there. But pretty soon I was out of visual range, and I harassed the nurses into telling me where Harvey was, double quick, so I could get back to the car. Sod Luke. I was in love, the real thing, hearts and stars and all.

Harvey had lost his neck brace and was lounging with his little girl friends, watching *Tweenies* on TV. Two of them were doodling on his full arm cast.

"Is there space for me?" I asked, and Harvey looked up and gave me his full-watt, all-American toothpastey smile. Then he clocked my outfit, and his face fell. "Jesus, what happened to you?"

I looked myself over. I was still all bloody. "I'm fine."

"But you're—"

"Not my blood," I said. "I'm okay."

He didn't look convinced. "I thought you weren't coming."

"I got held up," I said, and it sounded easy. "You ready to go?"

"I surely am." He kissed the little girls goodbye and promised to write to them.

"Paedophile," I said as we left.

"Aw, come on, they're sweet kids."

"Sorry. Bad day."

"It's only one o'clock."

"Yeah? Well, my bad day started on Friday."

Harvey backed off—well, as much as you can back off with a crutch. "Oh-kay."

We went out to the car park and he looked around for Ted.

"Did you take him in for repairs?"

"No. I just had a slight change of plan." I led him over to the Vanquish, and couldn't help a smile. "How cool is this?"

He stared. "My God. You are James Bond, aren't you?"

"Yeah. You should see me in black tie."

There wasn't much room to store his crutch, and we had to collapse it. Harvey winced as he pulled his broken ankle inside, but seemed to forget the pain as he looked around.

"This thing is awesome!"

"Yep."

"Where'd you get it?"

"Commandeered it."

"From...?"

"Docherty. He tried to kill me. So I shot him and put him in the lab lockup."

Harvey looked mildly frightened, a state which was heightened when he heard the rumble of the engine.

"Are you sure you can handle this?" he asked, and I gave him a look that has been making my parents back down to me for years. I was not to be messed with.

"So when did you realise the guy who was watching Angel is evil?"

"Yesterday morning when he blew up the house I was staying in with an Irish professor and his daughter."

"Are they okay?"

"Not really."

"Is—is Angel okay?"

"She's fine. She's somewhere safe." I'd got a text from her when she arrived, but I hadn't read it at the time, being otherwise occupied with Luke. I'd also had several missed calls on my phone from the Ace call centre, telling me that Docherty had booked, and then taken, a flight from Kerry to Stansted last night. But I hadn't listened. Stupid Luke had me deaf and blind to everything that wasn't him.

"Uh, Sophie?"

I let Harvey drag me back to the here-and-now. "Yeah?"

"What's the speed limit around here?"

"I dunno. Thirty? Forty?"

"Okay. It's just you're going about sixty-five."

Oops. I tend to drive slightly too fast when I'm angry. That's how I failed my second test.

Bloody Luke.

Harvey was watching me with concern. "So," he said cautiously, "apart from nearly getting blown up, how was Ireland?"

"I didn't tell you I went to Ireland."

"Angel did." Harvey looked like he might be blushing. "She, uh, came to see me once or twice."

"Something going on with you two?"

He shrugged, but I could tell the nonchalance was feigned.

"Just don't fuck her over, okay?" I said.

"What makes you think I'd do that?"

"I don't know. Seems like a guy thing to do." I ruthlessly cut up a white van. "Meet a girl, sweet-talk her into bed," I put my foot down a little, "spoil her for all other men," I swung across two lanes, "trick her into thinking you love her, then sleep with her and dump her. And make it look like her fault."

I got onto a bit of dual carriageway and floored the throttle. And found myself in the middle of next week.

"Am I guessing you've been having a rough time with Luke?" Harvey asked gingerly.

"He's a bastard fuckwit and the next time I see him, I'm putting him under the wheels of this car," I said, and then I remembered Tammy, and my eyes blurred, and I had to pull over.

"Sophie, are you sure you're all right?"

"No," I yelled, thumping the steering wheel. "I'm not bloody all right. Luke has no feelings for me, Docherty rejected me then tried to kill me, there is blood all over my floor from where I shot him and someone stole my car and ran over my cat."

Harvey nodded slowly. "Right. That is a bad weekend." He paused. "Is your cat okay?"

I shrugged. "I don't know. They said it was touch-and-go."

"They've said that about me before. Are you still going away today?"

Bollocks. "Yes. I have to go. It's important."

"Okay. Well, maybe me and the cat can recover together. We can eat grapes and watch bad daytime TV."

"You know grapes are really bad for cats?"

"Okay, I'll eat the grapes, she can watch the TV."

"Anything but MTV. It's too loud for her. She has sensitive ears," I said, and managed a smile.

"Okay," Harvey said gently. He reached over and touched my hand. "And you're right, you know. If Luke has no feelings for you, then he deserves to go under the wheels of the car."

"You're sweet."

"I never liked him anyway."

"He thought I'd left him for you."

Harvey looked at me sharply. "You didn't, did you?"

"No. He's just jealous."

"I'm flattered."

"Me too." *A god like Luke, getting jealous over me? You see, that's why I get so confused. Bloody Luke. I don't need him right now.*

Right, that's it. I'm just not going to think about him.
Ha!

I started the car up again and we set off once more. I showed Beckingham Palace to Harvey, who was very polite but didn't seem to know what I was talking about, but he did point out that we were driving on a road called Bonks Hill, which cheered me up a lot more.

By the time we got home, I was nearly smiling.

"This is a hell of a car," Harvey said as I helped him out.

"Yeah," I said, looking over it, "it really is." But not quite as good as the real thing. If you know what I mean.

I settled him in and explained about the locks and told him that I usually screen all my calls because I'm far too lazy to answer the phone, so he could do the same. Then I went to pack a bag for Cornwall. Angel had said she'd added me and Luke and Macbeth to the guest list, and that the party was so high-security that everyone attending had been sent a pass, like the ones we had at the airport, to be scanned on the door. Ours would be available when we turned up.

"Exactly how posh is this thing?" I called her to ask. "Can I get away with Monsoon or do I need to nick something again?"

"Nick something?" she asked, alarmed.

"Well, borrow without permission. You remember my friend Ella, her boss has a whole wardrobe of tasteless designer things..."

"Oh. Yes. Well, you can if you like, but I'm sure I told you it's a costume party?"

I stared at my wardrobe. God, she had, and I'd completely forgotten. "Right. Right. Is there a theme?"

"Not really. Just make sure it's a proper costume, no putting some hay in your pocket and saying you're the Last Straw or anything."

Dammit. "No. Okay. I'll see you later. I'm setting off in a bit."

Which was a complete lie, because I had to find something to wear first. I looked through my wardrobe and nothing presented itself immediately, so I made a snap decision and took the Vanquish off into town for some last-minute shopping. I always feel more inspired when I've been shopping. Plus, I needed a new watch. I was tired of it always being three-fifteen.

The idea came to me as I was parking up. I spotted a black Defender in the car park, all decked out with Halogen lights and stuff like the one in *Tomb Raider*, and I knew what I could do. I raced round the shops and eventually found what I was looking for: a green leotard. I already had khaki shorts and Doc Martens, so all I needed was a little rucksack and some brown hair dye. Sorted. My hairdresser would kill me, but I was sorted.

Harvey was very impressed when I came out in my outfit, and I was pretty cheered up, too. The leotard made my boobs look bigger (as if they needed it) which made my waist look smaller, and my legs weren't looking too bad after a bit of fake tan had been thrown in their direction. I even had thigh holsters to put my guns in, and they were real guns, too.

I called Karen to see if she'd got anything from Docherty, and she said that he'd been sullen and uncommunicative all morning. He'd asked for me, but I wasn't likely to go in. I'd let him cool down first.

I called the hospital in Tralee again, but there was no news on either of the Kennedys. I got the Interflora number from the phone book and arranged to have some flowers sent over. Then I turned and looked at Harvey, who was watching Kilroy with an expression of disbelief.

"Does he always talk like that?"

"Yes. And don't adjust the contrast, he always looks that colour, too. Harvey, about Janulevic..."

"He's a pawn for Docherty?"

"Well, I think so. Remind me what he looks like?"

Harvey shrugged. "Forgettable. Average."

"Brown hair, mid-forties maybe, good bone structure but skin like leather from too much sun?"

"Spent a long time digging in China," Harvey said. "How do you know all this?"

"I think he ran over Tammy."

"Tammy?"

"My cat." I said it almost without blinking.

"Then he knows where you live?"

"Docherty must have told him. I took his phone off him and everything," I said, gesturing to the carrier bag that held Docherty's wallet and phone and the various high-tech and illegal artefacts I'd found in his pockets. "So he must have told Janulevic before I got him." I drummed my fingers on the kitchen counter. "Luke thinks my car's bugged."

"But now he has your car."

"Yeah. Now he does." There was something bugging me, and I couldn't think what it was. It wasn't until I took my bag out to the car that I realised. There were spatters of petrol on the tarmac, and then a trail leading out from my parking space, in a three-point turn across the car park, and then out onto the road. I'd fired a shot at Ted's wheel and missed. I must have hit the fuselage.

I raced back in and grabbed my spare keys. "I'm going after my car," I said.

"How do you know—"

"Trail of breadcrumbs," I said, grinning, and started up the Vanquish.

I rumbled up the hill and through the village, following the spots of fuel. They led out towards Ugley in a clear trail, followed through the village, and then turned left onto a field and vanished. Damn.

Briefly I thought about dropping a match and seeing if I could set the trail alight, but I figured I might get into a little bit of trouble with the farmer. Not to mention I'd probably blow myself up. I'd have to go on foot and see if I could follow the tyre tracks.

I parked the Vanquish on the verge and set the alarm. I'm not having that nicked, especially when I'm not entirely sure where it came from. Then I set off across the fields, wishing I was wearing my boots, but I'd changed out of the Lara outfit into normal clothes to drive to Cornwall in. The ground was dry and crumbly, and my sandaled feet were soon coated with dust. There weren't any tracks to see.

Damn, when I wanted mud, did I get it?

I was just about to give up when I saw something glinting behind some trees. I got out one of Docherty's pistols, figuring now was as good a time as any to figure out how to use it, and crept towards the little coppice.

And there was Ted, looking like the feral car in *Harry Potter 2*, dented and smashed and scratched, but whole and lovely and magnificent.

I ran over and hugged his fender, and maybe it was my imagination, but he looked slightly pleased to see me.

Aw.

I told him I'd be back soon to pick him up, then I trekked back across to the Vanquish while I tried to figure out how to drive two cars home. Harvey couldn't drive, not with his ankle, and I wasn't about to call Luke—who also, I remembered, was not supposed to be driving. Stupid bugger. Although those few minutes he gave me might have helped Tammy a lot.

I drove home, thinking, and was just about to conclude that I'd have to call a cab or someone to tow Ted home for me, when I spotted Petr's bike in my courtyard.

Hello.

"Harvey," I said when I went in, finding him engrossed in a travel programme, "do you know how to ride a bike? I mean, like a scooter?"

He frowned. "Like that one outside? Sure."

"Show me."

It was simple, really, with the controls on the handles instead of on pedals, and after a couple of minor accidents and much amusement on Harvey's part I got the hang of riding around the car park.

"I thought you were going after Angel?" Harvey said, leaning on his crutch and watching me.

"Yeah, I am. I just need to get Ted first."

I made a fast stop at Total to get a can of petrol for poor leaking Ted, then rode up to the field and the coppice, stowed the scooter in the back of the car, and drove home, happy to have Ted back. For a brief second, I thought about taking him down to Cornwall—he deserved a nice long run after all he'd been through, and he was a Defender, and therefore subzero—but in the end the Vanquish won out. I tried to tell Ted that he had a hole in his fuel tank, but he didn't look convinced, and we both knew I was going for looks, not personality.

"I do love you more," I told him. "It's just that the Vanquish is better for this job."

Harvey was standing watching me. "You seriously talk to your car?"

"He's feeling unloved." I patted Ted's flank and went over to the Vanquish. While I was in town, I'd bought a carphone kit for both my phones, and I plugged in the Nokia. "Right, if my mother calls then *do not* pick up the phone. If she comes over, then tell her you're a plumber or something."

"With a broken arm?"

"Oh. Well, tell her—tell her anything, actually. Harvey, I'm all-out on this. If the vet rings then for fuck's sake call me, whatever the news is. Don't tell anyone I've left town, not even the postman. If there's a real emergency, Karen will know where I am. Do you have the office number?"

He nodded.

"Okay. Thanks for house-sitting for me." I went over and hugged him, and he put his free arm around me.

"Thanks for letting me stay. Say hi to Angel for me," he added wistfully, and I smiled. "In actual fact, will you pass on a message?"

I nodded. "Sure."

Harvey tilted my face up, and then he kissed me, very softly. "Give her that."

I blinked at him. "You want me to kiss her?"

"Yeah. And get someone to take a picture as well, if you can."

I opened my mouth to say—well, I don't know, really—but then I saw Harvey smile, his lovely hazel eyes sparkling, and I laughed.

"Okay. I'll see if I can get a pillow-fight out of her, too. How's that?"

He looked very excited. "It just might make my day."

I smiled and got into the car. "Bye, Harvey."

"Bye."

Chapter Fourteen

I pulled over at the services on the motorway roundabout so I could figure out how to work the CD player and hands-free phone kit, and once I had Garbage thrashing away on the speakers, I felt quite a bit better. Actually, I was feeling pretty good. Luke was still a misogynist bastard and Tammy was still horribly hurt, but I had faith she'd pull through. And who needed Luke, anyway? I had a vibrator in my bag and the car was like Viagra.

For the first time since I started driving, I wasn't afraid of the motorway. I sailed around the M25, other cars getting out of my way pretty sharpish, but they weren't as sharp as the Vanquish. I was queen of the road. I was a bloody superstar. Little children pointed at the car, boys in their tarted up Citroen Saxos gaped as I sped past in the fast lane. Lorries actually scooted out of my way.

I flew down the M4 and M5, and then it was A roads all the way to Falmouth. I got stuck at Indian Queens, where the traffic goes from four lanes right down to one in a very short space of time, but I was expecting it, and used the lull to call Angel and tell her I was on my way. I was a veteran of this route: ever since my brother acquired his loopy blonde dog, Norma Jean, we'd been taking dog-friendly family holidays in Cornwall. This was the first time I'd driven it, however, and I expected to be hell. But the car made it wonderful.

My phone rang several times with Luke's number displayed, but I ignored it. I even managed to resist the desperate urge to check my voice mail. See, *that's* self control!

I was about half an hour away from Tregilly Bay, the village closest to Pela Orso, when I got lost, having forgotten which tiny Cornish town to aim for, and had to pull over to look at the map. And while I was there I braced myself and listened to the voice mails Luke had left.

They were not pretty.

Basically he wanted to know when I was leaving for Cornwall so we could share a lift. He started off being cordial. He even asked about Tammy. But after a while he started to get mad and yelled at me a lot, telling me I was being unprofessional and a fucking stupid cow.

I put the phone down, took a deep breath and only just— with the help of a large chocolate injection and Garbage's "Supervixen"—managed not to send him a stuck-out tongue in reply.

I found my way to Tregilly Bay and parked up. The island of Pela Orso rose up from the sea, looking majestic. It was late afternoon, evening really, and the sky was just beginning to look dark. I got out my phone and used it to snap a picture of the castle, standing proud on the brow of the hill. Then I used it to call Angel.

"I'm looking at the house," I said. "How do I get across?"

"The tide'll be out for another half hour," she said, "so drive across." She gave me directions down to the quay, and I found a causeway going across the bay to the island. "Come right up to the house. You can put Ted in the garage."

I couldn't resist it. "I'm not driving Ted."

"What are you driving?"

"Wait and see."

I purred across the causeway, a million tourists staring at me, feeling very smug, then wound up the streets of the tiny little hamlet on the island, right up to the top where Macbeth stood at the gate, wearing black, looking forbidding.

"Holy shit." He pulled off his bouncer sunglasses to stare at the late sun bouncing off the Aston's gorgeous flanks. "Where'd you get that?"

"I talked very nicely to an Irishman."

"The one in the cell?"

"That's the bunny."

"Did you talk him nicely into going into the cell?"

"Well, maybe I shot him once or twice."

He shook his head. "You are a scary lady."

Tell me about it.

I looked him over. He was wearing a lot of gold chains—not his usual style. "Who are you supposed to be?"

"Mr. T."

I grinned. "Of course. Great outfit."

He handed me an electronic pass with a photo on it—the same awful digital photo that's on my gun licence, my red BAA pass, my military ID and my warrant card—and waved me through.

I pulled up at the front door of the house—a big Elizabethan affair with lots of crenellations and millions of wings—and waited for Angel to come skipping down the steps. She did, and her perfect little jaw dropped.

I gave a queenly wave and stepped out in best finishing school fashion.

"That's Docherty's car!"

"Yep."

"How'd you get it?"

I explained briefly about catching him—omitting the part where I bawled my eyes out—and losing Ted.

"Plus, I thought, big A-list party, I'll take the Aston." It gave me a little thrill to say it. *I'd* driven an Aston Martin. I'd *driven* an Aston Martin. I'd driven an *Aston Martin*.

Sometimes, I really loved this job.

"Well, I'm impressed," Angel said. "You look good in it."

I preened.

"Do you have your costume?"

"Yes, and I look good in that too."

"Glad to see you're feeling better."

"Driving that car is like getting laid."

"Speaking of which, Luke called. Boy, is he mad at you."

We started up the steps. "Well, I'm mad at him."

"He'll be here in about an hour. He called me to ask if I knew where you were and I told him you were probably on the M4. I'm not going to repeat his response to that."

"Oh, well. Traffic's bad at Indian Queens," I said cheerfully. "Probably that'll hold him up another hour or so. He might even miss the party."

"It's a ball, Sophie, not a party," Angel said severely, then grimaced. "Sorry. Had to put up with Livvy all day. I mean, I adore her and everything, but she does drive me mildly mad when she— Livvy! Have you met my friend Sophie?"

Livvy came gliding down the steps from the castle, looking airbrushed. She was tall and blonde, but not in the way I am. I have bad hair days and fat days and spot days. Livvy has only perfect, polished days. Every day. Even now, when her expression said "harassed" her makeup, hair and clothes said "personal stylist".

Cow.

"I think we met at Angel's birthday last year," I said, smiling bravely. Livvy gave me a swift up-and-down and turned to Angel with a "whatever" expression.

"Where the fuck is this crack security team of yours?"

Angel grinned. "Well, Mr. T's on the gate, and Luke will be here in a couple of hours—"

"A couple—" Livvy began, her perfect nostrils flaring.

"He'll be here," I said, grimacing.

"And Sophie is standing right here," Angel finished.

Livvy looked me over again. "You're in security?"

"Well, actually, I'm a government agent," I said, and she laughed.

"What, is that your character?"

Angel stifled a giggle.

"No, that's my job. My 'character' is being a PSA. I have military ID, if you want to see it?"

I wasn't that pissed off. I mean, when you think of government agents you generally think of people slightly more suave than me. Actually, Norma Jean would be more suave than me, and she wears a flea collar. When I told Harvey who I was, he laughed at me.

"Well, okay," Livvy said sulkily. "Do you know what you're doing? We have security people all over. Your...friend has been talking to them all afternoon."

I glanced over at Macbeth, who was indeed talking to someone in a parka that had the name of a security firm emblazoned on the back.

"Yeah," I said, "he's in charge of that. I'm more sort of surveillance. Undercover."

"Do you have your pass?"

I nodded and reached in my bag for it. Red BAA pass, green BAA pass, passport (you never know), driving licence, gun licence, warrant card, military ID card. Party pass.

Livvy and Angel stared at all the crap I'd piled into Angel's hands.

"I'll leave you to it, then," Livvy said faintly, and clattered off to talk to Macbeth.

Angel grinned at me and we started up the steps into the house. "So how was Harvey?"

I blushed as I remembered his message. "He's okay." I nudged her. "I think he misses you."

She smiled shyly. "I think I miss him too. God, Sophie, I only met him five days ago."

I shivered. I nearly slept with Luke three days after I found out his real name. I actually did sleep with him two days later. And look how that turned out.

"Well, he's a good bloke," I said. "He was very sweet about Tammy."

"What about Tammy?"

She didn't know, and I really didn't want to tell her, but she looked so sweet and anxious with her big blue eyes, that I sighed and started to tell her about the day I'd been having. But then we walked through the door into the main hall and sirens started bleeping all over, and people in security outfits rushed over.

"What'd I do?" I looked around in panic and realised I'd walked through a scanner. There was a belt beside it, just like at the airport, for scanning baggage, and my bag was taken off me and sent through, and I was pushed and pulled through the scanner again.

"We'll have to search your bag," I was told, as a woman started body searching me. I sighed and held out my arms. I set off the airport scanners on a daily basis. I reckon I have a magnetic personality, haha.

I watched them stare at the scanner monitor, then haul my bag out and go through the contents in disbelief. Revolver, illegal stun gun, matching pistols, Kevlar...

"Wow," Angel said, impressed. "You proper Stephanie Plum."

"I know," I said smugly. "Aren't I cool?"

"I'm afraid you can't bring any of this inside," the security woman said, and I shook my head.

"I'm afraid I can." I rummaged through the bag for my military ID, making her look nervous. "I'm a government agent." I turned to Angel. "You know, this is not very good for the undercover image."

"I won't tell anyone," Angel reassured me.

The security woman was on her radio: "Front door to party coordinator?"

Livvy's voice crackled over the radio. "It's a ball, not a bloody party."

The security woman rolled her eyes. "I have someone here by the name of Sophie Green, wants to bring firearms into the building. Claims she's Government."

"Let her," Livvy said. "Let her do whatever she wants." Ooh. Cheers, Livvy. "There's another one coming soon, er, I can't remember his name..."

"Luke Sharpe," Angel said, and I scowled.

"Don't let him bring guns in," I said. "In fact, don't let him in at all."

"What's he done now?"

"What hasn't he done?" I muttered darkly, as the security woman handed me back my bag and waved me off.

I followed Angel up to the guest quarters, where she showed me the massive room she'd be sleeping in, flanked by rooms for me and Luke, with interconnecting doors. I was quite glad Angel was sleeping in the room between us. Otherwise God knows what I might be doing in the middle of the night. As we walked I told her about the conversation Maria had had with Luke, about the fantastic night we'd had, and then the awful truth when Maria called me.

Angel made appropriate faces of sympathy and shock, she cheered when I told her about shooting Docherty and taking all his cool stuff, and she nearly cried when I told her about Tammy.

"She will be okay though, right?"

I shrugged as bravely as I could, which was to say not very. "Course she will. She's a fighter." But I didn't sound convinced, and I knew she knew that.

"Why don't you call Harvey to see if there's been any news from the vet?" she asked, a little too eagerly. "And then maybe you could ask him if he misses me, and then just casually drop into the conversation that I quite miss him too, and then you could say…"

"Why don't you call him?"

She looked shocked. "No. Far too soon for that."

I rolled my eyes. Since when were there all these rules about "too soon"? Or is that where I went wrong?

"I'm going to take a shower," I said, "and get all this travel dirt off me—"

"Does the Aston allow dirt in?" Angel asked.

"Well, not really. I think it sort of repels it. But it does tend to suck up chunks of the road as it goes along, like fuel I think. I could do with getting rid of the tarmac."

"So it's Aston Martins that are responsible for all those roadworks, is it?"

I left her to go to my own room—which was huge, opulent, plush, everything I've ever thought about stately homes multiplied by a lot—and had a massive claw-foot bathtub in the adjoining bathroom. I showered and shampooed, made myself smell all nice, carefully reapplied my fake tan (My shoulders and arms tan okay, but the backs of my legs don't. My mother has a theory that's the Irish part of me), and got dressed in my Lara outfit, with Pink on the stereo for added attitude. I did some makeup, spending about half an hour putting on some very complex two-coat mascara that was supposed to make me look like Catherine Zeta Jones, if the advert was to be believed, added some shades and plaited my hair high on my head.

I made a Lara pose for the mirror, gun in hand. Damn, I looked good.

I was dancing along to "Get The Party Started" when the door opened and Angel came in, phone in hand, wearing a black rubber wetsuit that was unzipped low enough for killer cleavage and made it quite impossible to wear any underwear. Her hair was tousled like she'd just risen up from the sea, her skin was bronzed, her eyes thickly mascara'd.

She looked just like her mother had in *Seakiss*, forty-five years ago, the film that made her career.

"Jesus," I said when she walked in. "God, Angel, I almost fancy you in that."

She grinned. "Likewise. Harvey said you had a hot outfit."

"Oh, he did, did he?" I said, looking pointedly at the phone.

"Well, you wouldn't call him, so I thought I would."

"Did he say anything about Tammy?"

"He said there's been nothing so far."

My shoulders slumped.

"No news is good news," Angel said, coming over and putting her arms around me—stretching up quite a way, because she really is tiny. "And patience is a virtue."

"Have either of those ever been true?" I asked, sniffing, determined not to smudge my mascara.

"I'm sure once or twice they must have been."

I sat down on the bed, and Angel came with me, still looking at the phone in her hand.

"Go on, then," I said, "tell me what else he said."

She grinned broadly. "He said he missed me. He said he wanted a photo—or else a live demonstration when I got back."

"As I recall, in the film the wetsuit comes off after about five minutes."

Angel blushed.

"Anyway," she said, "he said you had a message to give me."

Now it was my turn to blush. Maybe Angel went in for all that practising French kissing at boarding school stuff, but where I come from, girls who kissed each other were called dykes and never allowed to forget it.

"He, er, he, er," I floundered. Should I just tell her about it? No, because Harvey really wanted her to know how much he liked her.

Oh, come on, Sophie. You're not going to catch anything. No one will see.

So I lifted her chin, closed my eyes and kissed her.

And you know, it wasn't bad. She had a lovely soft mouth, and it was cool and minty, like toothpaste. And I'd boldly gone where many men would love to go. I'd kissed IC Winter's daughter.

Angel looked slightly stunned when I let her go. But she didn't look half as stunned as Luke, who was standing there in the doorway, bag in hand, eyes glazed.

"There is a God," he said, and I turned the colour of a strawberry.

"It's not what it looks like," I said desperately.

His bag thumped on the floor. "Are you sure? 'Cos if you left me for another girl I'm not sure I mind as much. So long as you let me watch?"

"Luke, don't you knock?" I said, standing up, flustered.

"No, and from now on I'm not going to." He grinned. "Can I have an action replay?"

"No," I said, and chanced a glance back at Angel.

"That was his message?" she whispered.

"Erm. Yes. He wanted a photo."

"Can I get a copy?" Luke asked, taking out his picture phone. What is it with men and lesbians? You'd think it would be a turnoff, the ultimate rejection. I mean, I don't get turned on by gay men. I think they're sweet. I wouldn't want to watch, though, and I sure as hell wouldn't want to join in.

Suddenly Angel smiled. "He wanted to kiss me!"

"Who did?" Luke asked.

"Harvey."

"I thought he—" He looked at Angel's glowing face, and stopped. "Never mind."

"You thought he what?" Angel asked.

"He's staying at Sophie's."

She nodded. "He wanted to kiss me." She threw her arms around me. "Sophie, you're an absolute darling!"

I blushed even harder, and Luke took a picture. "Cut that out!"

"Just one more?" he said. "I'll even send it to him myself. A gesture of friendship."

Angel and I looked at each other. "If it would make Harvey happy..." she said hesitantly.

"Believe me, it'd make him very happy," Luke assured us, and Angel stepped up on her toes and kissed me on the mouth. One kiss, and that's all it took. Like in *Friends*, where the girls snog each other to get their apartment back. Men are so damn easy.

Luke tried to persuade us the picture hadn't taken properly, but we ignored him, and five minutes later, Angel's mobile bleeped with a text. She read it, and smiled.

"What does it say?"

"I couldn't possibly tell you." If she smiled any wider, the top of her head would fall off. "I have to go and retouch my lipstick."

She wiggled off, and Luke stood there, shaking his head, looking far too happy for someone who'd just got out of a six-hour drive in a Vectra.

"Don't get any ideas," I warned.

"Too late. I am going to have *sweet* dreams tonight."

"Tonight you have work to do." I busied myself folding up my jeans for what was possibly the first time in my life.

"Since when did you get all bossy?"

Since you walked in and saw me kissing another woman. God, I can't believe I did that. Twice!

I am Twenty-first Century Woman. Look on me and tremble.

"Do you have a costume?" I asked, praying it'd be something really silly, but Luke winked and disappeared off in the direction of his own room, leaving me to run water over my wrists and press cold fingers against my flaming cheeks.

When he came back he was all in black: leather jeans and tight T-shirt, biker boots and a long leather coat. He'd slicked his hair back and there was a smudge of black nail varnish on his fingernails. On a lesser man, it might have looked gay. On Luke it looked flammable.

"And who's that supposed to be?" I asked, trying to keep my voice steady and failing quite spectacularly.

"You can't guess?"

"You don't look anything like him," I lied.

"Like who?"

"Spike."

Luke grinned and took a lazy step forward, softening his voice and hardening his accent. "William the Bloody," he quantified, looking me over hotly. "Pet."

I shuddered. I actually shuddered. Sod the Vanquish, Luke's all the turn-on I needed.

"So tell me more about kissing Angel," he said, and I snapped out of it.

"You should be so lucky."

"I caught the live show. Now I want the commentary. Come on," his eyes were dancing, "a step-by-step replay. Blow-by-blow account."

I stepped away. Luke followed.

"Stop it," I said.

"Stop what?" He looked smug, mocking, hot, his cheekbones so close I could have licked them. Not that I wanted to. Lick them, I mean.

Not much.

"This could qualify as sexual harassment."

"Bit late for that, love."

"Don't call me love."

"Just getting into character."

"Yes, well, don't." I looked at my watch. "Look at that, I have to go and meet up with, erm, with, erm," I snapped my fingers, "the coordinator..."

"Livvy?"

"Yes! Have to go and see her." I pushed past him, using every ounce of strength to avoid shivering with pleasure when his leather brushed my bare arm, and crossed to my bag on the far side of the room, keeping the bed between us. Not that the bed was much of a barrier.

"Have you met her yet?" Luke asked, as I strapped on thigh holsters and tucked the Heckler Koch pistols into them.

"Livvy? Yes."

"She's kind of a handful."

"You know her?"

"Yeah. Family friend."

"Polo parties? Hunt meets?"

"Something like that."

You know, when I was at school, kids went to the pub or underage clubs or places where ID wouldn't get checked. I didn't even know what polo was until I read Jilly Cooper. Talk about a different world.

"I saw the car out front," Luke said into the silence.

"The Aston?"

"Yeah. How's it drive?"

"Dreadful," I said. "Wouldn't recommend it. Even as a passenger."

"Nice try."

"Worth a shot."

"Speaking of which." Luke came over, and I thought he was going to goose me, but he took one of the guns out of its holster and looked it over. "Nice pair."

I looked up at him. "You'd better be talking about the guns."

He grinned. "Those too. You know how to fire these?"

I sniffed. "I'm not stupid."

"Never said you were. Do you know how to fire them?"

I gave in. "No. Please educate me."

His eyes flashed, and heat flared in me, and I had to shake myself.

"Disassembly," he showed me the levers, "safety, holding open." He flicked a catch and the magazine fell into his hand. "Fully loaded. The other one?"

I passed it over. It was fully loaded too.

"Twelve round box. The Yanks use them. Probably your friend Harvey knows his way around one of these."

"I'll bear that in mind."

"Was there anything else with them?"

I frowned, wondering how he knew. When I'd emptied Docherty's pockets, I'd found what I assumed was a silencer and another small module I didn't recognise. I took them out of my bag and handed them over. Luke screwed on the silencer and looked over the other piece, before fitting it on the underside of the barrel, making the gun look kind of square.

"Laser aiming module," he explained, aiming the gun at me, and a red spot appeared on my chest. "Damn helpful. It's a .45, so it can do a lot of damage."

"I know that," I said, because I'd seen it before. Luke handed the gun back to me, with the safety firmly on, and I unscrewed the silencer and popped it back in the holster, laser module still attached, feeling very cool and not a little bit scared.

"Hey," Luke said, as I put the silencer into my little backpack, with my Nokia and some lipstick. "Have you heard from the vet yet?"

Coldness ran through me.

I closed my eyes and turned my face away. I know it's a huge cliché but I didn't want him to see me cry. "Not yet," I said, and the words came out all right. No trembling or anything.

"She'll be okay," Luke said quietly. "She's like you. She's not going to let a car crash slow her down."

I smiled, slightly weakly, but I smiled.

There was a knock on the door and it was one of Livvy's minions, in a suit, looking nervous.

"Miss Green?" I nodded. "Erm, we were wondering if you could maybe move your car, because we need to clear the lawn for the 'copters..."

"When will they be arriving?"

"We just got a radio transmission, it should be about fifteen minutes."

I nodded and picked up my keys.

"Can I drive?" Luke asked hopefully.

"You got the lesbian kiss," I said, "you don't get the Viagra on wheels."

"Is that how Aston Martin are advertising it?"

He followed me down to the front of the house, and we both set the alarms off again. Luke rolled his eyes, ignored the panicking of the security people, and pulled me through the door.

"I saw Livvy arguing with her father in the dining room earlier," he said. "The Earl didn't want to take down all his guns and antique sword collection. Says the walls will look bare."

"Well, he's probably right."

"Yeah. And security in this place is tighter than Livvy's arse."

I forbade to comment on that, or on how he knew to compare.

I unlocked the Aston and got in, beaming stupidly. Gorgeous car, gorgeous guy, twenty-four bullets to hand. This was what I signed up for.

"Are you sure I can't drive?" Luke asked one last time as we got in.

"Sure," I said firmly, turning the key. "And no comments about riding, either."

"Well, now you're just bringing back memories."

I started the engine and tapped the throttle and watched the needle on the rev counter fly up to about eight thousand. Probably I shouldn't have brought Luke, I thought, familiar feelings of lust sweeping over me. People were staring, and I fastened my seat belt. Bumpy ride ahead.

The minion had told me I could park the car anywhere in the village—which comprised about four cottages and a tearoom. She'd looked disappointed, and I was, too, because the car looked like the sort of ornamentation a house like Pela Orso should have, but I didn't want a helicopter landing on top of it.

We growled our way down to the quay, where the car looked equally majestic, and stood outside, looking at it for a long while.

"Were you scared?" Luke asked.

"At first. A little bit. But I've been having a hell of a day."

"I heard. Are you okay?"

Not by a long shot. It only took the smallest thing—sight of a whisker, hint of an Irish accent, the scent of Luke's aftershave—to push me to the edge and leave me there, teetering. One more tiny flick and I'd be over, and there was no telling which way I'd fall.

"I'm okay," I said, and Luke smiled.

"Liar."

"We should go back."

"Stay a while. Do you want to get held up at the door while everyone gets scanned?"

Of course I didn't, but Luke in leather, plus the car, plus me feeling unstable, was not a good combination. But I stayed, leaning against the car's warm flank, looking out at the quiet water of the bay.

"Hey, you didn't happen to find a .22 on Docherty, did you?" Luke asked.

I shook my head. "Got a phone and the gun stuff. One of those scanner things like Macbeth has for getting codes off electric locks. Like your locks."

"Remind me to have a word with him about that. Where is all this stuff?"

I popped open the Aston's boot and showed him the carrier bag of stuff. "It wouldn't all go in my bag," I said, "and a Tesco bag looks so naff in this setting."

Luke smiled. "I am woman, see me accessorise."

"Damn straight." I looked at my watch. "We really should be going up."

Luke nodded. "There's a back door we could sneak in through."

"You don't think Livvy will have set slavering rabid wolfhounds outside?"

"Oh, yeah, probably. Okay. Ready to brave the front door, Lara?"

"Ready, Spike."

We set off back up the hill towards the house, where I could see the first helicopter landing. By the time we got there, it had spilled glittering guests all over the lawn: Marilyns and Henry VIIIs and Galadriels and Spidermen and Catwomen and Batmen, milling around excitedly.

"Spare me," Luke muttered.

"You don't like celebrity parties?"

"I usually end up staking out some fat guy's room," he replied. "Remember the Buckman Ball?"

"I've been trying to forget."

I spotted a few certified A-listers and made a mental note to tell Evie, the biggest starfan in the known world. And then I remembered I couldn't tell her, because I wasn't even really supposed to be here.

Luke touched my arm and I looked up.

"I meant it," he said.

"Meant what?" Still thinking about Evie, I wasn't concentrating.

"What I said." He shook his head. "What you heard."

I felt something twist inside me. "Can we not talk about that?"

He gave a noncommittal shrug, his face carefully blank. His undercover face. "Sure. Let's go in."

We joined the crowd of people at the door, all of them speculating about where they were. The house was lit up but the air was dark, and you couldn't really hear the sea above the noise of the people and the drone of the helicopters waiting to land. Macbeth was on the door and he waved us through a side gate without being scanned.

"Remind me why we're here again?" Luke asked, scanning the crowd in the lobby.

"To make sure no one tries to snatch Angel. Janulevic in particular."

"I thought you'd decided he didn't exist."

"Well, if he doesn't, then it was a random person who ran over my cat."

"Did you see his face?"

I nodded. "Not likely to forget it."

We split up and took different entrances into the ballroom, and when I got there I stood and stared. Livvy and her team had turned it into a cyberpunk dreamland. The walls and ceiling were entirely covered with white parachute silk that pooled artistically on the white marble floor, lit in bizarre bright colours from underneath. There was a bar set up in the middle of the huge room, dispensing drinks on four sides, and above it on a platform was a punky band in neon colours. Around the edges of the room were metal tables and chairs, all set with large jugs of iced water and lots of glasses shaped like lab beakers. It was all very surreal, kitsch, and cool.

I wandered round for a while, watching the room fill up with air-kissing celebs, avoiding the predatory reporter and photographers. It wasn't that I wouldn't like to be in the glossies, so much as I really didn't think Karen would be too pleased at the exposure. Not to mention what excuses I'd have to come up with if people saw the photos.

"Unknown beauty steals the show as role-model Lara Croft." "Robbie Williams wants to know: Who's That Girl?" Was Robbie even on the guest list? I had no idea. But a girl's allowed her fantasies.

Angel's guest list had mostly been prepared by Livvy, but it included her three best friends from boarding school: Livvy (of course), Penny and Charis. I'd seen Livvy in a funky boiler-suited approximation of a fighter pilot, all the better to cling to her radio and clipboard and PR paraphernalia. Charis, who I'd last seen at Angel's birthday party, dressed completely in black and purple, to match her hair, was wandering around in something green and flowy, her hair now blonde, some sort of woodsprite I think. I saw her with Angel and went over to say hello.

"Isn't this fantastic?" Angel gushed. "Livvy never tells me what she's planning. She's had someone on the door checking passes all day and I've not been allowed in."

"It looks great," I said. "Hi, Charis."

"Hi," she said shyly. "I like your outfit."

Charis is like the opposite of Tammy: looks really scary (most of the time) but is a complete pussycat underneath. Whereas Tammy looks like a baby kitten but is a scrapping ball of menace.

God, I hoped she was okay. When this was over I was going to catch a squirrel for her to kill, just to rebuild her confidence.

Just joking, okay? I couldn't catch a squirrel. They're vicious buggers.

"Listen," I said to Angel, "I need to tell you something." I drew her away from Charis and gave her a brief physical description of the man I who had run over Tammy. "I know it's not much to go on with everyone all dressed up, but I just thought you should know."

She nodded. "Thanks. I'll keep an eye out. Basically I want to be aware of anyone who's not a celeb, right?"

"Well, that does narrow it down." I looked around at the Who's Who that surrounded me. "A lot."

I moved off again, bumping into people whose faces I knew best from CD covers and Sunday papers, smiling and avoiding the roving photographers again. It was hot in the ballroom, despite the high windows open behind the parachute silk, and I grabbed a glass of water from the bar. Then I spat half of it out, because it was neat vodka.

"Bloody hell," I spluttered, and a model who I was pretty sure had just publicly come out of rehab shifted away from me pretty fast. Oh, if only I could tell the press what she'd been drinking.

I requested a large glass of very cold water, and while I watched the barman—topless, very fit, and painted all over in Day-Glo colours—pour it out, tuned into the conversation going on next to me.

"...So I told him, fuck him. If he can't even get me on bloody Parkie then what good is he? I mean, Paul McCartney's been on bloody millions of times, and what has he done in the last ten years?"

I flicked a subtle look in her direction. Soap star and ex-*Big Brother* housemate. I think.

"I know what you mean," the brunette moaned. "I tried to get on Ross but they weren't interested. Anyway, who wants to go on TV to be insulted? What I'm doing is launching in the States. They know how to treat a celeb over there."

"The way to get noticed over there is to get a sexy walker," the blonde confided. "Find out who's newly single and offer yourself up as a date. The papers'll get you, and that's your start."

"Well, it'd have to be a Yank bloke, because there is just no one available over here. They're all married or gay. Or," the brunette winked, "both. Remember Carlos?"

Who? Oh, yes, *Big Brother* again.

"Married with kids, yada yada yada, and also making moves on all the guys in the house. But, only at night or in the hot pool or something, so the cameras wouldn't see."

My my. You do learn something new every day.

"Hey, speaking of sexy," the blonde craned to see past the barman, "who's he?"

I diligently followed her gaze.

"Which one?"

"Well—both, but I meant the blond. I think Neo is engaged."

What were they talking about? I stepped to the side and looked over. And then I saw a marvellous Neo and Trinity, talking to someone in a long leather coat. Luke. With those stitches in his forehead he looked gorgeously dangerous, and my hackles rose up. I was not letting some two-bit soap star get her claws into my—erm, my colleague. Damn. I didn't have any claim to him at all, now.

"Wow, he is fit," the housemate said. "Actually, I saw him earlier."

"No, you didn't. Don't try and pull first dibs on him."

"But I did! Tell you what, we'll flip for it?"

The blonde dithered. Eventually she picked up a two-sided cocktail stirrer. "Pink, he's mine. Yellow, go get him."

The brunette nodded. I couldn't watch. I drained my water and strode over to Luke and put myself under his arm.

He looked down. "Hello."

"Hi."

"Erm, what are you doing?"

"How do you feel about soap trash and *Big Brother* housemates?"

He looked confused, but said, "Not particularly well disposed. Why?"

I indicated the pair, who were glaring at me so fiercely I thought I might combust. "They were flipping a coin over you. Well, a cocktail stirrer, but you get the idea."

"So you thought you'd rescue me? Aren't you sweet?"

I'm afraid I blushed.

"Oh, hey, I know you," Trinity said. "You work with Angel, right?"

I peered at her. She didn't look familiar. "Erm, yes. At the airport."

"I thought so. You look different with your hair like that."

Which was a polite way of saying, I look different when I'm sober. The last time I met Angel's friends I got really, really drunk.

"I'm sorry," I said, "I really don't remember you."

She grinned and took off her shades to reveal gorgeous violet eyes, and then I realised. "I'm Penny," she said. "We met at Angel's birthday party?" She touched her short black hair, which had been long and blonde last time I saw it. "I guess I do look pretty different. My agent sent me to John Frieda and told them to do something different and look what I got?"

"It suits you," I said, because, annoyingly, it did.

"Just as well, or I might have sued. Have you met my fiancé, Daniel?"

Neo took off his shades and held out a hand. "I think we have met. You were the drunk girl, yes?"

I blushed again. Penny bashed Daniel, who rolled his eyes. "Sorry."

"Don't be," Luke grinned, "Sophie's hilarious when she's drunk."

"Okay, change of subject," I said, and Luke laughed. "Aren't you hot in that outfit?" I asked Penny, who was, as I recalled, a model, and therefore looked perfect in her all-in-one PVC.

"I am slowly roasting." She grimaced. "But it takes about an hour to wriggle into this thing, so if I pee I'll miss the rest of the party. So I can't drink a thing."

"You have to suffer to be beautiful," Daniel told her, and she sighed.

"Sophie doesn't. Look at her, she's gorgeous, and she's wearing comfortable shoes, too."

"Actually they're a size too big," I consoled her, and quietly glowed from being called gorgeous by one of the beautiful people herself. Luke still had his arm around me, his leather sleeve hot against my bare shoulders.

"You do look pretty hot in that outfit," he said in my ear, and I shivered at the feel of his breath on my neck.

"The good kind of hot?"

"Oh, yes."

Excellent. "So what were you talking about?" I asked, rather blatant I know, but I was all out of subtle.

"You kissing Angel," Luke said. "Hey, you reckon you could go find her and show Daniel, 'cos he was pretty interested."

Penny rolled her eyes at me. I rolled them back.

"What is the big deal?" she said. "When I was in Milan, I snogged a girl for an ad campaign and no one batted an eyelid."

Yeah, right. A gorgeous blonde like Penny in Italy? The only way no one could have batted an eyelid was if no one saw the campaign.

"How come I never heard about this?" Daniel wanted to know.

"They didn't use the shots."

There you go.

"Show us how it went," he said, taking my hand and eagerly putting it in Penny's.

"No," we both said. "No offence, Sophie," Penny added, "but you're just not my type."

"I know," I said. "If I'm going to kiss a girl, she has to be tiny and blonde, like Angel."

Luke started looking around. "I saw her just a second ago—"

"Down, boy," I said, and Penny and I shared a smile.

Chapter Fifteen

As missions went, it was pretty uneventful. One of Livvy's It Girl friends threw up all over the floor and the cleaning team came in and vanished it away in seconds. A *Pop Idol* finalist (At least I think that's who it was. Me and Chalker spent the whole final drinking beer, throwing popcorn at the telly and ripping the piss out of the contestants) and his girlfriend had a screaming row and she yelled that she was leaving—only no one could leave, because the 'copters were all on dry land and the tide would be in until the early morning. Everyone had been allocated a room and people gradually drifted away until there were just a few left, slow-dancing to Tony Bennett. The band had long since packed up and gone to sleep in their van down in the village.

"Looks like that's it, guys and gals," Luke said. "No bad guy."

"It's a tough job," I said, clicking my fingers, "but someone has to do it."

He yawned. "What time is it?"

"Lara doesn't wear a watch."

"Well, neither does Spike. Livvy, what's the time?"

She lifted her nurse-style watch. "Four-thirty. It'll be getting light soon."

"Four-thirty?" I said. "It can't be."

"Time flies when you're having fun," Angel said, and we all grimaced at each other. We'd probably been the only ones at the party not drinking. And you know what? Celebrity parties without alcohol are really, really dull. Maybe they're dull with alcohol too, I don't know. At least you get to look at people through beer goggles. It's amazing how ugly these beautiful people are in real life. And they're all so sick of the sight of each other, their private lives are so public, that they have nothing to say to anyone.

Celebs are really, really boring.

"Right," I said, swaying on my feet. I'd hardly slept in two days and I was *knackered*. "Bed?"

Livvy nodded. "The caterers are coming back tomorrow for all their stuff and there's a cleaning team arriving at seven and, you know what? Someone else can deal with them."

"Good girl," Angel said approvingly. She tugged at the rather insecure zip on her wetsuit. "Bloody Brad Dennison kept trying to pull this down all night. And obviously I can't run like this..."

"Who's Brad Dennison?" Luke asked.

"He's in some boyband or other. Can't sing. Can't dance. Can't keep his hands to himself."

"Standard boyband, then," I said as we started up the stairs to our rooms. Livvy had her own room in the family wing on the other side of the house, and she said goodnight halfway up the landing, veering off in another direction. It had seemed cool when we went up to the third floor for our rooms to begin with. Now it seemed like torture, and I wasn't even wearing heels.

Although the three bedrooms connected, there was only one bathroom, and we let Angel go in first to peel off her rubber wetsuit and wash away the sweat. She'd looked incredible, but whenever I caught her eye, she was grimacing with discomfort. How do those dominatrices manage it?

I avoided Luke's gaze and shut the door to my own room, undressing in record time in case he decided to come in and talk to me. But he didn't, and when Angel came out of the bathroom I went in, washed away my makeup, and looked at my tired, pale face. I'd put bronzer on to compete with all the exotic tans out there, and now I looked wan and exhausted. Which I was. I was looking forward to sleeping so much I almost wanted to delay it so I could keep the anticipation going a little longer.

But not that much. I shuffled back into the bedroom, looked gratefully at the bed and fell facedown on it.

I woke when the hours were still pretty small, the very faint sounds of a guitar seeping in through the gap under my door. I listened carefully, years of living with Chalker having taught me to recognise a song by its bass line or drumbeat or sometimes, just by a couple of chords, and this song was one I knew well. It was on *Top Of The Pops* when I was a little girl, when bands still occasionally played live, before everything was manufactured, and when we used to take long car journeys it was always played on the tape deck. It was "Heartswings", Greg Winter's most famous, and possibly most lovely, song.

I tiptoed out of bed to listen at the door, and when that wasn't loud enough, gently turned the handle and watched Angel sitting with her back against her bed, playing for a few seconds before she saw me and stopped abruptly.

"God, you startled me. Did I wake you up?"

"Yes, but I don't mind."

"You said you were really tired."

I shrugged. Once I was awake, that was it. I wasn't going back to sleep now. "I'm okay," I said. "I can sleep tomorrow."

She strummed a few more chords, then shook her head. "If I play any more, I'll start crying," she said.

"Play 'Beautiful Girl'," I suggested, and then I did see a tear in her eye. "What?"

"He wrote that for me," Angel said. "When I was little. He hated all the lullabies he knew, so he wrote one for me."

Bloody hell. I wish someone had written a number one song about me. Maybe I could get Chalker to do one, "My Annoying Little Sister". Except I'm not very little.

"I always liked that song," I said. "I used to wonder who he wrote it for."

She shrugged and said nothing, blinking furiously.

"How old were you when he died?" I asked quietly, and she closed her eyes.

"Twelve."

Less than a year after IC Winter shocked the nation one last time by going and dying on us. God. Poor Angel. I don't know what I'd do without my parents.

I made a mental note to call them when I got home.

"I'd been at boarding school a year," she said, "I started about three months after Mum died, and I met Penny and Livvy and Charis, and I sort of forgot about it all. Well—not forgot, but started a new chapter. I'd been gearing up to living without my parents for a while anyway, but I sort of thought I might get so see them in the holidays."

"You saw your dad," I said.

"He used to come up at weekends too," she said, smiling tearfully. "He'd roar into the courtyard on his bike, which the headmistress hated, but from what I could tell she hated everything that was to do with the twentieth century anyway. All my friends fancied him. Charis had a massive crush on him and she was mortified when she found out he was my dad. I mean, imagine fancying your mate's dad!"

"I always thought your dad was pretty cute," I said, with hindsight, because I'd been a child when he died. But then I guess that's the magic of it—like Marilyn and James Dean and Natalie Wood, the Winters never did and never will get old. People remember them as young and beautiful, and they always will do.

"He was great, my dad," Angel said, and that nearly brought me to tears too, but I'd cried so much in the last couple of days I just couldn't any more. I'd found my limit. I'd dried up.

I should drink some water. This couldn't be good.

"What do you—" Angel began, but then the door opened and she jumped and dropped the plectrum inside the guitar. "Dammit!" She looked up. "Luke, you scared me. Make some noise when you open the door."

"I figured it might creak more. Is this one of those girlie midnight feasts?"

"No—"

"Is it a pillow fight?"

I rolled my eyes. "Do you see any pillows?"

"I see four, right there on the bed."

"Which is right where they can stay. Did you want something?"

"To see what you two were up to."

It was pretty obvious what he hoped we were up to.

Angel was still shaking the guitar, trying to get the plectrum out. "I hate when this happens," she said. "My dad used to be able to shake out a plectrum in seconds but I usually end up having to unstring it..."

She gave it one last shake and something fell out on the carpet.

But it wasn't a plectrum.

"What is that?" Luke said, coming over. He was wearing a T-shirt and boxers and he smelled warm and sexy.

"Is that a key?" I asked, trying to focus on the matter at hand.

"Looks like." Angel picked it up and turned it over in her hands. It wasn't small and it wasn't new, and all three of us frowned at each other.

"You got any locked doors in that church of yours?" Luke asked, and Angel shook her head.

"The only doors are on the stairs and I don't even have keys for them," she said.

"No secret compartments anywhere?" I asked.

"If they were secret, I wouldn't know."

"Priest holes or anything?"

"In a church?" Luke said, looking at me patronisingly. "That sort of defeats the object."

I scowled. "I'm tired, okay?"

Angel closed her hand over the key. "I'm tired, too. I vote we all go back to bed."

Luke opened his mouth and I jumped in quickly with, "To our *own* beds."

He looked moody. "You don't want to share with either of us?"

"No," I said, too tired to argue.

He sighed. "Sophie, can I talk to you?"

"In the morning."

"No, now." He took my wrist and pulled me through into his room. It smelled of him and his aftershave and I needed to get out, or I'd agree to whatever he wanted, so long as it involved both of us being naked.

"Look," he said, "about last night..."

Was it really only last night? It seemed weeks away. And yet, in emotional terms, only seconds away.

"It was a misunderstanding," I said wearily. "I was under the somewhat mistaken impression that you gave a damn about me—"

"I do give a damn about you," Luke said.

"Anything else? Or just a damn?"

"Sophie—look—we were both kind of stupid last night and—"

Kind of? I should get an award for it. "I get it," I said. "Really, I do. It was a misunderstanding. I'm sorry I bugged that conversation—which was actually Maria's idea, in case you're interested—"

"I know. She told me."

So why had he still yelled at me?

"So really it was just me being stupid and not listening properly. Newsflash, Luke: the only thing I'm really good at is fucking things up."

"You're good at other things, too," Luke said, smiling faintly, and I was too tired even to blush.

"I'm going to go to bed," I said, "I'm dead on my feet."

He walked over and reached out a hand to me, and I found myself arching towards it—*sod* my principles—and then he paused, not quite touching me, his eyes fixed on the window.

Then he walked over to the window, leaving me standing there, all cold and empty. I wrapped my arms about myself and turned to look at him. "What is it?"

"I thought I saw—*shit.*"

He dashed to his bag and started pulling clothes on.

"What? What did you see?"

"Someone down on the quay."

"So?"

"By the car."

"*So?*"

"They were aiming something at it."

I froze. "I'm going—" I said, but Luke shook his head.

"You stay here with Angel. Get your gun—any one of them you like—and your phone and don't go anywhere until I call you, okay?"

I nodded, somewhat reluctantly. I really wanted to go and check the car was okay.

Luke pulled me to him and kissed my forehead, and then he was gone, and I stood there, frustrated.

Then I went back through Angel's room, where she was sitting up in bed, looking confused.

"What did you say to him?"

"Nothing. He saw someone by the car. It's probably nothing, but he just went to check it out."

I looked at the sky outside, getting lighter and lighter, and then at the clock on Angel's dressing table, and sighed. I might as well get dressed.

It was colder in the house than I'd expected, but then early mornings always are. I remember sitting on the sofa at home in my Ace uniform, inhaling coffee, trying to get myself in a fit state to drive to work, and I'd be so cold I'd have a sweater and fleece on over my work shirt.

I pulled on the jeans and T-shirt I'd driven down in, added my fleece and the DMs, and strapped on a thigh holster for one of Docherty's guns. I emptied the clip from the other gun and slipped it into one pocket, put my phone in the other, and waited.

And then, five minutes later, the castle shook with a huge explosion.

I sat there, paralysed for a few seconds, and then I realised that Luke had been out there. The next thing I remember I was standing on the quay, staring at a blackened hole in the ground and the bits of car that were bobbing around in the sea.

Villagers came out of their houses, the punky band poured out of their van, party guests came streaming down the hill from the house, and I stood there and stared, my body apparently finding some liquid from somewhere and squeezing it out through my smoked-up eyes.

And then my phone started ringing. I pulled it numbly out of my pocket and stared at the display, but it didn't have Luke's number there so I hardly paid any attention as I lifted it to my ear and said, "Hello?"

"Sophie Green?" said a voice, a gravely, accented voice.

"Yes?"

"*Tvuj druh Docherty is bez citu.*"

I was still staring at the blackened, warped quay, not thinking at all. "What?"

"*Já explodovat jemu.*"

It took a few seconds for what he was saying to get to my brain. And then I felt very cold, all over.

"Janulevic?"

"*Ano.*"

I didn't know what that meant, so I started looking round and said, rather hopelessly, "Does anyone here speak Czech?"

No one listened, so I repeated it louder. And then I did a Bridget Jones and yelled, "*Oi!*"

And then everyone turned to look at me, and I asked quietly, "Does anyone here speak Czech?"

A girl raised her hand, and she looked vaguely familiar. One of those tennis starlets. I'd seen her earlier, dressed up as Barbie. She was very brown and toned.

"Can you please speak to this man and ask him what the hell he's talking about?"

She frowned and took the phone, and gabbled a bit of Czech, and looked faintly alarmed.

"What? What is he saying?"

"Are you Sophie Green?"

"Yes."

"Do you know someone called..." she stumbled over the name, "Docherty?"

"*Yes.*"

"This man says he is dead. He put explosives in his mobile phone. He just blew him up."

I stared at her. "Are you sure?"

She said something else to the phone, listened and nodded.

"He says you're next."

She handed the phone back and I took it, totally numb. Janulevic wasn't on Docherty's side. Did that mean Docherty was innocent?

Oh, *shit.*

"Is this all a joke?" the starlet asked. "Like your murdery mystery things? Agatha Christie?"

"No," I said. "No joke. Not funny." I was starting to shake. "Everyone go back up to the castle and get dressed and get in the helicopters and go home. Party's over. Go on, go. *Go!*"

They drifted away, shooting me puzzled looks, quite a few of them muttering about taking a joke too far, and I was left standing there, feeling cold with horror, staring at the bobbing waves and splintered boats. A few residents were poking about, saying angry things about the state of their property, but I wasn't listening.

"Sophie?" someone said from behind me, and I turned to see Penny standing there, huddled into little jersey shorts and a huge sweater with Team Masters printed on it. "Are you okay?"

I shrugged and nodded.

"What happened?"

"A mistake."

"Did something get blown up? 'Cos that's what it sounded like."

"Yes," I said distantly. "My car."

"Seriously? Was it a nice car?"

"James Bond had one."

"Jesus." She lifted up my face. "Why would someone blow up your car?"

"They were after someone else."

"Who?"

And then a voice came from behind me. "Not me, I hope," and I turned and saw Luke standing there, soaked through completely, looking utterly frozen and really pissed off, and I flew over and threw myself at him, sobbing with relief at the feel of him in my arms.

He closed his arms around me, wincing.

"Oh God, are you hurt? Did I hurt you?"

"No," he unclawed my fingers from his arm, "a bullet hurt me. You're just a reminder. Hey, Soph, if I didn't know better I'd say you were worried about me."

I slammed a fist against his chest. "Don't be so bloody flippant. I thought you were dead."

"Jumped in the water. Got pushed out a bit by the swell." He rubbed his forehead, which was bleeding where the stitches had opened up. "And I have bad news about the car."

"Really?"

"I think there's water in the carburettor."

I looked up at him, and he was smiling gently, and I smiled too.

"Okay," he said. "I think we need to get off this island and go talk to Docherty—"

"Erm," I said, and he looked at me. "About Docherty?"

"Yes?"

"The bomb was meant for him. Janulevic wired his mobile."

Luke stared at me. "And you know this how?"

"He just called me."

We walked back up to the house and I told him about the call. "He says I'm next. Maybe I ought to get a new phone."

Luke took the little Nokia out of my pocket and looked at it. "Did you get his number?"

"ID withheld."

"Any numbers in here you want to keep?"

"None that you don't have."

"Good." He tossed the phone up in the air over the cliff, borrowed my gun and shot the phone into a lot of small pieces. They fell through the early morning like little bits of confetti.

"Thanks," I said, taking the gun back. "Are you sure you're okay?"

"As soon as I get some dry clothes on I will be." He looked at me sideways. "You really were worried, weren't you?"

"Yes," I said, annoyed that he was right. "If you get killed I'll have to find a new partner. Or work with Maria, and that's just too Cagney and Lacey for me."

We went back up to our rooms and found Angel sitting on her bed, clawing at the sheets anxiously.

"Oh my God! Are you all right?"

We shrugged and nodded. "You didn't follow the rest of the household down to see?" Luke asked.

"Sophie told me to stay here."

"Did I?"

"Yes. You went really white, then you got your gun out and told me to stay here and ran off looking murderous."

Oh. Yes, now I thought about it, I might have done that.

Luke was looking very amused. "I'm going to take a shower," he said. "Want to join me?"

"No." Liar.

He went off, grinning, and I just caught a glimpse of him removing his shirt before he shut the door.

"Sophie," Angel said, "you're drooling."

I licked my lips. "God, Angel, I'm in trouble."

"Why? What happened?"

"I thought he was dead and it was like the world had ended. I have a serious thing for him."

Angel smiled. "Oh, that," she said. "We all know about that. I thought you meant that explosion. Was it an explosion?"

I nodded miserably. "The Vanquish has vanished."

She clapped her hand to her mouth. "What happened?"

There was a knock on the door, and I opened it to see Penny looking in. "Is Angel there?"

I pulled back the door and let her in.

"Angel, are you all right?"

She nodded. "Why wouldn't I be?"

"Well, you had the party moved down here because you were getting stalked, and then someone blew up Sophie's car..."

"They blew it up?"

I nodded. "Actually, it was Docherty's car. And it was his phone that exploded. The car just sort of went along with it." I shuddered. Imagine if I'd brought the phone into the house with me? It could have been in my bag, by my bed. I could have been dead by now.

I closed my eyes tight, and when I opened them my gaze fell on the guitar. The key. The key had something to do with this all.

"Angel, that key," I said, "can I see it again?"

She fetched it from her bedside. "I've been looking at it, but it isn't familiar."

I turned it over in my hands. It was big and heavy, a proper old fashioned Victorian kind of key.

"Maybe it's for a lock that doesn't exist any more," Penny suggested. "Like your front door. Didn't your mum have all the locks updated?"

My shoulders slumped. That could be it.

"But why would your dad put it inside his guitar?" I said. "Do you play that often?"

"No. It makes me too sad. I just brought it with me because I couldn't stand the idea of leaving it to—to whoever's stalking me."

I nodded. A security blanket. A very musical and not too comfy security blanket, but still.

"And he never mentioned anything about it to you? Or your mum? They never said anything?"

She shrugged. "Not that I remember."

The bathroom door opened, and Luke came out, wearing a towel and some water and not much else. I licked my lips without even realising it, and he looked the three of us over.

"Please tell me you were having a pillow fight," he said.

"Enough with the pillow fights," I said. "Do you ever think of anything else?"

His eyes met mine, and I guess I knew the answer to that.

He disappeared back into his bedroom, and Penny shook her head at me.

"What?"

"You. Eyes like saucers. Not that I can blame you. That man looks good half-naked."

"You should see the real deal," I said mistily, and they exchanged glances.

"So you are sleeping with him?" Penny asked uncertainly.

"Not at present." *But give me ten seconds to get in that room and things might change.*

"So you were, but now you're not?"

I nodded.

"Why not?"

I tried to remember, but right now it was damn hard.

Luke came back out, and I made myself look at something else. But I was still aware of him, still knew he was wearing the tight black T-shirt and leather jeans of his costume. Not a lot of men can pull off leather trousers, but Luke could.

Don't think about pulling off leather trousers, don't...

"That key," he nodded at it, "you think it's important?"

"Well, it's a secret. It could be important."

He nodded. "We need to go back. Get Docherty out and apologise to him—" I felt my face flush, "—and see if he knows anything about it."

"How are we going to get back?" I asked. "My car is rubble and yours will take until tomorrow."

"No, it won't," Luke began, but Penny suddenly leapt up.

"I have an idea," she said, and ran from the room.

We all stared after her.

"She's a model," Angel said eventually, and we nodded slowly.

"It's big, old key," I said. "Big, old lock." And then it came to me. How thick am I? "Angel," I said, "do you have a key to the crypt?"

Chapter Sixteen

Angel hailed me as a genius and even Luke looked pretty impressed. But as I was collecting my belongings, ready for a long trip in Luke's Vectra, I grumbled that it'd be quicker to walk back, and he quickly stopped looking impressed.

"Look, without referring to Jeremy Clarkson, tell me why you hate my car?"

"It's ugly and slow—"

"It's not slow."

"What's its top speed, then?"

"A hundred and fourteen."

"The Vanquish could do nearly two hundred."

Luke narrowed his eyes at me, and I remembered him whispering the same fact in my ear not so very long ago.

"It's a 1.6," I said, because I'd looked up these facts to use them against Luke. "It takes thirteen seconds to get to sixty—"

"Sixty-two," Luke said, and Angel watched us like a tennis spectator.

"What the hell are you talking about?" she said.

"Nothing," Luke said. "Go and get your stuff, Soph."

I made a face, but went off anyway. My dad had a Vectra for a couple of weeks once when his car got smashed up in an ice accident. It was the most uncomfortable thing I've ever been in, and I drive a Defender.

I packed up my bag and slung it over my shoulder and went back out into Angel's room, and was just about to ask if she was coming with us when the door came open again and Penny rushed in, towing a sleepy-eyed Daniel behind her. She was brandishing a set of keys.

"Daniel," she said, "has very kindly agreed to lend you his helicopter for the ride home."

I gaped. "You have a helicopter?"

"Three," he said, yawning. "Luke, I'm sure my dad said you were RAF."

"Used to be."

"Can you fly a helicopter?"

"I can fly anything."

Bully for him.

Daniel handed the keys over. "Silver and blue Bell with Masters F1 written on the side."

And then it clicked. "Daniel Masters, as in Mastercars?"

"Yep."

Bloody hell. This guy's dad makes cars that make the Vanquish look like Eastern Bloc dinky toys.

"What happened to your car?" he asked me. "Didn't I see you with an Aston?"

I nodded. "It got blown up."

"How very Stephanie Plum."

I turned to Luke. "See, he knows who Stephanie Plum is."

Luke raised his hands. "If I get out of this with both eyes intact, I'll read the damn books, okay?"

I nodded, satisfied.

Well, not really satisfied, not even by a long shot, but you know what I mean.

"Are you ready to go?" Luke asked, and I nodded.

We thanked Daniel and Penny and I called Macbeth to come and look after Angel for us. I couldn't see him objecting.

Then we went outside and stood looking across the lawn, past the border of rosebushes, to the sea far below.

"Tide's not out yet," I said. "How are we going to get across?"

"We could swim," Luke said, "but I've had enough of that for one day. Can you row?"

"Very well, but only if you want to go round in very small circles."

He rolled his eyes and we went down to the quay, where there were still a lot of residents poking about. One of the cottages had a hubcap embedded in the wall.

"Was that your car that exploded?" a woman with a mean face asked me.

"Yes," I said.

"Look at what it's done to my house! That's Grade II listed, that is. I want your insurance details. I'm not paying for this damage."

I sighed. "Look, I'm really sorry about your house, but frankly I don't actually give a crap."

She stared for a second, then screwed up her face, like a baby about to start bawling, but I turned away and ignored her. Luke was standing by a small dingy that bobbed about in the little harbour, watching me and shaking his head.

"Do I have a neon sign above my head that says 'Freaks Wanted'?" I asked, and he grinned.

"No, but you have one that's advertising for trouble." He stepped into the boat and held out his hand for me. I'm not very good with boats. I don't like the floor to be moving. I stumbled and fell into him and he pulled me upright, holding me for a few seconds.

"You okay?"

No. My heart was about to explode.

and quickly sat down, and Luke untied the rope ▪▪▪ ▪k the oars and pushed us away from the little crowd ▪▪ ▪ narbour, one of whom started yelling, "Hey, that's my boat!"

"Thanks," I called back, and we ignored him.

I actually had to look away after a while, because when Luke pulled on the oars his biceps bulged and I started to get dizzy. I needed to get some, and I needed to get some of him. And soon. As soon as we got home, I was locking him in my room and swallowing the key.

"Doesn't that hurt?" I managed to ask. "Your arm?"

"Yep," Luke said. "You can kiss it better later."

Hoo boy.

It only took a few minutes to row over to the mainland beach, pull the little boat up to dry sand, and then start across the beach with wet feet, feeling very Ursula Andress. Although with slightly more clothes and not so much tan, obviously.

Livvy had arranged for all the helicopters to be parked in an overspill car park on the edge of the mainland village. As we walked through the pretty streets, people were starting to come awake, old men with leathery faces going down to the harbour, a milkman whining around in his little truck, a florist getting in her van and driving off to the flower markets.

"I like this time of day," I said to Luke, and he looked as surprised as I felt. "I mean, not when I have to go to work, obviously, but when I can just look at the sun and smell the air. It's all clean and fresh."

He nodded. "This time of year, it's the only time you can be cool."

I disagreed. Luke was cool all the time. And, against all laws of physics, really, really hot.

"Do you really know Daniel Masters's dad?" I asked.

He shrugged. "Vaguely. Friends with my parents."

"I thought—" I began, then stopped. Luke looked at me sharply.

"What?"

"I—" might as well go for it "—I thought Maria said your parents were dead."

He gave a curt nod. "Car crash when I was seven. I didn't hear about until the next day. I was at school."

Jesus. "I'm sorry," I said, and Luke gave me a tight smile.

"Not your fault. Just don't ever get in a Morgan, okay?"

"I think it's fairly safe to say I won't."

We reached the car park, which was really just a meadow with a tariff board stuck at one end, and I stood for a few seconds, looking at the small fleet of helicopters. Livvy had obviously pulled in a few favours. Aside from Daniel's Mastercar 'copter, there were machines advertising football teams and banks, diamond companies and what we decided might be a polo team or two.

"Talk about millionaire's playground," I said, and Luke nodded.

"Pretty impressive."

We found the Masters helicopter, a very attractive machine in shades of blue and shimmering silver, and Luke opened it up. Inside were two seats looking out of the huge windscreen, and then a row of three seats behind. They were all finished in plush leather and it was all very impressive.

Luke took a seat at a bank of confusing controls and looked them over. He glanced at me. "Are you getting in?"

"I've never been in a helicopter before."

"So?"

I made a face. Obviously he didn't understand what a rite of passage it was. I climbed up into the cockpit.

"Where should I sit?"

"Wherever you like. Just not here." He put on a pair of headphones and switched on the radio, and as I tried to choose between the great view of both Luke and the countryside versus some much-needed sleep on the back seats, he radioed ATC and got permission to fly us back. He peered at the dash. "Hope we have enough fuel."

"What do you mean, you hope?"

He grinned. "I'm joking. It's a full tank. You ready? No walking about while we're in the air."

I strapped myself into the front seat. "Ready."

"Okay." He flicked about a million switches and the rotor blades started up with a whump, whump, above us, and then the engines got louder and whirrier, and we started to rise into the air.

My fingers were gripping the arms of the seat.

"You're not scared of flying, are you?" Luke glanced at me.

"No," I said, "I've just never been quite so close to the outside before."

"When I was learning to fly they took us up in little bubble 'copters with no sides in them."

"Like on *M*A*S*H*?"

"Yeah. Only without the stretchers."

We got up to a steady height and I made the mistake of looking down. "Oh, Jesus."

"What?"

"It's kinda high."

"Flying generally is."

"I'm not so good with heights."

"But you're five foot ten."

"So? This is a lot higher than five foot ten."

Luke smiled, but didn't comment. "Why don't you try and get some sleep? It'll probably take us a couple of hours to get home."

"It took me five to get here."

Luke glowered. "It took me seven."

"That's because your car goes faster when it's being towed."

"I hit rush hour, okay?"

I smiled and closed my eyes. "Whatever."

I had forgotten quite how tired I was, but as soon as I closed my eyes I settled into blissful sleep, lulled away by the whirr of the blades above us. As I drifted away I made up a mental to-do list: check key in crypt door, rescue Séala, find and stop Janulevic, apologise to Docherty, call vet, have sex with Luke, sleep.

It was only the last one I had any confidence about.

The quietening of the engine woke me, the same instinct that used to kick in on long car journeys when I was a kid, waking me in time to see our destination sliding up to meet us. Luke was taking off his headphones, his hair rumpled and sexy.

"Are we there?"

"Well, we need to cross the road, but yeah, we're there. Sleep well?"

My neck was cramped and I had pins and needles in some interesting places, but I nodded. "Very smooth flying."

"It's what I do. Well, what I did."

"Do you miss it?"

He shrugged. "I didn't think I did, but now I do."

We picked up our stuff and got out of the helicopter. Luke patted its nose, the same way I thank Ted after a long journey, and I had to hide a smile.

"So what's the plan?" I asked.

"Load up your gun, unlock the crypt, and let's see what we can find."

"Good plan."

"It's a shame you're not still in the Lara outfit. You'd fit right in."

"Well, you're still quite Spikey. You won't look out of place."

Angel's church reared elegantly from the trees, looking like a picture on a jigsaw puzzle I had as a little girl. There were birds singing and the road seemed a long way away. In fact, as we approached the creepy, half-hidden crypt, the whole modern world seemed a long way away.

"You ever been in here?" Luke asked.

"No. I don't think anyone ever has."

"Someone must have."

"Not anyone living." I took the key out of my little Lara backpack and started searching through the clinging foliage for a door. The crypt was made of stone, low-slung and crumbly where the ivy had dug in. There were things scuttling in the leaves, things hanging and flitting and leaving sticky trails. I shuddered.

"What?" Luke said.

"Bugs," I said, and he rolled his eyes.

"I could have picked a squaddie. I could have picked a copper. I could have picked a bloody ex-con, or even a current con, but no, I had to go and choose the girl who's afraid of flying and creepy crawlies."

"I'm not scared of flying," I said. "It's heights."

"It's the same thing!"

"No, it's not, if I don't know I'm high up I don't get scared. And I am not afraid of creepy crawlies. I just don't like them. And if you let that fucking huge great big spider there get anywhere near me, I will shoot you dead."

I had frozen completely at the sight of the creature, who was nearly as big as my hand and had a fat brown body with stripy legs. It looked like one of those horrible loud women who shout stuff out on talk shows. Bleurgh.

Luke shook his head at me and dug out a knife from his boot. He cut away the hanging curtains of ivy, sending the spider rushing away and revealing a small door set well back, down a couple of worn, slimy steps.

"You get the feeling no one has been down here in a very, very long time?" I said, and Luke nodded. "You get the feeling you should have your gun out?"

"Pretty much," Luke said. "God, I'm turning into you."

I scowled at him for that, but it was pretty halfhearted. I pulled my fleece around me a little closer and checked the gun at my side. Docherty's gun, with the laser sight. I was hoping I wouldn't need it, but the dramatist in me was imagining zombies and mummies and vampires in there. Although if they were Spike-like vampires, then of course I wouldn't shoot.

Everyone knows that doesn't kill them, anyway.

I got out the key, put it in the rusted padlock, and nothing happened. It wouldn't turn.

I looked up at Luke. "Of course, it could be another lock," I said, and he rolled his eyes and took over. But he couldn't turn the key either.

"It fits," he said. "How many other old locks like that are there around here? It's got to be this one."

"So why won't it open?"

"It's bloody ancient. Stand back."

I wondered what he was going to do, and then I saw him get out his gun and aim it at the lock.

I jumped away, there was a loud report, and then I looked back and Luke was chucking the wrecked padlock on the ground and shoving at the door. Once, twice, three times, and then it came open with a mighty creak, and he half-fell inside, and a massive cloud of dust and foul air flew out, choking me.

Chapter Seventeen

I was on the ground, coughing and spitting out dust, wiping it away from my streaming eyes, and Luke was leaning in the doorway, watching me.

"You didn't think to close your eyes?"

"Well, what if there'd been someone in there? Janulevic, maybe?"

"In a crypt that hasn't been opened for centuries?"

I stuck my tongue out at him, and only slightly ruined the effect by coughing some more.

"Are you ready?" Luke asked, and I hauled myself to my feet, nodding.

"Ready."

Luke got out a big heavy-duty flashlight that he'd got from the helicopter, and shone it inside. The steps went down another couple of feet, so that most of the dank little room was underground. I followed him in, cautious even though I knew there was no way anything living could be in there.

And in fact there wasn't even anything dead, either, apart from a couple of smelly rats in the corner of a small, brick-lined room, with a door at the far end. We looked at each other, and Luke got the key out. I shook my head and pushed at the door, which was pretty rotten, and it shambled inwards.

"Smart arse," Luke said, and I preened. He was standing pretty close, but for once I wasn't feeling horny. It's all right for

Buffy and Spike to get their naughty on in a crypt, but that was a nice, clean Hollywood studio, not a damp, dirty, dead-ratty hole.

The rotten door revealed a tunnel: narrow, low and very dark. It was hard to remember that outside it was daylight, a nice pretty summer's day. In here it was forever night, a cold, damp winter night.

"Ladies first?" Luke suggested, and I stared at him.

"You must be fucking joking."

"You're not scared, are you?"

"Of course I bloody am. Didn't you watch the *Indiana Jones* films? Or *Harry Potter and the Chamber of Secrets*? Nothing good ever comes out of dark, slimy tunnels."

"Wuss."

"And proud of it."

He shone the light into the tunnel. It reflected off curved brick walls, black with slime and dirt. The tunnel sloped downwards, and unless I was wrong, aimed for somewhere under the church.

Luke stepped inside, and when I hesitated, reached back and took my hand and pulled me after him.

It was hard to know how far we were going. After a few steps we were swallowed up in total darkness. There was nothing either forwards or backwards, just slimy black walls on either side, a steady sound of dripping, and our own echoing footsteps. It was cold in the tunnel, and damp, and we were breathing in white clouds.

"How long have we been in here?" I whispered after what felt like half an hour.

"About a minute and a half."

"Feels longer."

"That's because you're walking slower than my car."

So he did have a sense of humour about it. "Which is in turn because I don't want to go A over T and break my neck on this slimy floor."

"Sophie?"

"Yes?"

"Why are we whispering?"

I blinked. Because people in dark tunnels always whisper. "So the zombies won't hear us."

"Ah."

My heart was thumping so loudly, my blood thudding in my ears, I could hardly hear anything. I don't know why I was so afraid. I didn't even know what I was afraid of—but maybe that was the thing. I was scared of the unknown. Maybe Janulevic was hiding down here. Maybe it was Greg Winter's skeleton. Maybe Indiana Jones-style riches, glittering like the contents of Tutankhamun's tomb. Or maybe just some more dead rats.

Finally we got to another little door. There was a niche in the wall with some candles—some damp, extinct candles—and some very dead matches.

We stood and looked at the door for a while. It was about four feet high, and it reminded me of a door in my old schoolfriend Sarah's house. It was this ancient Elizabethan mishmash of about four minuscule cottages knocked into one, with staircases all over the place and intricately useless plumbing, and there was this one door that I was too tall for when I was seven. Honest to God, seven.

"Well," Luke said, still holding my hand, "what d'you rec?"

"I reckon I wish I was in bed with the covers over my head."

"Since when did you get to be such a coward?"

"Since I thought I was right about a lot of things and found out I was horribly wrong."

"Such as?"

Boy, he really wasn't showing any mercy.

"Docherty," I said. "You."

"You weren't wrong about me," Luke said quietly, but at the same time something scuttled behind me, and I jumped, and his hand tightened around mine.

"You think maybe we should go in?" I said, looking at the door. "Face our fear?"

"Speak for yourself," Luke said. "I've been potholing in Wales. This is a walk in the park."

"Watch out, macho alert."

He grinned in the darkness and handed me the torch as he lifted the latch on the little door, took out his gun, and pushed the door open with his foot.

The room was low and very dark, and so long the torch beam didn't reach to the other side. At a guess, it was maybe twenty feet across, with brick arches that were only just high enough in the centre for Luke to stand underneath. Along the walls were stone shelves, and I couldn't see what was on them to begin with.

"Storage?" I whispered.

"Yes," Luke went over to the nearest shelf, leaving me alone and vulnerable by the door, "definitely storage." He brushed away a cobweb, and I sucked in a breath, because what was on the shelf was a skeletal hand. And not just a hand, a whole body. And then I looked around, and saw through the thick, heavy layers of dust that every shelf bore bones, some neatly laid out in order, some in miscellaneous heaps.

"I thought Angel said this place was empty," I croaked.

"Apparently she was wrong."

I tried to calm myself. What was so damn scary about bones? These people were dead, had been dead for a very, very long time. I'd faced much scarier things than a couple of heaps of bones.

"How many do you think there are?" I said, creeping over to Luke and peering over his shoulder at the skeleton.

"God knows. I don't know how far the barony goes back. There could be hundreds."

I shuddered.

"What? They're already dead, Soph, they can't hurt you."

"I know. But dead things are always creepy."

"Says she living with a cat who turns her living room into a graveyard."

"I know, but they're fresh. They're like what you buy in a supermarket."

"So let me get this straight," we were moving along the ranks of dead barons now, "you don't find dead, ripped-apart squirrels creepy, but the bones of someone who died hundreds of years ago make you shudder?"

I nodded. It made sense to me.

"Women." Luke shook his head, and I scowled.

"So rows of dead people don't bother you at all? I suppose you're perfectly at home in a crypt."

"My parents are buried in one," Luke said, and I shut up.

There were dusty, corroded little plaques on the shelves, each announcing the baron and his dates. We passed the Henrys, Samuels and Johns of the seventeenth century, then the Edwards, Thomases and Francises of the sixteenth, right through the Williams, Edgars and Geoffreys of the late middle ages, after which the plaques started to get hard to read, and after a while, disappeared totally.

"Now tell me this isn't creepy," I said, as we ventured so deep into the darkness that the door wasn't even visible behind us.

"Maybe it is a little."

"Glad to hear it. I was starting to think you were some kind of android."

Luke frowned at me. "Remind me why we're here again?"

"The key. Which may not have even fit this lock."

"Marvellous."

"But, I bet it'd be a great place to hide something," I said. "Something like, I don't know, a mysterious ring with great powers."

"You really believe it has powers?"

I wasn't about to rule it out. "Janulevic does."

"What do we do when we find it?"

How the hell was I supposed to know? "Cast it back into the fires of Mount Doom?"

"You've been watching *Lord of the Rings* again, haven't you?"

"I could have been reading it."

Luke shone the torch at my face. "Have you ever read it?"

"Most of it."

He grinned and, the next moment, tripped over something, grabbing my arm for support.

"What the hell was that?"

"The third baron?"

"Funny." He aimed the beam at the floor. There was a large, solid iron ring set into the stones. If I looked carefully I could just see that the edges of a small trapdoor were visible.

"I am *not* going down there," I said.

"Could be fun," Luke said, but he didn't sound very enthusiastic. He knelt down, handed me the torch, and pulled at the ring. Nothing happened.

"Could be locked," I said.

"Do you see a keyhole?"

"Maybe it was locked from the inside. Maybe there's someone down there."

"They'll be in good shape, then. Help me out with this, Soph. My arm's bloody killing me."

I'd forgotten about that. I reached down and hooked two fingers from each hand around the iron ring. Luke counted to three and we both pulled.

The trapdoor sprung open, and we fell backwards. And I didn't give a damn about what was down there, or all the dead barons around us, or the dust or the slime: I was lying in Luke's arms and my heart was pounding.

"Hey," he said, brushing back the hair from my face, "you look hot when you're scared."

I frowned. Not the romantic line I'd been thinking of.

I pushed myself away from him and picked up the torch again. The trapdoor was small, maybe fifteen inches across, and the hole beneath it wasn't much bigger.

"There's something in there." I peered at the bottom of the hole, which was about two feet deep.

"You want to do the honours, or shall I?"

Reaching into a dark, forgotten hole to pick up an unnamed object wasn't my idea of fun. I could pull off the Lara Croft look, but I'd rather do without the dirt and the bugs and the general ickiness of your average tomb.

"I'll let you," I said. "Someone has to hold the torch."

Luke gave me a look, but he gamely reached into the hole and brought out a small, carved wooden box. It had a little lock on the front, but a long time in the ground had corroded the metal. It opened easily.

"It's like pass the parcel," I said, looking at the dusty velvet wrapping inside. Luke held out the box and I, mindful of nasty wriggly things, very gingerly reached in and lifted the velvet aside.

There was a ring, a large, man's ring, set with tiny little jewels in a complicated Celtic design. The whole thing was gorgeously made, every surface covered with intricate patterns.

"Wow," I said, impressed. "Do you think that's what I think it is?"

"I think it might be," Luke said, and took it out. "It's big."

"Irish kings had big fingers."

"You really reckon it's that old?"

I frowned. "Well, it's called Séala, so it's supposed to be a seal. But you wouldn't put stones in a seal ring. Maybe it was reset."

Luke took it out and slid it onto his thumb. "Maybe it's not the same ring."

And then a voice came from behind us, a gravely, foreign voice, and we both spun around to see the man who had run Tammy over standing there, holding a gun against Harvey's temple.

"Hey," Harvey said. "How about that, you're here too."

"Harvey? What are you—what's going on?"

He gave a very tense smile. "This is Dmitri Janulevic. He showed up at your apartment and said he knew where you were and I was going to come along and help him."

"How did he know?" Luke asked, at the same time I asked, "Help?"

Janulevic garbled something and I glanced at Luke. He shrugged in incomprehension, but Harvey apparently understood. He shifted on his plaster cast, grimacing.

"He's been monitoring the cameras you set up at Angel's. You all left the church unattended so he could hack in."

"But—Maria?" I said in horror. She was supposed to have been watching it.

Janulevic chortled nastily and said something. Harvey winced.

"He sent her a telegram her mother was dying. Maria left."

"I'll fucking kill her," Luke muttered.

"He saw you coming and watched you go in the crypt. Then he came and got me for, uh, translation purposes."

Janulevic said something else, and Harvey flicked his eyes at me. "He wants you to know it's not personal, he just wants the ring."

"What ring?" Luke said, and I willed myself not to look at his hand, which was hovering by the gun at his side.

Janulevic snapped something, and Harvey translated, "He says drop your weapons. Both of you. And, Sophie, your bag too."

I glanced at Luke. He gave a small nod, and I unbuckled the holster holding Docherty's gun. God, why hadn't we gone to get him out first! The gun went on the floor, and then Luke's joined it, and I added my little backpack to the pile.

"Hands up."

I raised my hands.

"He wants to know what's in the box."

"Nothing," Luke said swiftly. "We dug it up but it's empty. Someone else must have got here first."

Harvey relayed this to Janulevic, who shook his head and babbled something that came back to us as, "He says you're lying. Luke, he wants to see your ring."

"What ring?"

Harvey rolled his eyes. "On your thumb?"

Luke held up his hand. "It's a family ring. We all have them. A signet ring. It's a British thing."

Harvey said something to Janulevic, who shook his head crossly.

"He says that's the ring he wants."

I cleared my throat. "I thought he was after a seal ring? This one has stones in it. You wouldn't put stones in a seal ring."

"Wouldn't you?" Luke asked, sotto voce.

"Well, no, because you'd use the ring for sealing letters and you wouldn't want to get wax in all those diamonds, would you?"

Luke and Harvey looked impressed. Janulevic didn't. He glared at me and jabbered something in Czech. Harvey's face fell.

"He says you need to shut up."

"Good luck," Luke muttered, and I glared at him.

"Actually, what he said was ruder than that, but you get the idea. I don't think he likes you, Sophie."

"Well, he's not exactly my favourite person, either." My arms were beginning to cramp. "What does he want?"

"*Ta* Séala," Janulevic said, and we didn't need a translation for that.

"We don't know where it is," I said.

"We don't even know what it is," Luke added.

"What about Ireland?" Harvey translated.

My nostrils flared, and I glared at Janulevic. "You tried to kill me in Ireland."

Janulevic sneered something else, and Harvey said, "He thought he had. But you're persistent."

"I'm hard to kill," I said, feeling brave, and then the next thing I knew Janulevic had fired his gun at me and my head exploded with pain, and I thudded to the floor, stunned and bleeding.

"Sophie," Luke yelled, and grabbed hold of me. He probed my temple, felt my neck, my wrist, then he closed my eyes and cradled me in his arms. There was blood on my face, hot and sticky and seeping into my eyes. God, I'd been shot in the head and I was dying.

And then, "She's dead," Luke said in disbelief. "You killed her."

Hold on a sec. Dying, maybe, but surely someone with Luke's combat medical training should be able to tell the difference between dead and dying?

Or at least show a little more remorse.

Bastard.

I started to open my eyes, but he pressed them shut again. "Sophie," he said, holding me close, "God, Sophie." And then in my ear he whispered, "Play dead," and laid me on the ground.

Janulevic jabbered something else, and I wished I could see what was going on, but maybe I didn't need to because I heard Harvey's voice, properly miserable, saying, "He says get up. Luke, I'm sorry. She didn't deserve to die." Janulevic said something else. "He says get up or he'll kill you too."

Slowly, Luke moved away from me, and I realised as he did that there was no light coming in through my eyelids. He'd laid me down behind the beam of the torch, which was lying on the ground.

God, he was clever.

I opened my eyes a crack, and realised I was in total darkness. I could see Luke, standing a few feet away with his hands still raised. There was blood on them and on his face. My blood. I blinked, and it hurt. I couldn't even tell where I'd been shot. I could be bleeding to death. I'd already had one head wound this week. Two was just ridiculous.

"Is that how you killed the professors?" Luke asked Janulevic, his voice hard, and I wondered if he'd be this calm if I actually had been killed. Would he give a damn? Or would it just bugger up the mission?

Janulevic sneered something in reply.

"He shot some of them," Harvey said. "But only a few so the bullets wouldn't be matched up."

"Like we matched up the bullet that killed Petr Staszic and the bullet that shot me?" Luke said. "And the bullet that shot Greg Winter?"

Janulevic smiled a horrible smile when he heard Greg's name, and when he'd got the full translation, laughed a little. He said something that made Harvey flinch.

"He says you're smart. He says he's had this gun a long time. Almost as long as he's been searching for the seal."

"Why Greg?" Luke asked. "He didn't have it."

"Not when he was killed. But he'd had the ring. He hid it somewhere. Janulevic's spent seventeen years looking for it."

"What if it doesn't exist?"

Janulevic got mad when he heard this, and blabbered on for quite a while. I moved my hand up to my face, very slowly, and tried to feel where I'd been hit. Rationality was creeping back in and I knew, if I was still alive, then it couldn't be a bad wound. Everyone knows head wounds bleed worse than they actually are, right?

Right?

Luke was looking at Harvey for a translation.

"He's pretty sure it exists," Harvey said.

"That's all?"

"A lot of insults to you. He wants the ring."

"It's not a seal ring. You heard Sophie. Not with stones in it. It's a family heirloom."

Whose family? I wondered, spotting my gun lying not far away. If I moved very quietly I might be able to stretch over and get it.

"He says it's a magic ring," Harvey said, and asked Janulevic something. But Janulevic shook his head. "He won't say what it does."

But Luke already knew, and I knew, and I wondered, if I had that ring on my finger, would I be making a wish?

Hell, yes.

But what wish? This was Luke, right, so his heart's desire would probably be to finish the mission safely. But maybe, just maybe, he might be hoping that I was okay. After all, I must've looked pretty bad. I had blood all over me. He could be wishing that Maria got back here in time and took Janulevic out. He could be wishing for Angel's safety or even Tammy's recovery, although I didn't think that was very likely. He could be hoping that he and I would work things out. Or he could be hoping that I'd get my hands on that gun.

The laser sight lay next to the gun, and I reached it first and used it to pull the pistol over to me. But it rattled on the ground, and I couldn't move properly to pick it up, my head was swimming, and I lay very, very still, just in case Janulevic heard the noise and looked over.

But Luke, gorgeous darling Luke, spoke up loudly. "Why do you want it, Janulevic? What's your heart's desire? Total world domination's a bit James Bond. Financial freedom? Wouldn't it be easier to play the lottery? Or is it arms you're after? Why not try the Middle East. I hear they've got some excellent stuff. American, too, so you know it's quality."

Harvey relayed this, in a slightly amazed tone of voice, to Janulevic, who started spitting angrily, especially when he heard the American bit, and he began ranting in reply before Harvey had finished, his little eyes fixed on Luke.

I used up all my strength to reach over and grab the pistol, snap the laser sight in place, and cover the beam with my hand. Then, reeling from the effort, I shakily aimed it.

"...taking over his ancient culture, slamming McDonalds on every street corner, turning Prague into Pittsburg and Brno into Boston," Harvey was reciting, looking pissed off, and I nearly smiled as I sighted down the barrel, removed my hand from the laser sight, and trained the little red dot on Janulevic's trigger hand. "His heart's desire is to eliminate the—" Harvey ground his teeth, "—the scourge that is America, to claim back what they have taken and undo the damage they have inflicted."

I squeezed the trigger, there was a flash and a bang, and Janulevic's .22 clattered to the ground. Janulevic clutched at Harvey for support, but Harvey kicked him away, and when he was clear, I aimed again, the dot on Janulevic's head this time.

"Luke?"

"What are you waiting for?"

For your assurance that killing this man is the right thing to do. That I won't lose my soul like I thought I was going to do last time I shot someone. That Janulevic deserves to die for what he's done. That you're really sure I need to do this.

The red dot shook as I trembled.

Luke turned to look at me, and I saw it in his face: there wasn't anyone else about to make my decision for me.

So I made my choice.

And fired. Janulevic was dead.

Harvey stared in amazement as Luke picked up the torch and knelt by me. "Are you okay?"

"Not bad, to say I'm dead."

"You were faking it?" Harvey said incredulously.

I looked up at Luke. He raised an eyebrow. "Just this once," I said, and he grinned and kissed my forehead. "What did you wish for?"

"Wish?"

"You were wearing the ring. It's supposed to grant you your heart's desire. What was it?"

Harvey and I both looked at Luke, who looked nonplussed.

"That you'd shoot Janulevic," he said.

Figures.

Chapter Eighteen

Another trip to the emergency department, where one of the nurses waved at me and asked how I was getting on with those stitches in my calf. Janulevic's bullet had ripped through my ear, which hurt like hell, and would probably leave a scar. Great. Another thing to lie to my parents about.

Luke took me home and told me to rest, which was never going to happen, especially as whenever I turned on my side, pain shot through me. I threw all my bloody clothes straight in the machine and managed to take a shower without getting my big fat ear bandage wet, although I wasn't sure about how well my hair had been washed. I got dressed, looked through my mail, and picked up the phone to call the office and tell Karen I'd be in later to make a report. Luke had already called her about the body, and now he'd gone off to help her with moving it out of the crypt.

She wasn't yet back at the office, so I called her mobile and left a message on voicemail. Then I flumped idly down on the sofa, and it was quite a while before I realised my answer phone light was flashing.

"You have one new message. Message one: Hello, this is Julie from the Stansted Vet's Surgery. I'm calling for Sophie Green? You brought a cat in to us yesterday, by the name of Tammy. I would have called you yesterday but I'm afraid we had a computer failure and lost your number."

Fear gripped me. My nails dug in my palms. Why didn't she just go ahead and say it?

"I just wanted to tell you that Tammy...will be fine."

I let out a huge long breath of relief.

"It was touch and go during the night, but she made it through to this morning, and now she's quite bright and perky."

I grabbed the phone and dialled so quickly I got it wrong the first time and had to try again. "Can I come and see her?"

They said I could, and I grabbed my bag and my keys and rushed out of the house. Ted sat there, looking weary and battered, a bit like me really, but solid and sure and not about to give up. He sounded happy when I started him up, and seemed to enjoy the short ride up to the vet's.

Tammy was languishing in a little cage with a soft, furry blanket and a catnip toy. She was wrapped around with lots of bandages, her ear was split and half her lovely multicoloured fur had been shaved off to make way for rows and rows of stitches. I felt tears come to my eyes, and when she lifted her head and mewed at me I nearly broke down.

Okay, so maybe I was overreacting. But Tammy's my baby, and I'd been neglecting her quite a bit recently, and if it wasn't for me having such a stupid, dangerous job she'd never have been in danger.

"It's okay, Tammy-girl," I said, reaching through the bars to stroke her little head. "They said you're going to be fine. Lots of TLC. Milk and cream with every meal. And the nasty man who hurt you has been—" I was about to say shot, but then I realised the staff were probably listening, and changed it to, "dealt with. And, sweetheart, I'm so sorry, because this is all my fault, me and my stupid job."

Tammy licked my fingers and started purring.

"And," I gulped, "if you want me to quit then maybe I will."

"I do hope she doesn't want you to," came a voice from the doorway, and I nearly fell off my chair, because Luke was standing there, watching me. He'd washed the blood from his hands and face and changed his black T-shirt for a grey one, but he still had the leather jeans on and he still looked really, really hot.

"I thought you were supposed to be resting," he said.

"I—I couldn't. They called me and said she was okay, and I had to come and visit..."

Luke nodded, and came over and bent down to look at Tammy. She offered him a tiny squeaky miaow, and he smiled.

"I think she likes you," I said, and he grinned.

"I think I like her, too." He reached out and touched my face. "Are you okay?"

I nodded. "But you'll have to speak to my left side, because I can't hear very well through this bandage thing."

"Sophie," Luke said, and then he stopped, looking frustrated.

"What happened to the ring?" I asked, into the silence.

"Karen has it. Sending it to the British Museum. They can argue over who it really belongs to."

"Did you get Janulevic sorted out?"

He nodded. "Czech authorities are glad to get him back. Harvey said they sounded quite embarrassed."

"As well they might." I studied him. His face was tight, worried, tired. "So you'll acknowledge that Harvey has his uses?"

"He can speak Czech. That's about it."

I rolled my eyes. "He'll keep Angel off our hands."

"Oh, yes. Anyone who gets you two kissing can't be all that bad. Even though I think you've had your chance, now."

"What do you mean?"

"I mean, he's just got on a plane to go down to Newquay to meet up with her."

Aw. How romantic. "So he'll be able to deliver the kiss in person this time."

"Yeah." Luke looked disappointed. "Macbeth wants a copy of the picture. And so does Docherty."

Gulp. "You've spoken to him?"

Luke nodded. "He was pretty pissed off. Says you owe him an apology." I grimaced. "And a new car."

"Doesn't he have insurance for that kind of thing?"

Luke looked at me like I was mad. Not that I wasn't used to it.

"Okay, so probably not. But he's not getting a hundred and fifty grand off me."

"I think he was looking for a different kind of payoff."

I met Luke's eyes. "He's not getting that, either."

He was silent a bit, looking at me. Then, "Do I get it?"

My fingers started trembling. The vet's ward smelled of disinfectant and cat food, and the faint, warm scent of Luke's skin. "Don't you know the answer to that?"

"No."

Me neither. Truth was, if he asked me again I'd give in. I'm weak, okay?

Luke sighed. "So where did we go wrong?"

"I wanted a grown-up relationship and you wanted casual, filthy sex."

Luke was silent a while longer. Then he said, "Maybe we could work on that."

"I don't think—"

"How about a grown-up relationship with a not-so grown-up man, and not-so casual but still reassuringly filthy sex?"

Now what am I supposed to say to that?

About the Author

Kate was born in 1982 and still hasn't grown up yet. She lives in England with her family and two cats who are her babies in every sense. Except, obviously, the biological one. She's been writing since her teens and is damn glad it's finally taking off since this means she won't have to go back to working airport check-in any more. Kate is single but aspirational (Prince William likes Kates, right?) and asks all potential dates to send in pictures of themselves and their Aston Martins.

To learn more about Kate Johnson, please visit www.katejohnson.co.uk. If you have a MySpace, please look up Sophie (Yes, she really does have her own Space.) and add her as a friend at www.myspace.com/sophiesuperspy. Send an email to Kate at katejohnsonauthor@googlemail.com or join her Yahoo! group for news about Kate and her alter-ego Cat Marsters at http://groups.yahoo.com/group/catmarsters.

Look for these titles

Now Available

The Twelve Lies of Christmas
I, Spy?

Coming Soon:

A is for Apple

Life is just a series of events with consequences. On their own they wouldn't add up to much, but when you put them all together you never know where they'll end up taking you, or what the outcome will be once you're there.

Thirty Lessons
© 2007 Mary Eason

The last thing Paige Wilder is looking for at thirty-eight is another bad-ending relationship. Paige believes she has it all—good friends, a challenging career in publishing and the perfect little companion named Sammy.

Unfortunately from the moment Paige meets Jude, even before she realizes he is going to be one of those bad-ending relationships, she knows her life will never be the same again after the lessons he has to teach her.

Jude Martin has made some promises to himself. He will never return to New York City, never work for his father and never, under any circumstances, will he fall in love again. So why is he here, in New York, running his father's publishing house and trying to convince a woman who is just as determined as he is to give him a second chance?

Available now in ebook from Samhain Publishing.

Cosmos, gays and guns, it's murder on a girl's love life.

A is for Apple
© 2007 Kate Johnson

Book Three in the Sophie Green series.

Cosmically inept spy Sophie Green is dispatched to the Big Apple on the trail of an invisible man. What she finds is an artist, a conspiracy, and some very large men with guns.

Meanwhile, her gorgeous partner, Luke, is getting worryingly intimate. Can it really be time for him to meet her parents?

Sophie, spy extraordinaire, isn't overwhelmed just yet. Until she's informed of the new terms of her assignment. No longer Sophie Green: Spy, now she'll become Sophie Green: Teenager.

Yep, she's being sent to the scariest place on earth. Back to school.

Available now in ebook from Samhain Publishing.

GET IT NOW

MyBookStoreAndMore.com

GREAT EBOOKS, GREAT DEALS . . . AND MORE!

Don't wait to run to the bookstore down the street, or
waste time shopping online at one of the "big boys." Now,
all your favorite Samhain authors are all in one place—at
MyBookStoreAndMore.com. Stop by today and discover
great deals on Samhain—and a whole lot more!

WWW.SAMHAINPUBLISHING.COM

hot
stuff

Discover Samhain!

THE HOTTEST NEW PUBLISHER ON THE PLANET

Romance, fantasy, mystery, thriller, mainstream and
more—Samhain has more selection, hotter authors, and
everything's available in both ebook and print.

Pick your favorite, sit back, and enjoy the ride!
Hot stuff indeed.

Samhain
Publishing, ltd

WWW.SAMHAINPUBLISHING.COM

GREAT cheap fun

Discover eBooks!

THE FASTEST WAY TO GET THE HOTTEST NAMES

Get your favorite authors on your favorite reader, long before they're out in print! Ebooks from Samhain go wherever you go, and work with whatever you carry—Palm, PDF, Mobi, and more.

Samhain Publishing, Ltd.

WWW.SAMHAINPUBLISHING.COM

Printed in the United States
105148LV00005B/133-135/A